My
not so
Wicked
Boss

Dedication

To Lisa Jo, the newest love in my life. Thank you for making me a grandma.

Chapter One

DON'T CRY. DON'T cry. Don't cry. It wasn't the end of the world. I stared at the email from the vice president of the bank, who didn't have the decency to tell me in person that he wasn't going to promote me to the position of client services manager. Even though I'd jumped through all the hoops and had been an employee longer than Stephen. Stephen, who I trained to be a personal banker like myself. Stephen, who barely knew the difference between a credit card and a debit card. Stephen, who was walking toward my desk in his new suit wearing a gloating smile and a ridiculous comb-over to hide his bald spot. Stephen, who had a huge piece of spinach wedged between his two front teeth.

"Aspen, I just wanted to say that going against you was stiff competition, so this win means even more to me."

Wow. For that, I wasn't going to mention the spinach. Or the coffee dribbled on his white shirt.

"In the end, the best man won. I hope there will be no hard feelings. Especially since I'm your new boss." He guffawed to himself.

I pressed my lips together, not knowing what to say. He wasn't the best *man* for the job. All he had was a degree from a highly touted university and a mother who was on the bank's board of directors.

He waited for my reply, but I had nothing. All I could think of was my daughter, Chloe. I wanted to be able to finally move us out of our tiny apartment and say *yes* to more of the things she wanted, even needed, like braces. I almost had to take a loan out just to pay for her junior high school fees.

Don't cry.

When I said nothing, he blankly stared at me for a moment longer. "Well," he clapped his small, oddly shiny hands together, "now that we've cleared all that up and moved on, I need you to help out today in private banking." He smirked. "Now."

I wasn't surprised by his behavior. I knew he would be the worst sort of boss—authoritative without any skills. He would make himself look good on the backs of others. My back. I stood without a word, only taking the time to log out of my computer and grab my satchel before I marched across the marble floor to take the elevator to the second floor. It was rubbing salt in my wounds to have to help the wealthier part of our customer base today. At least the solo ride on the elevator gave me time to compose myself. Tears pricked my eyes, but I stifled them with shallow breaths.

Evelyn, the sweet receptionist—who was old enough to be my grandmother and planned to work at the bank until her dying day—greeted me with a smile on her cute, chubby, aged face as soon as I stepped off the elevator. "I was hoping they would send you up here today when Valerie called in sick."

"Thanks, Evelyn. Should I take the floater's office?"

"I have it ready for you."

When I walked past her desk, she stood and took ahold of me. "I heard the news," she whispered in my ear. "I can't believe they promoted that little brownnoser over you."

"Me either." I had to stave off the tears again. I was afraid I was never going to catch a break.

She tipped my chin with her crinkled finger. "You keep your chin up. Better doors for you are waiting to open. I just know it."

I sighed, not sure. I was told if I finished my degree that the job would be mine. Now all I had to show for my degree was student loan debt and the long hours I spent late into the night doing homework and taking online classes so that I didn't take even more time away from my baby.

I settled into the desk chair, at least thankful I had an office today. Downstairs, we were in cubicles. Apparently, if you didn't make a lot of money it was okay if you discussed your financial needs and private information for the world to hear. I reached into the desk drawer, grabbed my extra nameplate, set it on the mahogany desk, and logged in to the computer. While the computer started up, I stared at the framed picture on the wall in front of me of a beautiful mountain scene with our bank logo and slogan obscuring it, "A Better Bank for a Better Life." *Lie,* was all I could think.

I didn't have time to wallow. Before I knew it, Evelyn was bringing back my first customer of the day. I sat up tall and plastered on a fake smile when I saw her coming. Evelyn was fanning herself as she walked toward me with a Cheshire grin. I wondered why until I saw a man trailing behind her. Not only *a* man, but *the* man. At least, I thought it was him. If not, I was going to start believing in doppelgangers.

I stood and, for the first time in forever, my heart raced, and not because I opened the electric bill. This was a different kind of pulse; one I had forgotten existed. I didn't like men as a general rule, unless I was related to them or I had been friends with them circa high school. I made a few exceptions if my friends happened to be married to them and were bearing their children, which was happening more and more lately. Beyond that, I didn't have much use for men.

But this man I had kept by my bedside for over a year now.

Evelyn made it in before him. The man in question happened to have a little someone with him. That little someone was giving him fits, as little people often do. But what a cutie the whining boy was. He had dark, curly hair like the man who was now kneeling in front of him. Did he have a son? For all my admiring of his picture and reading the books he wrote more times than I was willing to admit, I had forced myself not to learn more about him, except that he was single and loved to play polo. I only knew those tidbits because of my friends.

"Listen, mate, if you're good here, I promise we will go get ice cream afterwards. Does that sound good? Can you do that?" The man in question's sexy British accent wafted my way, making my pulse tick up even more.

The handsome boy, dressed like a tiny royal in shorts, a sweater with a collared shirt underneath, and dress socks up to his calves, nodded and took the man's hand. The man was also impeccably dressed in slacks with a dark blue button-up that brought out his aqua eyes.

Eyes I'd stared into too many times.

Never did I think I would get the opportunity in real life. Not that I wanted it. Okay, maybe I thought of having dinner with him a time or two, but it was only to discuss how brilliant his latest book was. That wasn't exactly true either, but now was not a time to fall into one of my daydreams about him. Honestly, though, I would have loved to ask him how he dreamt up the complex character of Isabella Jones. I felt connected to her, almost as if I knew her in real life. We shared similar backstories—both middle children, once upon a time uninhibited, but life had gotten to us, making us reserved in nature and a tad snarky. I also wanted to know when the sequel to *Silent Stones* was coming out. It had been two years. How long could it take to write a book?

Evelyn, still fanning herself and red like she was having a hot flash, cleared her throat. "Aspen, this is Miles Wickham—"

Miles Wickham? I expected her to say Taron Taylor. I guess I was wrong. He wasn't the man on the cover of the book that held a place of honor on my nightstand. I told my heart it could stop racing, but Mr. Wickham's piercing eyes caught hold of mine. They widened as if he were surprised to see me, as if we were already acquainted. Then he tilted his head and began studying me from every angle. I wasn't sure what to make of it, but I reminded myself I was at work and to focus back on Evelyn.

"—he's here to open a checking account. I thought you would be perfect to help him." Evelyn gave me a covert wink. She was always trying to set me up with someone, including most of her grandsons.

I walked around the desk a bit shaky and held my hand out. "It's a pleasure to meet you, Mr. Wickham." I had to stop myself from smiling. All I could think of was wicked Mr. Wickham from *Pride and Prejudice.*

Mr. Wickham held out his own masculine hand, still studying me. He swallowed hard. "The pleasure is mine, Ms.—?"

"Parker," I stuttered like an idiot. Men weren't supposed to have an effect on me. It was the British accent, I told myself.

"Ms. Parker." He spoke my name with reverence while keeping my hand in his. "I feel as if we've met before."

I looked at Evelyn, not sure how to respond. Not sure if I could. There was suddenly less oxygen in the room, or so it felt. Evelyn's excited eyes said to say something flirty. I didn't remember how to do that. More importantly, I shouldn't be doing that. I was a professional and I didn't like men.

I found some air and pulled my hand away from his. Oddly, it made him smile as if that's what he expected.

"I think I would have remembered if we had," I finally managed to say, which, unfortunately, did sound flirty even though it was true. I *would* have remembered him if we'd met before. To cover up my blunder, I knelt carefully in my pencil skirt in front of the little guy who had to be all of three. "And who are you?" I asked.

"I'm Henry," he replied. Forget the sexy British accent, his adorable one was ten times better. He held up his bear. "This is my teddy, George." His teddy bear looked well-loved with matted-down fur and his bowtie askew.

I shook George's paw. "It's nice to meet you, George."

Henry giggled, making me wish Chloe was a toddler again, or for another little one running around. I would have had another baby in a second if I could afford to and, you know, if it didn't involve the opposite sex.

"We are going to get ice cream," he said so grown-up like.

"That sounds yummy. What kind of ice cream do you like?"

"Butterscotch." He smiled.

"I'll have to try that flavor."

Henry nodded and I stood to find Mr. Wickham gazing thoughtfully at me. He wasn't helping with the pulse racing thing.

"I'll leave you to it." Evelyn wagged her brows before exiting.

"Please have a seat." I waved to the chairs in front of my desk, trying to maintain my composure.

Mr. Wickham took a seat, but Henry had other ideas; he followed me to mine.

"Henry, come sit next to me," Mr. Wickham kindly directed.

Henry grinned mischievously while shaking his head *no*. He held his arms out to me. One look at his big brown eyes with lashes to die for, and I could hardly refuse. "Do you mind?" I asked Mr. Wickham.

"Not at all. My nephew is . . ." he swallowed. "Is a precocious tyke."

I didn't think that's what he was going to say, but no matter. I picked the little guy up along with his bear and set him on my lap and wondered why he had his nephew with him. Bringing a toddler to a bank wasn't usually a wise choice.

"He's adorable."

"He gets that from me." Mr. Wickham deadpanned.

I started to respond with my normal sarcasm toward the opposite sex, but I stopped myself. "What can I help you with today?"

Mr. Wickham leaned forward as if he were trying to get a better look at me. "I'm going to be in the States for a while and my financial advisor recommended I open an account here to make things easier."

"We have a few options. Let me get you a brochure and we can go over those and see what best fits your needs."

Henry didn't want to be forgotten. "I'm three." He held up three fingers.

I wanted to kiss those cute fingers but thought that was even more unprofessional than holding him on my lap. "You are a very big boy for three."

He puffed out his chest.

I reached into the desk drawer for the brochure. "What brings you to the States?" I tried not to stare at the handsome man. I couldn't get over how much he looked like Taron Taylor. He was even British, which was strange. I had to say, though, that I was relieved he wasn't my favorite author. I had promised my girlfriends if I ever met him,

I'd try to get to know him. I'd known the odds were in my favor of that never happening, so I'd agreed to appease them. They worried I was going to die an old maid. The odds were highly in favor of that, considering I hadn't been on a date since my ex-husband left me and our daughter twelve years ago.

"I have some personal and business matters to attend to." He kept it vague on purpose, given his stiff body language.

It didn't offend me that he didn't divulge anything personal. I could relate. I slid a brochure of our different account types across the desk. "Here are—"

"My mummy and daddy are gone," Henry wailed unexpectedly.

My head shot up and caught Mr. Wickham's defeated eyes. He sighed and hung his head. Meanwhile, I tried to comfort poor Henry, who began to cry into my bosom. I wrapped my arms around him, hoping his parents were on vacation or something, but Mr. Wickham's demeanor said otherwise, and it broke my heart.

"My sister and her husband were in a car accident," Mr. Wickham spoke low, refusing to finish the rest. I could guess. "Come here, Henry." Mr. Wickham stood to retrieve his grieving nephew.

"No!" Henry refused, snuggling further into me.

Mr. Wickham looked at a loss of what to do. "I'm new at this."

"It's fine. I don't mind keeping him, if it's all right with you."

He sat back down, relieved. "I was only supposed to be the fun uncle."

"I'm very sorry for your and Henry's loss." I stroked Henry's dark curls.

"Thank you, love." He suddenly seemed uncomfortable. "Do you mind if we move along? I have several appointments to attend to."

"Not at all." I kept one arm around Henry, who was shuddering against me. Poor baby. I used my free hand to point at the brochure. "If you could tell me a bit about your goals and profession, I can make a solid suggestion on the right account for you."

He rested his hands on his legs and leaned forward. "Would you believe I'm an international bestselling author?"

I gasped.

"Are you all right, love?"

"Yes," I squeaked. "You wouldn't happen to use a pen name, would you?"

His left brow raised debonairly. "As a matter of fact, I do. Taron Taylor."

The bated breath I had been holding came out in a rush. "Oh."

His lips curled up. "Have you heard of me?"

I nodded and, unfortunately, I could feel my cheeks burn.

"A fan," he said, ever so pleased. "I love fans."

"I never said I was a fan," came rushing out of my mouth before I could stop it. I didn't want to be rude to him. It was a conditioned response to men. A defense mechanism, if you will.

He didn't believe a word or seem to take offense. "Which book is your favorite?" He flashed me a disarming smile.

It was enough to almost make me blurt out how much I loved *Silent Stones*, but I stopped myself. "I think our platinum premium account would suit you," I suggested instead of answering.

He laughed this deep, rich laugh. "Aspen, was it? I like you."

I tucked my long, brown hair behind my ear. "Um, the account has a competitive APY, no fees, online and mobile banking—" I started to ramble, amusing him more.

"Sounds brilliant."

"I'll need your passport, individual tax identification number, and—"

His phone rang, interrupting me. He held up his finger. "One moment please. I must take this." He answered and walked out but kept me and his nephew in his line of sight. He kept smiling at me and shaking his head like he couldn't believe this was happening. I had the exact same thoughts, but wondered why he felt that way. And why did he think we had met?

Henry had cried himself to sleep against me. I stroked his baby-soft brow. "I'm so sorry," I whispered. I had to keep myself from tearing up. When I looked back up, Mr. Wickham or Taylor or who-ever he was, was now pacing, running his hands through his gorgeous hair. I mean, his hair. It was just hair.

"What the bloody hell am I going to do now? I don't have time for this." His voice, while raised, was discreet given he wasn't in private. I still couldn't believe he was here, and that I was holding his sweet nephew. I shifted him on my lap, trying to get more comfortable. It was amazing how much heavier they felt as they slept. I missed these days, though Chloe and I did snuggle on the couch when we watched our favorite shows and stuffed our faces with popcorn.

Mr. Wickham paced and paced some more, talking more quietly. "Stella, I can't just pick someone off the street." He glanced at me and his nephew before abruptly stopping. His lips curled and his eyes brightened. "Let me call you back. I think I have an idea." He hung up without another word and shoved his phone into his pocket. He walked back in, his lips pressed together, assessing me even more than he had previously.

"Ms. Parker, do you like your job here?"

"Um . . ." That was an unexpected and uncomfortable question given the morning I'd had.

"Hesitation," he said, pleased. He shut the office door and leaned against it.

I couldn't help but stare at him. The picture on his book cover didn't do him justice. Which was ridiculous. Because my second thought was that this was inappropriate. Closed doors had become something of a taboo. You'd be surprised at some of the salacious stories that had circulated around the bank.

I bit my lip. "Mr. Wickham—"

He pushed off the door. "Please call me Miles." He took his seat back, grinning between me and his nephew, who, by the tender look he gave him, he was obviously fond of. "You see, Aspen, I'm in a bit of a bind. I came here because of my sister's last wishes and to work on my novel."

I wanted to say it was about time—I needed that book—but instead I attentively listened.

"She loved Carrington Cove," he said wistfully.

"I grew up there. It's a beautiful place." My parents still lived there. Chloe and I lived in Edenvale because it was cheaper and closer to work.

He clapped his hands together. "Splendid. I think a bit of kismet is at play here."

"I'm not following you."

He gave me a charming grin. "I'm in need of someone who can be both a nanny to my nephew and a personal assistant to me."

I laughed, startling Henry, who I quickly soothed back to sleep. "You're kidding, right?" I looked around for a recording device. "Did my new boss put you up to this?"

"I assure you, I'm not having a laugh at your expense. I'm in earnest, and somewhat desperate."

I blinked an inordinate amount of times. "No. No. I'm not a nanny." And I certainly couldn't be his personal assistant.

He stared down at his sleeping nephew. "You seem to have a magic touch when it comes to wee ones."

I shrugged. "I wouldn't say that, but I have a daughter."

"How old?" he asked.

"Twelve."

His brows raised. I knew what he was thinking. *You look too young to have a child that age.* He was right, but I would never regret it even if it meant having the most worthless ex-husband in existence. Chloe was the best thing that had ever happened to me.

He cleared his throat. "Excellent," he stammered as if he was unsure what to say to that. "You have plenty of experience then. Exactly what Henry and I need."

"Listen, Miles, you don't know me. I have a degree in business management, not child development."

"I would do a background check on you, of course. And I need a savvy business mind."

"I don't think I'm the right person. Maybe I could ask around for you." I looked down at sweet Henry and my mother's heart wanted nothing more than to see that he had the right person to take care of him.

Miles slapped his hand on the desk. "Whatever you are making here, I'll double it."

My head popped up. Our eyes locked.

"What do you say now, Ms. Parker?"

Oh. Wow. I leaned back, stunned. "Can I think about it?"

Chapter Two

THREE SETS OF eyes stared at me on the bleachers, waiting for me to speak. My eyes were set on Chloe talking animatedly with her soccer team at the park after practice. They were enjoying the last warm evenings we would have as September wore on. She was at the center of the decision I had to make. My beautiful girl whose carefree spirit lighted my world and her heart of gold that reminded me I must have done something right despite all our challenges, financial and otherwise. I smiled, watching her twist her golden-brown ponytail like she always did. We shared the same hair and eye color, however her green eyes shone pure and trusting. Mine were marked with caution tape.

Emma, one of my best friends from high school and Chloe's soccer coach, interrupted my gaze. She placed her hand on my knee. "Did you get the promotion?" she asked.

I turned my gaze from Chloe and faced the best friends a woman could ask for, Emma, Jenna, another long-time friend from high school, and Shelby, the Southern belle who had crashed our party a year ago. Funny we all thought we would hate her, but none of us could imagine our lives without the perky blonde now.

I rested my hand over Emma's clammy one. Poor thing was dying from morning sickness. I sighed. "They gave it to Stephen."

All their eyes widened while shaking their heads. Each disappointed for me and confused. Not only had I complained about

Stephen's incompetence for months, but they had each seen the slimy man.

"We can bury that weasel easily," Jenna said, always willing to dispose of a body.

Shelby placed her hand across her ever-growing chest. Pregnancy had the opposite effect on her. She was even perkier, if that was possible, and her voluptuous chest was expanding, to her husband's delight, I was sure. Those two couldn't keep their hands off each other. I'd seen some pictures, but that was another story.

"Well, I will march down to that bank tomorrow and inform them that my husband will be taking his business accounts elsewhere." She sounded reminiscent of Scarlett O'Hara. Losing Prescott Technologies would be a significant loss to the bank, but it wouldn't help my cause. In fact, it might cost me my job if they found out why.

I smiled at my fearsome friends. "I appreciate your willingness to go to jail or disrupt your husband's life on my behalf, but . . ." I bit my lip, "losing the promotion isn't what I wanted to talk to you about."

Each leaned back with narrowed eyes.

Emma rubbed my bare knee. "Everything okay?"

"Let's just say I had an interesting proposition today."

"Did Cory the teller manager ask you out again? You should totally say yes." Jenna grinned. "I know he laughs like a hyena, but he's hot."

I rolled my eyes at her. "Cory's given up and moved onto nicer, greener pastures." They all did. I made sure of it. Best to push them away before any hurt or hopes occurred on either end.

"You're as sweet as can be," Shelby patted me, "most of the time." She giggled.

"I'm not sure about that." I wanted to be nicer.

"Well, what is it?" Jenna was growing impatient.

I let out a deep breath. "I'm going to tell you, but you have to promise not to freak out on me or tell me what I should do based on who it is. And along those lines, I don't want to hear any 'this is fate' crap."

They were all thoroughly confused now and wore perplexed looks.

"Do you promise?" I was going to make them swear. I was already freaked out enough about the prospect of working for Miles. Miles, who had done his best to convince me. Even offering more money after he found out how little I made at the bank.

They all nodded eagerly.

"Okay," I swallowed, "today, a man named Miles Wickham—"

"As in *Pride and Prejudice*'s Mr. Wickham?" Emma interrupted.

"Yes."

Shelby's beautiful blue eyes began swirling with possibilities. "Is he British?" They all knew I had a thing for the BBC and British men. It was the accent and the way they carried themselves. It was different than American men.

"He is," I breathed out. "Remember, you promised me no conjecturing."

They all grinned slyly, telling me they were doing exactly that. I hadn't even told them the half of it, which gave me no hope for an unbiased opinion now. To their credit, they tried to suppress their smiles.

"Anyway," I continued, "he came into the bank today to open an account. And he happened to have his adorable three-year-old nephew with him, and the little guy and I hit it off." I thought back to how sad he was to say goodbye to me. His tears broke my heart and made me want to take the job even more than the money. "So much so," I paused, "his uncle offered me the position of his nanny." I left out a lot of details—on purpose.

If I thought my friends looked perplexed before, they were downright puzzled now.

Jenna pursed her lips. "That's weird."

"You're not considering it, are you?" Emma asked.

"Well, kind of. The money is good. Like, really good."

Shelby pressed her lips together and thoughtfully stared at me as if she knew there was more to the story. It wasn't surprising, given her wealthy background. "Who is this man?"

That got Emma and Jenna thinking too.

"That's a good question," Emma added. "You wouldn't up and

quit the bank for no reason, even though they treat you like crap and we've all been telling you forever you deserve better. So why this guy?"

I should have listened to them, but the bank was stable, and they had promised me that promotion. They were obviously liars. I cleared my throat. "It's not about the man. It's the opportunity and his nephew Henry is the sweetest thing." I rubbed the back of my tense neck. "And I would also be Mr. Wickham's personal assistant, which would look good on a resume."

"How personal?" Jenna blurted. "Are we talking—"

"No," I interrupted her dirty mind.

"Wait." Emma squinted. "Why would it look good on a resume?"

I tucked some of my long, curled hair behind my ear. "Here is the part where you absolutely *cannot* freak out."

Their smiles said they were waiting to totally freak out.

I guess there was no hiding it. "Miles Wickham is an author. A famous one, in fact."

Jenna was already on her phone googling him.

I beat her to the punch. "You might know him better as Taron Taylor." I braced myself before they all accosted me with hugs.

"Holy crap!" Emma exclaimed.

"Mylanta! I knew in my heart you two were meant to meet." Shelby gripped me the tightest. She was a hugger.

"Dang it. I got so excited my boobs are leaking." Jenna pulled away from us and surveyed the damage while reaching in her bag for some tissue. Breast milk spots on her shirt had been her nemesis since her ten-month-old, Elliott, was born. She swore she produced enough to sustain a dozen children.

I untangled myself from them. "You are all liars. You promised me you wouldn't freak out."

They laughed at me but were all stunned. Believe me, I was too. It was all I thought about all day. We all sat in silence for a moment while they stared at me with wonder in their eyes.

"So, why is he here with his nephew?" Emma rested against me. Pregnancy was kicking her butt. She'd lost at least ten pounds since she found out at the beginning of last month.

I put my arm around Emma. "It's awful. His sister and brother-in-law died in a car accident a couple of months ago."

Gasps and hands over hearts were their responses.

"His poor nephew, Henry, crawled onto my lap and cried himself to sleep over it." Tears pooled in all our eyes.

"That's kind of sweet, though," Jenna commented.

"It really was," I agreed. "He's adorable."

"Like his uncle?" Shelby grinned.

"His uncle seems to think himself adorable."

"So, you flirted with him." Jenna wagged her brows.

"I did no such thing," I defended myself.

They each rolled their eyes.

"Anyway, Mr. Wickham is here because his sister and brother-in-law owned a place in Carrington Cove up in the Bluffs." It was the swankiest of the swanky in Carrington Cove, which was saying something of the once-upon-a-time small town that had turned into a tourist's dream and resort town.

Emma lifted her head. "Really? What were their names?" Emma's dad, Dane Carrington, owned half of Carrington Cove and knew the other half. He and Emma also ran a dude ranch there.

"Sophie and Kevin Mahoney. Kevin was originally from Denver, I believe."

Shelby fanned her misty eyes. "Oh goodness, I knew her. She came into the boutique a few times." Shelby owned M&M'S on Main, a clothing boutique in Carrington Cove. "Such a beautiful woman with the best taste in clothes. We talked quite a bit when she was in over the summer on holiday, as she called it. She was an interior designer. I knew she was from London, but I had no idea she was related to your Mr. Wickham."

"He's not mine."

"Yet." Shelby patted my knee.

"He's a potential employer," I reminded them all. I was never telling them about the pulse racing thing or the little zing it gave me when he shook my hand. Or those few strands of gray in his dark hair that made my fingers ache to run through his mane.

"Give us the details on this job." Jenna was flapping her shirt trying to dry it off.

I was happy to discuss anything that didn't involve my friends conjecturing about what this could mean for my nonexistent love life. "It's pretty involved. I would do everything from taking care of Henry to answering fan mail and keeping up with his social media accounts. Maybe even some proofreading." Which excited me. I needed to know what happened to Isabella, who'd gone missing at the end of the book with only a cryptic letter hinting she'd disappeared on purpose. But I had a feeling it wasn't her that left the letter.

Emma pursed her lips. "How many hours a day would you have to be at his house?"

I bit my lip. "Well . . . if I took the job, he would want Chloe and me to move into the guest house on his property." He promised it would all be on the up and up. He kept odd hours as a writer and wanted someone to be there for Henry if need be.

"What?" Their heads ping-ponged between me and Chloe at the park.

There was no doubt about it being a big deal. "I know, but most nannies live with their employers, and Chloe's best friend lives in Carrington Cove and she's always begging me to move us back so they can go to school together." We had lived with my parents until Chloe was nine. While she had good friends where we lived now, her closest group remained in Carrington Cove. I had always felt guilty moving her away, but I couldn't live with my parents forever, and Carrington Cove was out of my price range. Taking this job could change all that. It could change so many things. I gazed at my daughter. More than anything, I wanted to do right by her. This job could be the key to that.

Shelby took my hand. "Have you vetted this man?" It was funny how they were all gung-ho about me dating him, but living on the same property was a different story. Believe me, I knew.

"Are you sure he isn't hoping for some side benefits?" asked Jenna, who now had tissues plastered to her chest.

I smacked Jenna's arm. "Of course not, but regardless, I'm going to do my research. As part of that, he invited me to dinner tomorrow night to discuss any questions or concerns I may have." I had a list.

"Dinner for two?" Jenna asked not so coyly.

I rearranged a tissue for her. She'd missed a spot. "He will be bringing his nephew, thank you very much." He obviously didn't have anyone to care for him, hence the job offer. Apparently, whoever called had informed him that his nanny wouldn't be joining him in the states since her boyfriend finally proposed to her after she told him she was moving several thousand miles away. Not sure if that marriage was going to make it. Why had it taken a major life change for him to commit? Oh man, I needed to stop being so jaded toward the opposite sex, but men made it so easy sometimes.

"A little hanky-panky under the table is great." Emma nudged me.

"I'm not going to fool around with a potential employer, or anyone, for that matter."

"I don't know, fooling around with your sexy British boss sounds kind of nice," Jenna sing-songed, making everyone laugh, including me, but only because it was a ridiculous notion. Me and my favorite author? It was never happening.

"Believe me, ladies, if I accept his offer, it will be strictly business."

Chapter Three

WHILE I SAT in bed contemplating my life, I kept staring at Miles's picture on his website, though he was called Taron there. I had scoured the internet trying to find out as much about him as I could. What I'd gleaned so far was he was forty years old, never married, raised by a single mom, and-based on how many women were draped all over him in the pictures he was featured in—he loved women. The women seemed to adore him too. They all looked at him as if they would sell their souls to remain permanently by his side. I could hardly blame them. He was dashing and he had this enigmatic smile that made you want to know what he was thinking. I should stop thinking like that. I needed to look at him as a potential employer, not future boyfriend material.

"Hey, Mom." Chloe walked into my room with a towel on her head, freshly showered after soccer practice.

"Hi, baby girl." I patted the ever-empty space next to me in my bed.

She took the invitation and jumped in bed with me, snuggling into my side. I put my arm around her, breathing in not only her clean scent, but her goodness. I was the luckiest of moms.

She leaned her head on my shoulder, eyes fixed on my laptop screen. "Who's that guy?"

I gave Miles one more glance before I closed my laptop. "Funny you should ask." I reached for the book on my nightstand and handed it to Chloe, making sure to point out Miles's picture on the back copy. "He goes by Taron Taylor, but his real name is Miles Wickham. I met him today at the bank."

Chloe touched his picture. In it he looked like a brooding author with his hand under his chin. "That's cool. He's hot."

My brow furrowed. "What do you know about men being hot?"

"Mom." She rolled her eyes. "I know lots of hot boys at school."

"Oh, really? Who?"

She blushed, making me worry. I was hoping for her not to notice boys until she was thirty and had the sense to stay away from them all together. It was a pipe dream, I know. When she didn't answer, I became more concerned. "Do you like someone?" *Dear God, please no.*

"Kind of," she squeaked.

My heart dropped to my feet. "Does he have a name?"

"Alec." She grinned.

"How do you know Alec?"

"We have the same lunch. He's in ninth grade."

All the air whooshed out of my lungs like I'd been sucker punched. That's how I met her father, except I was a sophomore and he was a senior. I had to remind myself Chloe wasn't me. "That's nice," I lied. My baby was only in seventh grade. No one should be looking at her, especially older boys.

"It's no big deal. I've never talked to him."

I breathed a sigh of relief, for now.

"But one of his friends told Ginger to tell me that he thinks I'm pretty."

That was it; we were for sure moving back to Carrington Cove. "That's sweet, but can I give you some advice?"

"Okay," she resigned herself.

I kissed the top of her towel. "I know you think I'm old, but it wasn't that long ago that I was in your shoes. And I wish someone would have told me to wait for a boy who is brave enough to tell you himself how he feels about you." If only I'd known. Leland was like this Alec. He played the cat and mouse game with me my entire sophomore year, having his friends tell my friends or me how much he liked me, but he didn't ask me out until the last day of school. Then all summer long he strung me along until he left for college. He broke more of our dates than he kept. His excuses ranged from having to work to his parents grounding him, but looking back, it was always another girl. I was just too naïve to realize it.

He played the same game with me every summer until I graduated. Like a lovesick puppy, I always chased after him whenever he showed me any attention. All because he was beautiful, angsty, and could play a guitar. Every girl I knew wanted him. Then I finally went off to college and started dating a nice guy named Matt. When Leland found out, he came chasing after me, telling me how much he loved me. I was foolish enough to believe him, but the truth was he didn't want anyone else to have me. That's how we got Chloe. There I was, pregnant and married at nineteen, baby at twenty, divorced by twenty-one. Never once did I regret having her. I squeezed my girl tighter.

"Mom, it's no big deal."

She was probably right, but I knew there would be a day when it was going to be a huge deal, and I wasn't ready for it. Just like I wasn't ready for the choice I had to make. "Baby girl, I need to talk to you about something important."

She lifted her head and looked up at me. She barely had to lift her head; she was almost as tall as me now. A few more inches and she would surpass me at five foot eight.

I tapped her cute button nose. "The man on the back of this book, Mr. Wickham, offered me a job today."

Her face scrunched. "What kind of job?"

"He wants me to be his nephew's nanny and his personal assistant."

Chloe's face looked more than unimpressed. "He wants you to be a babysitter?"

I pulled her to me and hugged her tight. "It's a little more detailed than that, but sort of, except this is better paying than any babysitting job. In fact, it's a lot more money than I make now at the bank."

That got her attention. She popped up and out of my arms. "Like how much?" Her eyes began to swirl with all the possibilities. "Could I finally get a cell phone?"

"It would definitely be enough for you to get your own cell phone."

She squealed and kicked her legs. "Yes! Take the job."

"Before you get too excited, kiddo, I don't know if I *should* take the job."

Her mouth fell open like I was crazy. "Why not?"

"Because, honey, I don't know this man, and it would mean you and I would have to move back to Carrington Cove."

Her green eyes, so like my own, widened while she got up on her knees, making my bed bounce. "You mean I could go to school with Brooke?" Her BFF since she was in preschool.

I nodded.

She grabbed my shoulders and shook me. "You have to take this job. Please, Mom."

I placed my hands on her perfectly smooth cheeks. "I'm thinking about it."

"Think hard," she begged.

"I'm having dinner to discuss the job further with him tomorrow night after I drop you off at Grandma and Grandpa's, and we'll see how it goes."

She flung herself on my bed with her hands clasped together. "Oh please, oh please, oh please," she repeated over and over again.

I couldn't help but smile at her and want to make her wish come true. After all, she had made almost all of mine come true, even before I knew to wish for something as wonderful as her. She changed my life, making me less selfish and more aware. She kept me from being bitter about her father. Even now, as Leland was threatening to intervene in our lives once again, Chloe reminded me that she was worth any price, even facing her father.

Unfortunately, facing him was a possibility. A couple of months ago, he called out of the blue after having no contact with us for three years, to tell me he was remarried with a baby and he wanted Chloe in his life. According to him, he was a better man now, all because his new wife taught him what love really was. Leland never failed to shove the knife that he'd stabbed me with so many years ago in deeper. Everything was always my fault. His excuse for cheating on me was I was always too tired to have sex with him whenever he wanted because I was busy taking care of our daughter. He didn't pay child support because it wasn't his fault I didn't use birth control. And now he felt the need to remind me that he never loved me.

He was real father-of-the-year material. If only I could legally keep him from seeing Chloe. I didn't want him to flit in and out of her life, hurting her more than he already had when he disappeared again. And I knew he would. Which got me thinking. If I did take this job, I could finally hire a lawyer to sue him for all the back child support he owed his daughter. But gazing at Chloe, I knew that the choice I had in front of me would be solely based on what was best for her. I only had to decide what that was.

Chapter Four

I PACED OUTSIDE Cove Café on the cobbled sidewalks of Main Street in Carrington Cove in the fading evening light, telling myself to go in. It was only dinner. I didn't have to accept Miles's job offer.

It wasn't only that though. My pulse was racing again, and not because I was nervous about a huge life change. For over a year now, I had imagined an evening like this. Dinner with Taron Taylor, where we would sip wine and discuss *Silent Stones* and his plans for the protagonist, Isabella Jones. I bit my lip and wrung my hands, thinking about the other things I had imagined. I wasn't supposed to meet the man I had fantasized about smiling across the candlelit table at me before he leaned in and ran his thumb across my lips. His smile would turn from playful to smoldering with each brush of his thumb before he would whisper my name as if I were a secret he wanted to keep all to himself.

I would draw close enough to share his breath. Anticipation brewed and then bubbled over as our lips teased but never touched. Then just as we couldn't stand the sweet torture any longer, I would tell myself he would eventually disappoint me. I would force myself to either wake up or stop daydreaming. Each make-believe meeting ended the same. And there had been many of them. I knew how ridiculous it was to fear even fantasized intimacy, but it was better than being disappointed or disillusioned, especially by the man who wrote such beautiful words.

Words that had made me laugh, cry, even reflect.

In her heart was hidden the deepest desire to love and be loved, but the wound that locked her fragile heart had not healed with time. No, time had only proven to her how right she was to hide the key that would unlock the beguiling gift she held within herself. A gift to bewitch the soul of any man. But not any man would be capable of finding the key to her heart she had buried deep within her damaged soul. He would need to be courageous if he dared to trespass the path to her very essence, obscured by time and thorns. He must be willing to pay in blood and patience. For the overgrown thorns hid not only the key to her heart, but the loveliest roses waiting to bloom under the gentle touch of the man patient enough to prune and care for the garden within her. For that man, she waited to grow with. For him she would give not only the map, but take the journey with him.

I stopped my pacing under the striped awning of the Cove Café. His words haunted me. In some ways, it reflected me. I felt damaged and ached for someone brave enough to try and push past my defenses. To give me the time to trust them even though I knew how unfair that was. But unlike Isabella Jones, I didn't possess her bewitching powers. I couldn't even keep the attention of my husband when I had one.

I brought my clasped hands up to my mouth and breathed in and out, trying to convince myself to walk in and face the man who was making my pulse race. Echoes of Chloe's encouragement, begging, and her crooked little smile lent me some bravery. She'd already picked out the mobile phone she wanted.

She wasn't the only motivator. I thought of Stephen's gloating attitude today when he demanded I take a customer wanting to open a CD after we'd already closed the bank. Did I mention Stephen went home after he barked his last command? To add insult to injury, the customer was difficult, lecturing me for twenty minutes about the bank's pathetic interest rates, because I had control over those. To top it off, I couldn't open the new account because he forgot his ID. For that, I got another lecture about poor customer service.

Forget the pay raise I would receive if I took this new job, seeing the look on Stephen's face when I gave my notice would be far more satisfying. First, though, I had to open the door and face Miles Wickham. I took one more deep breath of the crisp autumn air, smoothed out my blush cardigan, and reached for the door, reminding myself that if I could survive the mood swings of a pre-teen, I could do anything.

I let the breath out once I entered the establishment. The smell of the freshly baked breads they used for everything from bread bowls to grilled cheese sandwiches tickled my nose, flooding me with memories both good and bad. This was a favorite hangout during high school, not only for Emma, Jenna, Brad, and me, but Leland too. He would sit in the corner booth brooding while he scribbled out lyrics on napkins. I found it so mysterious and alluring. He knew it too, which was why he would only glance my way until I came to him. Never once did he come to me.

The young hostess grabbed my attention. "Would you like a table, or to sit at the counter?"

I shook thoughts of Leland out of my head, figuratively and literally. "I'm meeting someone."

That someone stood and waved, catching my attention from, wouldn't you know it, the corner booth. I took it as the universe's way of warning me, until he picked up his nephew and began to walk toward me, smiling. *He was coming to get me?*

Little Henry lit up when he saw me and immediately began to wiggle out of his uncle's arms. Miles let him go and watched the tot run straight to me. Before I could catch Henry in my arms, I caught a glimpse of Emma and Sawyer from the corner of my eye. I turned to find not only the aforementioned couple, but Brad and Jenna and Shelby and Ryder all there gawking at me unabashedly. I would deal with them after I scooped up the most adorable boy, dressed to charm in his shorts and tights.

If Henry were the only consideration, I would accept the job on the spot. It was as if my heart directly linked to his. He obviously felt the surreal connection too by the way he wrapped his tiny arms around my neck. But then he yelled, "Nanny," leading me to believe his uncle had coached the tyke. Perhaps Henry didn't feel as connected as I thought—or maybe even hoped. Either way, I didn't know how to respond. I looked at Miles and locked eyes with him. I could tell he was trying to suppress his guilty smile, leaving no doubt he was using Henry's adorableness to his advantage. Obviously, I was a sucker for the kid.

Miles stepped closer, his guilty smile turning debonair, making me feel like I was having a series of mini strokes. That wouldn't do. How could I work for someone who caused such a physiological response? Don't even get me going on how his aqua eyes drew me in. Or his cologne. Whatever it was, I needed to find out and stay away from it at all cost. His spicy, warm smell was more than likely brain numbing. I had a laundry list of all the trouble intoxicating scents had gotten me into, starting with a tattoo my parents still didn't know about and ending with becoming a single mother.

As I looked closer at Miles's eyes, I was startled to see they were filled with remorse, like he knew he'd placed me in difficult spot. I had expected to find arrogance. Instead, I found I was more uncomfortable with his concern than Henry's declaration.

"I may have been a bit presumptuous," he stated.

I swallowed hard. His accent wasn't doing my heart any favors. "More than a bit."

"Please forgive me," he sincerely begged.

His apology completely threw me off. I wasn't used to men admitting they were wrong, so much so, I didn't know how to respond. Instead, I did the intelligent thing and stared blankly at him, unfortunately, with my mouth hanging open. That had to be attractive.

He tilted his head, studying me like he had at the bank. "Hmm," he muttered as if he totally got me, which was off-putting. "Why don't we see what we can do to make Henry's proclamation a reality."

I got my vacant stare under control and responded, "I wonder where he got such an idea."

Miles's melodic laugh filled the café. "I do like you, Aspen. Come, let's sit." He waved his hand toward the corner booth.

That action had Brad, Sawyer, and Ryder jumping up like some chivalrous cavalry. Did they think Miles was luring me away? I supposed that meant I needed to make introductions. I gave my friends a wry grin. The women were all laughing and tugging on their husbands, trying to get them to sit down. I admit I was touched by their concern.

"Miles, would you mind meeting a few friends of mine first?"

Miles looked in the same direction as me. "Ah. I see your mates have come to check me out. Let's not keep them waiting."

"I didn't know they would be here," I sighed, somewhat embarrassed.

"No worries, it speaks volumes about the kind of person you must be."

"And what kind is that?"

He gave me good once-over in my "motherly" outfit consisting of a cardigan and black ankle pants. I'd even started wearing granny panties for the fun of it. I think he was more interested, though, in the way his nephew clung to me. "As far as I can tell . . . lovely," he admitted reluctantly.

I had no words, but my cheeks said it all. If I had to guess, I would say they were a nice shade of crimson. I covered it up by rubbing noses with Henry, who giggled. "Are you hungry?" I asked him.

"I want pizza!" he loudly voiced his preference.

I tapped his nose. "I don't think they have pizza here, sweetie."

Henry's lip began to quiver.

Miles immediately cringed while huge crocodile tears leaked out of Henry's gorgeous brown eyes.

"I'm mucking up this job," Miles confessed with a heavy breath. "He won't eat anything my chef prepares. I promised him pizza tonight."

Did he say chef? I would come back to that later. I wiped Henry's cheeks and kissed his forehead. "My parents are good friends with the owners. I'll see what I can work out." Surely they had what they needed in the kitchen to make pizza.

Miles's broad shoulders, which had sagged in defeat, lifted, nicely showcasing his charcoal button down. "See how much we need you?" Miles was laying it on thick.

The entire exchange between Miles and me had not been lost on my friends, judging by how wide all their smirks were. When we arrived at their table near the hearth, I shifted Henry to my hip. My curves were at least good for something. I missed a toddler there.

Six sets of eyes darted between the beyond cute boy in my arms to the ridiculously handsome man standing next to me smiling with ease at my friends.

"Miles, these are my friends, Emma and Dr. Sawyer King." I pointed to an ashen Emma, who had probably recently vomited given the only thing it looked like she had touched of her dinner was her bread. Normally she could eat the men under the table.

Sawyer stood up to shake Miles's hand. Emma remained seated, smiling through her obvious discomfort. I hoped she felt better once her first trimester was over.

"It is a pleasure, Dr. and Mrs. King." Miles took Sawyer's hand, giving him a firm handshake.

Emma used all her energy and waved. "We don't stand on cere-mony around here. Please call us by our first names."

Everyone at the table nodded to concur, which was funny since Shelby was famous for Southern manners and used them all the time on us. I kind of loved it when she called me Miss Aspen.

Ryder and Shelby, aka the world's most attractive couple, stood up next. Ryder resembled a Hollywood star with his masculine build and tanned skin marked with tasteful tattoos. His bride beaming by his side was more gorgeous than him. Her long blonde hair shone like a crown while her blue eyes sparkled like jewels. Pregnancy had been kinder to her than Emma. It had appeared to only enhance her beauty and appetite. Shelby was now eating like a teenage boy. Her plate showed a half-devoured bacon cheeseburger and only a few fries left. She had confessed to sneaking potato chips into bed with her every night. Her thin figure didn't reflect her new snacking habits one bit.

"This is Ryder and Shelby Prescott. Shelby owns a clothing boutique in town and Ryder is the owner of the Worlds Collide app."

Making introductions drove home how successful my friends were. I tried my best to not compare myself to them, but times like these were glaring reminders of how backwards I had lived my life. My friends had all graduated from college—except Ryder, but despite that, he owned a multi-million-dollar tech company. They each had successful careers before getting married and starting a family. Even my goofball friends Jenna and Brad, who introduced themselves, owned a comedy club that did well. I didn't think they'd ever getting rich off it, but it paid the bills and they loved it.

That was all I wanted. To do something I loved that paid the bills with a little extra to give my girl all she deserved. Was that too much to ask?

I stared at Miles, who was going through the handshaking rounds, politely inquiring more about each person, and wondered if taking this job would set me on the same path as my friends. Not like being a nanny was a career changer, but being able to put on a resume that I was Taron Taylor's personal assistant could look good and open doors. Maybe I could even love it.

Miles flashed me a grin as soon as the introductions and pleasantries were over. I smiled back before I could stop myself. A few more grins erupted because of it. Emma, Jenna, and Shelby were practically giddy over it. Before they said anything embarrassing, I bounced Henry on my hip, drawing attention to him. "This is Henry."

"I'm three." He held up his fingers as if he knew he would get asked that question.

All the women went doe-eyed over the cutie. The kid was going to be a heartbreaker when he grew up. I couldn't help myself and kissed his cute fingers, making him giggle.

Jenna decided it was time to stir some trouble. "So, Miles, did Aspen tell you we just read *Silent Stones* for our book club? On her recommendation, of course."

My soon-to-be ex-friends did a horrible job of stifling their snickers.

Miles's eyes widened about as much as his big fat grin that was directed toward me. "She failed to mention that when we last met." He was kind enough not to linger on me or embarrass me further. He turned his attention toward the table. "I do hope you enjoyed it."

"It was a tad on the squeamish side, but delightful," Shelby drawled. Only she would call it delightful. Brilliant was more like it, but I kept that to myself.

"We are looking forward to the sequel," Emma commented.

"Yeah, when is that coming out? It's been awhile." Jenna was never one for tact.

Miles ran his hand through his thick dark hair, leaving a trail of misplaced curls. "I'm working on it." He focused on me. "It is why I am hoping to convince your lovely friend to accept my job offer tonight."

Henry jumped in again, this time declaring loudly, "I need to use the toilet."

Miles chuckled. "That is my cue. Excuse me. It was nice to meet all of you." He took a reluctant Henry out of my arms. "I'll be right back." He winked. It may have caused a flutter somewhere deep down inside of me. I wasn't exactly sure. It could have been gas for all I knew. I hadn't had flutters in a long time.

Once Miles and Henry were out of sight, I leaned on the table. "What are you all doing here?"

"Eating." Emma played coy.

Jenna fanned herself. "We came to check out the Brit for you. Wow. He's something."

Brad looked highly affronted. "Excuse me?"

Jenna kissed his cheek. "Do you think you could get an English accent?" she teased. I think.

"What's up with women and Brits?" Sawyer asked.

Emma rested her head on Sawyer's shoulder. "You can blame Jane Austen, but no worries, baby, I'll take you any day over the dashing Brit."

That didn't make Sawyer feel any better. His brow raised. "Dashing?"

"I meant . . . well . . . that perfectly describes him." Emma laughed.

Sawyer rolled his eyes but kissed his wife's head anyway.

Ryder, in Ryder and Shelby fashion, pulled his wife onto his lap. His hand landed on her still flat abdomen. He gently rubbed it. Those two had hands for days for each other. "I'm not worried." He nuzzled Shelby's neck.

Shelby threw her arms around Ryder. "I do have to say I prefer a Southern drawl, but," she faced me, "I do believe the handsome Englishman is enamored with you. He couldn't keep his eyes off you."

I pushed off the table and shifted my feet. "That's because I was holding his nephew."

Brad snorted loudly. "The dude is totally into you." He looked to the other men at the table to confer. Sawyer and Ryder nodded in agreement.

"Little Henry seems to be taken with you too." Shelby patted her heart. "He's just precious."

"He is," I agreed.

Jenna leaned forward. "The real question is what do you think of Mr. Sexy?"

Unfortunately, Jenna's description of him was spot-on.

Chapter Five

"I'M SORRY ABOUT my friends." I helped get Henry situated in his booster seat. He insisted on sitting next to me in the booth.

"Not to worry, love. It's good you have excellent mates. And I do love to meet *fans*."

My attention switched from Henry to Miles, who was gloating.

I tucked some hair behind my ear. "I love *Silent Stones*," I conceded. "It might even be my favorite book." It absolutely was, but I felt like I should leave some room for doubt.

His beautiful aqua eyes danced in the dim lighting. "Why was that so hard for you to admit?"

The complete answer was complicated and would only be shared with someone I knew I could trust. Mr. Wickham, as kind as he seemed, didn't qualify. "Um . . ." I picked up a crayon and began coloring with Henry on the children's menu. "I didn't want you to think I was only interested in this position because I was some crazed fan." I offered part of the truth.

He chuckled. "I have known many crazed fans, and you don't qualify. I thank you for that."

I looked up from my stellar coloring job—my blue bear was going to be a masterpiece. "Are crazy fans a problem for you?" I hadn't thought about that aspect.

"Back home in London, once in a while a daft fan will get it in her head that she fancies me, and she'll do something ridiculous like kiss me unexpectedly or hand me her knickers."

My brows shot up. I bet they weren't granny panties. "What do you do when that happens?"

"It depends on how good the kiss is and how sexy the knickers are."

I manifested my disappointment by sighing audibly. Though I should have expected his response.

Miles hung his head. "That was an ill-fated joke, I see."

I bit my lip, sorry I had jumped to a conclusion. "I'm—"

Henry interrupted by holding up his picture. "Look what I made."

I was happy for the distraction. I took Henry's picture and admired how he had scribbled over the forest scene. "You did such a good job."

Henry beamed with pride.

I ruffled his curly locks.

"Aspen," the most alluring voice spoke my name.

My eyes lifted, meeting Miles's.

Miles wore a thoughtful gaze. "I'm not sure what sort of man you are used to, but I promise you, while under my employment you will be respected, and I will make sure no harm comes to you or your daughter from any of my fans. If it makes you feel any better, hardly anyone recognizes me in America." He sounded relieved by that fact.

"Thank you," I whispered.

The smile returned to his face. "I hope this means you will accept my offer."

"I have some questions first."

His laughter reverberated between us. "I figured you might."

Our server showed up before I could ask any. I had already worked out the pizza situation for Henry before we sat down, so only Miles and I had to order. Miles ordered a veggie wrap, which didn't surprise me. His physique was lean, and the glow of his skin said he took good care of himself. I, on the other hand, needed some comfort food, so I went with the grownup grilled cheese on homemade sourdough bread and tomato soup.

Henry made sure to get more of my attention by handing me a crayon. "You color."

I was happy to be bossed around by a three-year-old. I took the yellow crayon and filled in the sun while Henry continued his reign of terror with the black crayon.

"You're good with him," Miles commented.

"Are you trying to persuade me?"

"Very much so." He tapped on the table. "Why don't you ask your questions."

My coloring became more like a few strokes here and there while I faced my potential employer. I took a breath and began my interrogation. "Well . . . first off, why were you given custody of . . .?" I pointed to the adorable boy now chugging apple juice from a sippy cup.

"Ah, you read up on me."

I nodded, unashamed.

"That's good. We should be honest and upfront with each other considering the amount of time we could be spending together in the very near future. Tell me what you've read, and I will tell you the *real* story."

I had come across some interesting tabloid type articles about his family and the fight over Henry, so I wasn't sure what was true or not. Honestly, some of it was straight out of Shelby's soap opera life. Family feuds and vast amounts of wealth. "I read something about a custody battle and your father, Baron Greaves, intervening." Miles was part of Britain's aristocracy, though I couldn't figure out why he and his father had different last names. "Does that make you Lord Wickham?"

Miles let out a derisive laugh. "Darling, they don't pass down titles to bastard sons."

Before I could digest that tidbit, Henry slammed his sippy cup on the table. "Bastard!"

Miles pinched the bridge of his nose and let out a heavy sigh.

I pressed my lips together to make sure I didn't smile or laugh. "If you haven't figured it out yet, children are like magnifying mirrors, they reflect the best and the worst of us. Always the worst at the most inopportune times, though." I gave him a sympathetic smile. I had been there more times than I wanted to remember. Like when Chloe told an old boss of mine at a company picnic that I called him a douche bag. Thankfully, upper management agreed with me and fired him not long after.

"Henry." Miles gave him a stern look, ready to reprimand him.

"May I give you some advice?" I interrupted Miles.

"Please, I'll take any you have."

"Don't draw attention to it. If you do, he's bound to repeat it."

Miles sank back into the booth, looking worn and at a loss. He rubbed the back of his neck. "Thank you. You must question my sister's sanity leaving me her child, like the rest of my family."

"You do seem like an unlikely candidate." I tried to keep my tone lighthearted to spare his feelings that for some reason I cared about even though I didn't know him. Though in my mind we'd had many conversations. The way Miles's face dropped told me I'd failed, making me feel awful, so I followed up with, "But a mother's love is fierce; she must have seen something in you that maybe you don't even see in yourself."

The corners of his mouth lifted. "You're just trying to make me feel better."

"That's not really how I roll." It hadn't been for a long time.

"You're not like anyone I've ever met . . . well, except," he paused, "never mind. Why don't we get on with the Q&A before I make another blunder with the lad."

The lad in question gave me a huge cheesy smile while I contemplated who Miles thought I reminded him of.

"Where were we?" Miles drew my attention back to him. "Ah, yes, my scandalous family."

"I don't want to pry." Maybe I didn't want to pry, but if I was being honest, I wanted to know what made this man tick and where his beautiful words came from.

Miles waved away my reluctance. "This is well-known fodder and I'm not ashamed. If you did a little more digging, you would find it anyway." He played it off as if he didn't care, but there was a hitch in his timbre that said, although he had resigned himself, he did care a great deal about it. He leaned forward. "You see, Sophie, Henry's mother, was my half-sister. We didn't know of each other's existence until we were young adults. In fact, my father didn't know about me until I was almost university age."

I tilted my head. "Were you given up for adoption?" That would have explained the different last names. Except he had said bastard son, so then I felt inept for asking such a stupid question. But we didn't really say things like bastard son in the U.S.

Miles threw his head back and laughed. "That's not near scandalous enough. No, darling, think more along the lines of an affair and a long-kept secret. Otherwise known as me."

My eyes popped before I could dial back my reaction.

Miles didn't seem to mind by the twinkle in his eye. "Intriguing, is it not?"

I dropped the crayon I wasn't really coloring with anyway, most definitely intrigued. "How do you keep a child a secret?"

The smile he wore so easily faded. "The better question is *why*?"

I found myself clasping my hands and resting them on the table as I leaned toward him, wanting to know exactly why. Miles moved in closer, his hands gliding across the overly shellacked wooden table, landing a fingertip away from mine. My hands retreated a few inches back, while his remained steady as did his eyes fixed on me. Locked in his gaze, for a moment I felt as if we were playing out my daydreams. Something familiar crackled between us. In his eyes, I could see he felt it too.

I rubbed my lips together, nervous. His gaze went right through me. When I couldn't stand it any longer, "Are you going to tell me why?" came falling out of my mouth in whispered tones like I was flirting with him. I wanted to kick myself. This wasn't one of my daydreams.

He nodded slow and deliberate. "First, though, I will tell you how Henry—" Miles threw his nephew, who was continuing his crayon assault on the coloring page, a thoughtful glance that carried with it a touch of loss "—came into my care. As I previously mentioned, Sophie was not made aware of my existence until we were adults."

"But you knew about her?"

"Yes . . . and more." He began to absentmindedly tap his index finger against the table. "I do believe I came as a nasty shock to her and my two other half-siblings—Amelia, the youngest, and our older brother, Charles, the Greaves heir. But Sophie, who was three years my junior, was gentle and loving in nature and sought me out while we both attended Oxford. At first, our relationship was merely superficial and probably mostly based on curiosity, but then she forced me," he grinned to himself, "to meet her once a week at a local pub for drinks. From there, brotherly and sisterly affection began to grow. We became the best of mates." He cleared his throat to cover the emotion that accompanied his words.

I felt his pain so deeply I found my hand reaching toward his to give it a comforting squeeze. Before my hand fell upon his, I came to my senses, and it awkwardly froze right above his. Unfortunately, none of this went unnoticed. Miles's thoughtful expression waited patiently to see what I would do. His hand stayed still as if he welcomed the gesture, but his eyes said he wasn't sure about it. I agreed with his eyes; it was inappropriate behavior for a "job" interview. If one could call this that. I felt more like I was interviewing him. I think if it were up to him, I would already be signing an employment contract.

I withdrew the affection I had carelessly tried to offer, with cheeks burning brightly. He did the kind thing and didn't draw attention to it. He chose instead to pretend to be interested in the sights and sounds around us in the crowded café until my hands were safely gripping my ice water the server had brought when he'd taken our order. I let the cold from the glass seep through me, begging it to put out the fire that had spread across my face.

Miles went right back to his story as if nothing awkward had passed between us. "As the years passed, we both ended up in London. At one point, for a short period of time, we shared a flat while I was a struggling writer, driving a taxi to make ends meet. She, on the other hand, was well on her way to becoming one of the most sought-after interior designers in the city. I had refused her offer at first," he said fondly, "taking it as pity since she always felt guilty that she had the advantages of the Greaves name and wealth. But once again, she got her way. For as demure as she was, she knew how to bowl me over."

My almost numb hands fell away from my glass. "But if your family knew you existed by that time, why didn't they help you too?"

He took a long drink of his water while he thought about how to answer me. "We are coming to the crux of the story. I promise I will enlighten you."

Henry started getting wiggly and began to whine about how long it was taking for his food to arrive. To keep him entertained, I took my doodle notebook, as my mom called it, out of my bag. She'd said I'd had one since I was two. "Do you want to help me draw a picture of George?" His bear and faithful companion was seated next to him in the corner.

Henry nodded vigorously and armed himself with the brown crayon.

I used a pencil from my bag and began to outline George's body. Henry, who like any three-year-old I had ever met, was impatient and started coloring the picture of his friend before I was even halfway finished.

"You're an artist." Miles admired my scribbled-on artwork.

"Hardly." The only classes I'd ever taken were in high school. My only claim to fame was when I won the blue ribbon at the district art festival my junior year. My parents were so proud, they had the charcoal drawing I did of the old abandoned mine above Carrington Cove framed. It still hung on the wall in their home office, near the shelves where my parents saved every award my siblings and I had ever won. Granted, my siblings occupied most of the shelves. There were a few soccer championship trophies of mine scattered amongst the many academic accolades my older sister and younger brother had received over the years.

My siblings deserved the recognition. Vanessa, my older sister, was a clerk for a federal judge in Washington D.C., and my little brother, Troy, was just hired by NASA in Florida. At least I gave them a grandchild. Mind you, it wasn't how they hoped, but they loved

Chloe like she was the air they breathed. My siblings, though each married, had yet to fulfill my parents' wish for more grandchildren. They and their spouses were more focused on their careers right now.

Miles angled his head to get a better look at my simple drawing. "You have talent."

I didn't argue with him. I was anxious for him to finish his story. I went back to absentmindedly drawing for Henry while he continued to color everything I drew.

Before Miles continued, I saw him flexing his fingers as if he was trying to prepare himself for the painful memories he was about to share with me. Once his fingers relaxed, he began again. "Sophie," he said her name with such love, "was determined to be better than her family, *our* family," he conceded. "Especially when it came to her husband and son. She wanted Henry to live a life outside of family secrets, lies, and propriety. I've always lived outside the 'familial' rules." He smiled to himself, but it only lasted for a moment. His handsome face soon turned somber. "So . . ." he had to take a deep breath, "after the accident . . ." his voice cracked.

I had that urge again to reach out and comfort him, but this time I stopped before I made a fool of myself.

Miles steadied himself. ". . . my sister lived for a few hours." A sheen of mist covered his eyes.

My free hand flew to my mouth.

"It was then," he hurried to say what he needed to, "that I found out she and Kevin had made me the executor of their estate and guardian to Henry."

Henry looked up at me and I brushed back his hair. My heart ached for him and his uncle.

"She made me swear I would bring him here and raise him better than she could. An impossible task."

I wanted to ease his pain. I thought for a moment before leaning forward. "She paid you the highest compliment and honor. I would believe her."

He too leaned forward with hope in his eyes that what I said was true. "Will you help me honor my sister's last wishes?"

Chapter Six

I KEPT NERVOUSLY staring up at Miles between each bite. He was doing the same. We hadn't said much after our food had arrived and his plea for help. Meanwhile, Henry was enjoying his cheese pizza, at least what was making it into his mouth. He refused to let me cut it into smaller pieces. He wanted to eat it like a big boy. Thankfully, I had thought to tuck napkins into his collared shirt. I'd never seen a young child so properly or expensively dressed.

Miles set his veggie wrap down and wiped his mouth with his napkin. "I've frightened you."

I lowered the spoon for my tomato soup and rested it in my half empty bowl. "Not at all. But you've given me a lot to think about." Not that I didn't feel the weight of what he was proposing, but it didn't scare me. Scary was finding a note on your kitchen table from your husband announcing he was leaving, and you were on your own. I imagined Miles might be having some of those same feelings now. There was nothing as terrifying and wonderful as raising a child.

He cocked his head. "What are you thinking?"

I looked between him and Henry, who gave me a messy tomato sauce grin that melted my heart. My eyes landed on his uncle, who did some other things to my heart that scared me. I was kind of hoping my heart would stay permanently dormant where men were concerned. This way I was sure to never get it broken again. Miles's thoughtful stare, however, had my heart skipping beats. I rubbed my heart, not sure what to think. It stung like a numb foot once you began to move it to get the blood flowing again. Was it wise to work for a man who elicited such a response?

"Well," I bit my lip, "I have a few more questions." That seemed like the easiest way to answer.

He leaned back. "You want more details about my sordid family affairs?"

"Yes, I mean no, I mean . . ." I sighed, feeling foolish.

Miles seemed to enjoy how flustered I was by the playful arch of his brow.

"What I meant to say was, I only need to know if it will impact my employment. If there is a custody dispute, I don't want to be out of a job." And from the little Miles had told me, I didn't want him to lose Henry either—little Henry, whose eyes were becoming very heavy now that his belly was full.

I caught the poor baby mid nod and wiped his sweet face off before I placed him on my lap. His eyes fluttered several times, trying to fight off the sleep his body so desperately wanted. Miles and I both laughed softly at his feeble attempt to stay awake. I employed a tactic I used to use on Chloe when she was a toddler. I stroked Henry's brow and nose until he could resist no longer and peacefully rested in my arms.

Miles's gaze was filled with both admiration and envy. "You are a natural. Sophie was too. It was as if she was born to be a mother."

I shifted Henry, pulling him closer to me. "It's the best thing that has ever happened to me, and why I need to know exactly what I'm getting into."

He pressed his lips together. "And you shall know everything, but first, I suppose I should ask you a bit more about your own situation. Your daughter is twelve, correct?"

"Yes."

"Where is her father? If you don't mind me asking."

My entire body tensed just thinking of Leland. "Supposedly Texas. Why?"

"You don't know for sure?"

"He hasn't exactly been involved in Chloe's life, so it's not relevant." I couldn't keep the bite out of my tone.

He put his hands up. "I apologize if I've hit a nerve. I'm only inquiring to see what limitations you have in case I were to move back to London."

"What do you mean by 'limitations'?"

"Well, if things work out the way I'm hoping they will, I would want you to continue to work for me there."

I gasped. I had dreamt about visiting the UK since I read my first regency novel as a teen. I imagined garden parties with handsome, eligible men of good fortune (of course) who would want to be my suitors. That turned into a love affair with the BBC and PBS Master-piece Theater. Both allowed me to be in love vicariously, not only with the handsome men that starred in their shows, but with the UK itself. I'd always thought one day, after Chloe had graduated from college, I might be able to save enough money to visit, but never had I thought about living there. And most definitely not with someone who I had already had some vicarious dates with.

Miles narrowed his eyes. "Would that be a problem for you?"

I sank back against the booth, careful not to jostle Henry too much. "I don't know," I answered honestly. My mind was spinning with the possibility.

"Would your ex-husband prevent it?"

"I doubt it; besides, I have physical custody of Chloe." Leland did have visitation rights, but if he ever took me to court, I would bring up the little matter of all the child support he owed.

"Is there someone else?"

"No," I laughed.

Miles tilted his head. "You're single?" He swallowed.

"Is that a problem?"

He drummed his fingers against the table. "I admit I was hoping you weren't."

"Why?" I was absolutely perplexed.

He stopped tapping his fingers and cleared his throat. "We are now getting to those scandalous details I promised."

I was all ears.

"You asked before how you keep a baby a secret. In my mum's case, you never tell anyone you're pregnant and you leave town."

"She told no one at all?"

"Not a soul. Not even her own parents."

"Was she afraid?" I remember how scared I was to tell my parents I was pregnant. I knew how disappointed they would be, especially given who the father was. They hated Leland, for good reason.

He looked up as if he was consulting someone before he met my gaze. "She was ashamed," he admitted heavily. "You see, she was my brother's nanny."

Oh. My eyes popped.

"Yes," he responded to my reaction. "Quite scandalous, don't you think?"

I remained still. Not sure how to respond to the rhetorical question.

He pressed on regardless. "The *esteemed* Baron Greaves," Miles hissed, "was having a torrid love affair with his very young and beautiful nanny." Miles began flexing his fingers again. "Mum, God rest her soul, loved him and didn't want to cause him any complications," he scoffed. "She took on the burden of raising me alone."

That pricked my heart. "I'm sorry about your mother."

He waved away my condolences, not wanting to dwell on it.

I didn't press the issue further. "How did he find out about you then?" I hesitated to ask given his agitated state. It was apparent he didn't think too highly of his father.

"Mum," he sighed. "She always wanted what was best for me. We always managed to scrape by, but she said that wasn't the life I was intended to lead. It was her wish that I attend Oxford and live my dream of becoming a writer. She made that happen," he lowered his voice, "by telling my *father* the truth."

"How did that go over?"

He laughed sardonically. "Not well, as you can imagine."

I lowered my head. I could imagine all too well. Leland blamed the pregnancy on me. I broke up with him that night. If only I'd had the good sense to keep it that way. But no, he came crawling back with a tiny diamond ring begging me to marry him. I was so foolish and afraid. I wondered who would ever love me once I had a baby. Then, not even my own husband did. I promised myself after Leland left for the last time I would never think so little of myself again.

"Did he blame her?" I asked quietly.

"For keeping me from him, yes."

My head tilted up, surprised by his response. "He wanted you?"

Miles shrugged, looking off into the distance. "Perhaps, but he disliked the inconvenience of a," he lowered his voice, "bastard son. His wife, Imogen, was none too pleased."

"Did they divorce?"

He barked out a laugh. "No darling, my father's title and wealth were worth staying in a bloody loveless marriage. She was more put out that he hadn't done a better job of keeping his philandering ways a secret."

"So she knew the entire time he was unfaithful?"

"Of course she did."

I hated being so nosy, but I was intrigued. "If she knew he was cheating and didn't care, why did your father tell her about you?"

Miles let out a slow breath. "I'm not sure, perhaps for spite. He claimed to have loved my mother and was devastated when she disappeared. He always suspected that Imogen had driven her away."

I stared down at Henry, trying to make sense of Miles's sad tale, but I don't think there was any sense to be had out of it.

"You are wondering why my father stayed, are you not?"

It bothered me that he could read me so well. I looked up and found him peering at me as if he too were concerned with how well he could read me. But his concern was quickly replaced with a warm smile.

"I am curious," I admitted.

"Tradition and unwritten societal rules keep my father and Imogen miserably together. It is one of the reasons why Sophie sought out the American."

"Did she love him?" fell out of my mouth.

"Very much. Kevin showed her a way of life she never knew. I hate that they both perished, but it was merciful they went together." He clapped his hands and gave me a pointed look. "You are probably wondering why I'm sharing all this with you. I have good reasons for doing so. First, you need to know that as much as my siblings Amelia and Charles, and even their *dear* mother, Imogen, have made their arguments that they are better suited to raise young Henry, my father, for all his faults, has silenced them on the issue. Henry is to remain in my care as Sophie and Kevin wished."

That was a relief if I decided to take this job. But what came out of his mouth next left me unsettled.

Miles leaned back and gripped the table all while tenderly looking at me holding his sweet nephew. "Aspen," he whispered my name as if he wanted to keep it a secret for only himself just like I had imagined him doing many times in my dreams. It made me hold my breath, waiting to see if he would lean in next. When he did, I bit my lip. It drew his attention toward my mouth. I could almost feel this thumb gliding across my lower lip. He raised his hand almost as if he was imaging the same thing, but his hand dropped, and he steeled himself. "Aspen," he spoke again, this time in less hushed tones. "I must admit you are fetching, very fetching, indeed."

I swallowed hard and blinked an inordinate amount of times. Normally, I would have stopped him right there and told him I wasn't interested, but the words never came. More disconcerting was there would have been no truth in them had they been spoken.

"If circumstances were different, I would have invited you to dinner for strictly personal reasons, but . . ." he forced himself to say, "I need to think about someone else for a change, like Sophie reminded me. I must think about Henry." He sat up straight as a pin. "If you agree to work for me, I promise you we will have a purely business relationship. For the sake of Henry, I will not entangle myself in a scandal with his nanny."

Every muscle in my face worked to create a full-scale frown.

Miles returned it with a pressed-lip smile. "Please do not take offense. I'm not implying that you would even entertain the thought. For all I know, I repulse you."

I wish.

"I only want to be upfront with you. As such, I will require that as part of your contract, you will agree that there will be no romantic entanglements between us. This is as much for your protection as it is mine."

There was no way to hold back the incredulous look on my face. "You must think very highly of yourself." Now I was sounding like my old self.

He chuckled. "On the contrary, it is you I think highly of."

I stared down at Henry's angelic face, not sure how to respond. And, admittedly, I felt stupid. For a moment, I had let myself fall victim to his charm. Worse, I welcomed it.

"What do you say, Aspen, will you come work for me?"

I contemplated his offer while stroking Henry's curls. My heart said I was meant to take care of this little boy. Almost like a voice that spoke to my heart pleading for me to. For a second, I thought it was Sophie. What a crazy thought.

But what about Henry's uncle and his contract? Another little voice asked, why does that bother you? You don't like men. *Or do you?* it taunted. Great, now even my subconscious was becoming prickly. But it was right. Maybe this was the perfect situation for me. More money, free rent, and a contract guaranteeing I wouldn't have to worry about any unwanted advances. *Unwanted?* my annoying subconscious asked. Seriously, she and I were going to have a talk about her attitude.

I looked up and found Miles waiting anxiously for my reply. I flashed him a smile. "We are a match made in heaven."

Miles's shoulders dropped. "Darling, believe me, I wish we—"

"You misunderstand me," I interrupted him before he made me second-guess myself. "I meant that 'romantic entanglements,' as you call them, have only caused me grief, so I avoid them at all costs."

He released a heavy breath. "I should have known."

"How could you have?"

"You remind me of someone close to my heart," he admitted reluctantly. "But that is neither here nor there." A sense of loss lingered in his words. "Do you accept my offer?"

"I do."

Chapter Seven

"HE'S MAKING YOU sign a contract that says what?" Emma walked slowly beside me in the crisp morning toward the soccer field for warmups before the game. She had just finished puking behind her jeep.

I carried the bag of soccer balls for her. Normally Sawyer would have, but one of his patients had an eye emergency this morning, so he was at their clinic in Carrington Cove. I was glad for the time with her. "That there will be no romantic *entanglements*," I exaggerated, it was such a funny word, "between us." I decided to leave out the reasons why for now. Someday I would share them all with my friends when there was more time.

Emma snorted. "What does that even mean?"

I shifted the heavy bag on my shoulder. "Basically, that we will have a business-only relationship."

Emma blew into her hands to warm them up. It was chilly this morning. "Well, that's too bad. From the way you two behaved last night, we all thought you might decide to play house instead."

I stopped and set down the bag. "What are you talking about?"

She took ahold of me to steady herself. Her baby meant business. "The sexual tension at your table last night was crazy hot. It's why we didn't bother saying goodbye to you. The way he looked at you and the way you would blush and lean in was like watching a rom-com play out in real life. We all thought for sure you had finally met your match. That the dashing Brit would be the one to finally get to you."

"I have no idea what you are talking about." I snatched up the bag and slung it over my back, offering my arm to Emma as a support.

Emma leaned into me. "You are such a liar."

I totally was. "It doesn't matter, because come Monday morning, I'm going to sign the contract his barrister is drawing up, and I'm going to make more money than I thought I ever would and give Chloe everything she needs," my stupid voice cracked.

"Hey." Emma rubbed my arm. "What happened last night?"

"Nothing," I lied . . . again.

"Aspen, it's me."

I leaned my head on hers, so grateful for our years of friendship. "It's just, I feel dumb. There was a moment when he admitted that he was attracted to me and wished he was free to ask me out. And maybe for a microsecond I kind of hoped he would." After all, no one had ever called me fetching. It felt like more than telling someone they were beautiful. It was like saying you encompass my senses. Ugh, listen to me. I seriously needed to quit watching British regency period shows.

Emma found in her the strength to grab my shoulders and shake them. "Then why in the world did you agree to take this job? He could find another nanny."

"Besides my awful track record with men, I feel like I'm supposed to be his nanny. There is something about Henry. I feel like he needs me."

"What about what you need?"

"I don't need a man."

"They're kind of nice." Emma giggled.

"You're still in the honeymoon phase."

Emma smooshed my cheeks. "Listen to me, it's not that. And I'm sorry, I don't care what you say. You never had a 'honeymoon phase' with Leland, so you don't even know what that means. But by the way, they're fabulous and you deserve one. Regardless, though, I saw the way you looked at Miles last night. Your sparkly eyes said you missed whatever it was that was igniting between the two of you."

I closed my eyes and tried to blow a breath out, but Emma's hands made it sound more like I was blowing raspberries, which made us both laugh. She dropped her hands and took my arm back.

"Em, this job could be a game changer for me and Chloe."

"I get that." She leaned more into me. "Just make sure you don't forget it's not the only game you could win."

I was about to ask her what she meant, but her assistant coach, Gwendolyn, who was basically a trophy coach, waved at us from her lounge chair in her skintight designer jeans with sky-high leopard-print boots. "Ladies," she called, "I asked Mario," her Latin lover and husband number three or four, I couldn't remember, "to run to Star-bucks and get us all hot chocolate. Isn't that nice?"

"Do you know what would be nice?" Emma grumbled. "If she actually helped me coach." Emma's tired eyes lit up. "Now that you work for Miles, does that mean you would be free to help me coach?"

I thought about it for a second, excited about the prospect and the doors taking this job would open for me not only professionally, but personally. I could finally be the kind of mom I'd always wanted to be, volunteering at the school and, of course, being more involved in the sport Chloe and I loved so much. "I would love to. Just let me make sure it's okay with Miles if I bring Henry to practice with me."

Emma threw her arms around me. "You know, I think this job is going to be the best thing ever."

I thought so too on Sunday when I brought Chloe with me to Miles's home to see where we would be living and to sign my employ-ment contract. When we entered the gated community up on the mountain above Carrington Cove, Chloe's eyes widened as she took in all the magnificent homes, each with their own distinctive look. One was reminiscent of a castle, another a lodge, but Miles's home was in a class of its own. The steel, wood, and glass house was the crown jewel of the neighborhood. It was set up above the other homes as if it was meant to be their shining light. I would imagine in the dark it was just that with all the floor-to-ceiling windows the house boasted. I couldn't believe we would be living in such dream surroundings.

I turned down the radio with my sweaty palms feeling a little self-conscious driving up the long driveway lined with large pine trees in my old Subaru that had tears in each seat. I may have grown up in Carrington Cove, but my parents lived in the older section on a couple of acres that they bought back when Carrington Cove was a one street-light town. My dad was a geologist for a local gas and oil company and had provided a comfortable life for us, but he was never going to be wealthy. Though they could sell their house and property for a small fortune now, thanks to the extensive growth Carrington Cove had seen over the years. I didn't see that happening. Mom and Dad loved it here. Besides, this is where Chloe was, and she was their life. Even though my parents were wary about me taking this job.

Mom had done her own research on Miles, even going as far as writing a report for me. She was dad's unofficial research assistant, so she lived and breathed digging for information. I had a nice fifteen-page report that she had spiral-bound and laminated. I'd shoved it in my glove compartment after skimming through it and laughing. It was filled with pictures printed off the internet of him and her hand-written captions that were all questions like, "Don't you think he's a little old to be wearing such tight jeans?" The answer was no. He looked amazing. Other captions included, "He's forty, why isn't he married?" She also listed all his books and ranked them by critical reviews and how much money they had made. *Silent Stones* was on the top. She had informed me she would be reading every book and doing a book report on each one. Oh, how I loved my silly mom. Dad, I believe, was holding out judgment until Mom came to her conclusions. I think he thought it couldn't be worse than marrying Leland, and it meant that Chloe and I would be closer, so for now he was tentatively giving his approval.

I glanced at Chloe to find her eagerly peering out the window with her hand over her mouth, amazed by the grandeur. "Can I invite Brooke over here?"

"Of course. But you know we won't be living in the main house."

"Who cares. I bet the guesthouse is awesome too."

We were about to find out. We pulled up in front of the four-car garage that was attached to the house by a covered walkway. The contemporary rustic home loomed large, but not as big as the decisions I had made in the last couple of days.

I wrapped my arm around Chloe as we made our way to the front door. I admired how the landscape around the house stayed true to the Rocky Mountain scenery. Wild roses and boulder raspberry shrubs dotted the landscape among the junipers and Rocky Mountain maples. However, my favorite were the aspen trees my parents fondly named me after. They said when I was born, my hair shined golden like the leaves of the aspen in the fall. My hair had darkened over the years, but I loved that story.

I gave Chloe one good squeeze before I rang the doorbell. It wasn't too long before I heard the pitter patter of little feet and Henry's adorable voice yelling, "Nanny is here!"

Chloe grinned at me.

Miles opened the door and my stomach swooped. He looked too handsome in a form-fitting gray turtleneck and those jeans my mom had commented about. I barely caught his smile before I turned my focus on Henry. He was the safe option. No swooping, only some heart pricks where the little guy was stealing it piece by piece.

Henry ran to me and I bent down and picked him up.

Chloe was immediately drawn to him too. "He's so cute." She took his chubby hand.

"I am cute," Henry was quick to agree, making Chloe and I giggle.

"I'm cute too." Miles didn't want to be left out.

My eyes lifted to find his already peering at me. I reminded myself and my swooping stomach this was strictly business and to play it cool. "Hello," I greeted him.

"Hello, lo— I mean, Aspen," he stuttered. Apparently, I wasn't the only one who needed a reminder. "Please come in. It's a bit nippy today."

Chloe and I entered the grand home, but before I could admire the gorgeous place, I made introductions. "Miles, this is my daughter, Chloe. And, Chloe, this is Henry." I bounced him on my hip.

"It is a pleasure to meet you, Chloe." Miles gave her a warm welcome.

Chloe seemed intimidated by him and tucked some hair behind her ear. It was then I remembered she thought he was hot. Which he was. She, like always, recovered quickly and found her footing. I adored that aspect of her, along with so many other things that made her wonderful. "It's nice to meet you too," Chloe politely responded before turning right back to Henry, who was happy to garner all the attention.

"Can I get you anything to drink?" Miles offered.

Chloe and I both declined.

Miles bounced on the balls of his bare feet as if he was trying to get rid of some nervous energy. "Well, shall we take a tour before we go over the contract?" he asked me. "My barrister made the changes you requested."

He sent me a copy yesterday and I was taken aback by the clauses about travel. I supposed I should have expected that he would want me to travel with him at times with Henry, but this was a different world for me. I requested that if I needed to travel with him, it be no longer than three days. I didn't want to be away from Chloe for even that long, but it seemed reasonable. Miles offered if it needed to be longer, he would only ask me to accompany him if it was during Chloe's school breaks and he would arrange for her to join us as well. I thought it was a sweet gesture. I also requested that the initial contract be for a year. Miles agreed that would be good for both of us. I knew this meant he could easily terminate me after a year, but my plan was to save as much money as possible and do a good job so that he would be willing to at least give me a good reference. So, in the event we parted ways, I would still be better off than I was now.

"I'd love a tour." I glanced around the magnificent home. Stone walls dramatically showcased the height of the room. The white oak floors and neutral palette of the furniture and walls added warmth. The simplicity of it all made it stunning. It was easy to see why Sophie was such a sought-after interior designer. She had left her mark and it was beautiful.

Miles seemed grateful to have something to do other than stare at me. He headed straight for the great room with floor-to-ceiling windows that gifted us with a pristine view of the nearby mountain peaks. The low-profile furniture around the stone hearth with a fire burning in it added to the peaceful feeling of the room. I also noted how impeccably clean it was. It didn't look like a three-year-old lived there, or anyone really. Maybe he had a housekeeper as well as a chef.

"I want you to both feel at home here." Miles looked between Chloe and me before pointing out the window. "You can see the guesthouse from here."

Chloe and I eagerly joined him at the window with Henry still on my hip. Henry was happy to add his fingerprints to the unspotted windows. I noticed how that made Miles cringe, but he didn't say anything. I almost told him he should get used to smudges on everything, but I figured he would soon learn it all on his own.

The guesthouse was more like a stone cottage set back behind the large yard that was covered in fallen leaves and accented by large pine trees. It also boasted magnificent windows. I couldn't wait to see the inside.

"Sophie," Miles always paused when he said her name, "hired an architect from Scotland to design the guesthouse. She had seen something similar on holiday in the Highlands. I hope it will be adequate."

Adequate? He should see my cramped apartment with water-stained ceilings. Chloe and I smiled at each other, both thinking the same thing before I responded to Miles. "It's perfect, as is your home."

"It doesn't feel quite like my home. I'm used to living in a flat with views of the city," he responded wistfully.

I got the feeling he wasn't planning on making this his permanent residence. Which probably meant I would only be working for him for the year. As dreamy as it sounded to live in London, assuming he would even want me to continue working for him, I wouldn't put my career over Chloe. Which meant I needed to learn everything I could in the coming months to make my resume shine.

As we walked up the floating staircase, the stairs made me nervous for Henry. They weren't exactly child friendly. He could easily get stuck between the steps or possibly fall through with little effort on his part.

"We can play with my toys," Henry informed me on the way up the stairs.

"What do you like to play?" I thought that was a good thing to know.

"Trains and puppets!" he shouted, making his voice echo through the open home.

"Henry," Miles turned around, "what have I told you about shouting inside?"

Henry buried his head in my chest, unwilling to answer him.

Miles's eyes filled with regret. "It's hard for me to work if it's noisy," Miles felt the need to explain to me.

I kissed the top of Henry's head. "We will get our shouts out outside, won't we?"

Henry nodded his head against me.

Miles gave me a grateful smile before leading the way.

I was beginning to see how unprepared Miles was to raise a child. I could see why his sister thought it was important for him to care about someone else besides himself. I believed men in general were selfish by nature. Not to say they were that way on purpose, but for some reason, it seemed like women naturally were able to see what needed to be done and they intuitively knew how to nurture. For men, in my unfortunate experience, it was something they had to learn, and many of them chose not to. There were exceptions. Sawyer, for one, made Emma's needs a priority. He could even anticipate her wants and needs before she expressed them. My father was another good example, but Mom said it took years for him to get that way. That's how I saw Brad. He was becoming less selfish since Elliott was born.

I hoped Miles would allow Henry to change him.

I stopped in my tracks when we got to the nursery. The walls came alive with a scene of dancing trees, perched owls watching over the children, and an enchanted forest in the depths beyond. I even spied a tiny boat full of red-tailed foxes floating down a winding river.

Henry wriggled out of my arms and took Chloe's hand to show her his collection of books and his wooden train set displayed on a large wood table. He showed Chloe how to push the train and make choo choo noises, and was delighted when Chloe mimicked him. His giggle was intoxicating.

Miles spoke, drawing my attention back to him. He kept his distance with his hands in his pockets. An unspoken uneasiness lingered between us. Maybe he was embarrassed for sharing so much about his family. Or perhaps he regretted telling me that he found me fetching.

"Do you think Chloe could watch Henry for a few minutes while I speak to you in my office?"

I didn't think that would be an issue other than I feared to be alone with him. He made all my dormant senses flicker back on—like he pushed the power button on an old computer and my operating systems were slowly but surely coming back online. My brain was trying desperately to manually override the system. I didn't have any use for flutters and raised pulses. I certainly didn't need the longing for slow kisses. I had forgotten how much I missed them. I needed it to stay that way, but every time I looked at Miles, I found myself aching for warm lips—his lips.

No. No. I couldn't afford to think like that. I wouldn't think it.

"Sure," I stammered, trying to get thoughts of kissing Miles out of my head. "Chloe, would you mind playing with Henry for a bit?"

She looked up from the train wreck Henry just initiated and grinned. "Nope."

"Thank you, we won't be long," Miles added.

I followed Miles out the door and down the hall, taking note of all the black and white photographs of London that graced the walls. "Are these yours?" I asked.

Miles stopped and admired one of the River Thames. "They are. My *friend* took these and gifted them to me before I left."

Friend? Was this a woman friend? "Sounds like a good friend."

He rubbed his lips together. "She can be when she chooses."

So it *was* a she. I got the feeling there was more to the story, but I didn't ask. I was determined to not only keep our relationship all business, but I meant to keep him at arms-length, just like every other man in existence.

He gave the picture one more good look and sighed absent-mindedly. "Shall we head to my office?"

I nodded and followed, but not before catching the signature—PW with a heart around it in the corner of all the photos. Interesting.

Miles pointed out his bedroom, guest room, and gym on the way to his office that honestly blew me away. The entire back wall was a window with the most gorgeous view of the nearby meadow. Not to take anything away from the beautiful landscape, but it had nothing on the large free-standing white board filled with the outline of his book. I tried not to stare, but Isabella's name and her being held captive jumped out at me. I knew it.

Miles flipped the whiteboard around. "Sorry, I'm not ready to share her story with anyone yet. And I'll need you to sign an NDA before I do."

I found it intriguing that he called it *her* story. It sounded almost as if he were talking about a loved one. "Of course." I turned my gaze back to the window. "I didn't mean to pry."

"Not to worry. I shouldn't have been so careless. I'm not used to sharing my space."

My head drifted in his direction. He was laying out what I assumed was my contract on his desk. "Are you sure you want Chloe and me living here?"

He set the papers down and, instead of looking directly at me, his eyes roved down the length of me. I looked down at my long sleeve tunic and leggings wondering if maybe I'd dripped food on them. I would have hoped my daughter would have mentioned that. I didn't see any stains. So why was he staring at me so intensely? And why wasn't he answering my question?

"Aspen," he did that name whispering thing again that made my senses go into overload. "I . . ." he looked between me and the contract and back to me again. He clenched his fists and inhaled and exhaled enough to make his shoulders rise and fall. "The answer to your question is yes, Henry needs you." He sounded determined. But he asked me in return, "Are you having second thoughts?" Did he want me to say yes? I swore his eyes were half pleading with me to say exactly that while the other half begged me not to change my mind.

My thoughts, as always, turned to Chloe and what this job meant for her. It didn't matter that I would have to bury deep any stirrings for Miles I might have. Or that for the first time in several years I could picture myself searching for the key to unlock the bolt on the door to my heart. Once again, the key would remain safely hidden.

"No." No second thoughts here.

Chapter Eight

I WAS GETTING a lot of strange stares from my coworkers—my soon-to-be ex-coworkers—when I walked into the bank Monday morning, late, with the cutest three-year-old boy dressed in shorts. I really needed to talk to Miles about getting this little man some pants. I didn't see any in his drawers when I got him ready. The autumn days and nights could get downright cold here. It could even snow. But then again, it was Colorado, so there could be days where it was warm enough to swim outside. You just never knew.

Today was the perfect day, though-sunny, light jacket weather, and I was quitting. Yep, I wasn't even giving two weeks' notice. It was the first rebellious thing I had done in years, and it felt oh so good. Almost as good as that spring break trip to Florida where I inherited the tiny heart tattoo on my butt. Well, maybe. Miles gave me a hefty signing bonus for starting right away and the balance in my bank account did make me feel pretty euphoric.

I headed straight for my cubicle and set Henry on my desk while I filled my bag with the few personal items I'd kept there. The framed picture of Chloe and me doing our best duck faces was really all I cared about. Henry took the picture from me and pointed to Chloe. "I love Co-ee."

Chloe was already in love with him too. He was seriously

adorable. He cried yesterday when we left. And this morning when I showed up early to start my duties as his nanny, he was all smiles and full of hugs and kisses. His uncle, on the other hand, was relieved to finally get some time to write. I had to say I was happy to give it to him. I needed that book.

"Do you want to hold the picture for me?" I asked Henry.

He hugged it to his chest.

I had just placed my stash of protein bars in my bag when overly shiny Stephen appeared in my cubicle. His comb-over this morning looked more like a swirly Q plastered to his forehead with gel. I pressed my lips together so I wouldn't bust out laughing. I was so going to snap a picture of it and send it to my friends.

Stephen smacked his lips, making a sound that made me want to wretch. "You're late," he said with way too much satisfaction. "And," his beady eyes landed on Henry, "this isn't bring-your-child-to-work day."

The idiot didn't even realize Henry wasn't mine, though I would claim him in a heartbeat, especially after he pointed at Stephen and said, "You have a tail on your head."

There was no holding back my laugh. Henry joined in and giggled too, repeating to me, "He has a tail on his head." He was right. It did look like a rat tail.

Stephen turned so red he almost looked purple. He ran his hand over his hair, which only made it worse. He had used so much gel it made his hair stick straight up. While he tried to smooth his hair down, he spluttered, "I'm going to have to write you up for this."

"You do that. I quit." Wow, did that feel amazing to say.

Stephen's jaw dropped. "Is this some sort of practical joke?"

I picked up Henry and gave him a squeeze. "Looks like the joke's on you. You may have to do some actual work until you can find my replacement. Good luck with that." I grabbed my bag and strode right past Stephen. "By the way, you have spinach in your teeth . . . again."

He covered his mouth with his hand and muttered, "I hope you don't expect a good reference."

I laughed as I walked away. "Believe me, I would have never asked you for one. In your last email, you spelled absences *abscesses*. And no, I won't be 'comming' to the training meeting. You might want to invest in a spell checker." How he graduated from college I had no idea.

"For that, you're fired," he yelled.

I waved to him from behind while two of the other personal bankers stood, envious, and silently clapped for me. We all hated him. I bowed as best I could with Henry in my arms.

After I was done grandstanding, I kissed Henry's head. "Let's go say goodbye to Evelyn." She was the one person I would miss. We hopped on the elevator and Henry insisted on pushing the button for the second floor. I never quite understood why kids loved to push the elevator's buttons, but Chloe had as well. She'd had a meltdown when she was four at the doctor's office because I accidentally forgot and did it myself. After her exorcist event, I never touched another button until she was ten.

In Evelyn fashion, she was all smiles when I got off the elevator holding my new charge. Evelyn grinned wider when she recognized Henry. "Is this who I think it is?"

"I'm Henry," he was quick to answer in his adorable accent, leaving no doubt who he was.

Evelyn came around her desk in a happy tizzy. "Please tell me you and the debonair Brit are dating? I had a feeling about you two."

With a shake of my head I dashed her hopes. "Sorry, but," I paused for dramatic effect, "I'm his new nanny and personal assistant."

She playfully smacked my arm. "You're kidding me."

"No. I just told Stephen I quit."

She placed her hand across her heart. "Oh, I would have loved to see that." She wrapped her arms around me and Henry. "I knew there were better doors for you to open. But I'm going to miss you, sweetie." She kissed my cheek. I was sure she left a red lip stain. She loved her lipstick.

"I'm going to miss you too. I wanted to make sure I came to say goodbye, and," I reached into my bag, "I wanted to give you this." I held out a framed sketch I had drawn a while back of the sunflower fields near the bank that she loved to comment on. I was going to give it to her on her birthday next month, but this seemed like a good time.

She took it and tears immediately welled up in her eyes. She pulled me to her. "You are a talented, sweet woman. Thank you, dear."

"You're welcome," she had me choking up. "I'm going to miss you."

She patted Henry's cheeks and then mine. "You will be missed, but I'm happy for you. You deserve better than this place has treated you. I do hope the handsome Brit will realize what a gem he's getting."

"Not sure I qualify, but so far so good." The money was amazing, and did I mention he gave me a luxury SUV to drive? I was sure it was his sister's, but he said as long as I worked for him, it was mine to drive. He probably didn't want me carting around his nephew in my eyesore that now sat in his garage.

"Oh, honey, you are a rare find. Make sure he treats you as such."

"He has to be better than the wicked boss I had here."

She nudged me with her elbow. "If you're lucky, he'll be a tad wicked."

I rolled my eyes. "It's not going to be like that between us." I had signed a contract guaranteeing it. No need to mention that, though.

"I wouldn't be too sure. I saw the way he looked at you."

I had noticed too. "Well, I better get going. I need to get Chloe registered for school in Carrington Cove." She was home with my mom now who was helping me pack. The plan was to move what little furniture I had into my parents' garage since the guesthouse was fully furnished. It was going to be like living in Pottery Barn. I would need to keep reminding Chloe and myself it wasn't going to last, so not to get used to it.

Evelyn tilted her head. "You had to see he was attracted to you." She wouldn't let it go.

"It's strictly business, I promise you." Addendum A in the contract clearly stated it. *To avoid impropriety or scandal, there will be no romantic involvement between the two parties for the period outlined in section two. Both parties willingly agree to these terms . . .* Blah, blah, blah.

"Let me know how that works out for you. Strictly business," she laughed to herself. "I give you two months before you start getting down to business."

"Evelyn." I blushed.

"Mark my words, honey." She gave me one more pat. "Keep in touch."

"I will."

Henry waved bye-bye and we headed downstairs to turn in my ID badge and walk out for the final time. As soon as we got off the elevator, we were approached by the harried Vice President, Mr. Stanley. Otherwise known as Mr. He-wouldn't-know-a-good-employee-if-she-bit-him-in-the-butt. I was honestly surprised to see him so out of sorts. Normally he strutted around in his designer suits trying to look as distinguished as possible. He was one of those men who loved mentioning how many times a week he played racquetball and that he only ate whole foods. I would give it to him—you wouldn't know he was well into his fifties except his hair was more silver now than brown.

"Aspen," Mr. Stanley said, relieved. "I'm glad I caught you. Can we speak for a moment?" He eyed Henry carefully.

"What about?" I was playing it cool.

He cleared his throat. "I just heard the unfortunate news that you've decided to leave. I hate to lose such a valuable employee."

Valuable? I wanted to laugh, but all I could do was stare at him blankly.

He tugged on his collar. "Why don't we talk in my office about your career goals and what it would take for you to stay."

Henry was starting to fidget, so I set him down and took his hand. The wonderful way his hand felt in mine gave me all the courage I needed. "Mr. Stanley, you never appreciated how valuable I was to this organization, and sadly, neither did I. But now that I do, I see I'm worth more than this place."

Mr. Stanley stared, dumbfounded.

"Here's my badge. Have fun with Stephen." I turned with the biggest smile on my face and never looked back.

Chapter Nine

AFTER PUTTING HENRY down to sleep, I knocked on Miles's office door. It had been a long day and I was ready to call it a night. I had forgotten how much work it was to take care of a toddler. They were hardwired to get into everything and had no fear, which was a dangerous combination. On top of taking care of Henry, I had to get Chloe into school and pack up all our clothes, which were currently in disarray in our new home. I had left Chloe to at least put hers away while I brought Henry back to put him to bed. He didn't go willingly, which made me sad. I would have thought he'd be anxious to see his uncle who we had only seen briefly this morning. Miles said he kept weird hours, but he hadn't mentioned how long.

"Just a minute," Miles called.

I could hear him turning his whiteboard around before he answered the door. You don't know how badly I wanted to sneak into his office and read every word on the board. I mean, I signed his NDA, so I wouldn't tell anyone. Though I'm sure my friends would ask.

Miles finally answered the door and my stomach swooped again. I hoped I would become immune to him soon. It didn't help that his chiseled features were sporting sexy stubble and his countenance lit up when he saw me.

"Aspen."

Why did he have to say my name so tenderly? I held up the baby monitor, trying not to think about it. "Henry is sound asleep." After four stories and a song, but I didn't bring that up. "But I wanted to make sure you had this in case he woke up and you didn't hear him." I had to admit I was kind of concerned that Miles wasn't the most attentive parent and was having a hard time adjusting to his new role.

Miles took the monitor. "Thank you. How was he today?"

"Busy." I smiled. "But he's an angel. You're a lucky man." I hoped he knew that.

Miles ran his hand through his tousled curls, looking unsure. It pricked my heart, but I couldn't exactly blame him. He'd been through a lot in the last several weeks. Anyone would need time to adjust.

"Well, good night," I said when he didn't respond. I turned to go.

"Aspen, would you like to come in for a minute?" he asked nervously.

I pointed down the hall. "I should get back to help Chloe unpack."

"Yes, of course . . . but," he paused and rubbed the back of his neck, "I would really like to discuss a few items I need taken care of tomorrow."

"Oh. Okay."

"I promise to only be a few minutes." He opened his door wider, inviting me in.

I skirted past him, making sure I stayed as far away from him as possible. I didn't need any whiffs of his intoxicating cologne. It was bad enough I had to be subject to his good looks and heavenly accent. Not to mention his beautiful words. I had already put *Silent Stones* in its place of honor on the nightstand in my new room.

Miles squinted at me as I passed by, probably wondering what was wrong with me, but didn't point it out. "Please have a seat." He waved toward the two simple wooden chairs that matched the style of the home in front of his neatly organized desk.

I took the one closest to the door and he surprisingly turned the other toward me and sat down close enough that our knees practically touched. Why couldn't he have taken his own chair across the desk from me? There was no avoiding his mind-numbing scent now. I gripped the edge of my seat and started taking shallow breaths.

Miles raised a brow over my behavior. "Am I making you uncomfortable?"

I placed my hands in my lap and lied. "No. Nope. Not at all." How many times did I need to convey that? I was such an idiot.

Miles's lip twitched, but I could tell he was holding back a full-blown smile. He leaned forward and rested his hands on his legs. "I'm happy to hear that. I do hope that you will be comfortable here. Does the guest house have everything you need?"

That and more. I planned to take a long, hot bath in the soaker tub tonight. We hadn't had a tub since we lived with my parents. And I could go on for days about the stylish and comfortable furniture. Reading in bed was going to be so much more pleasurable now. And the extra space alone was a treat. It was three times the size of our apartment. "It's perfect. Thank you."

"Please let me know if you require anything else."

The only thing I needed right now was some distance between us. Each debonair word he spoke was making the numbing agent around my heart fade, leaving a stinging effect I wasn't too fond of. If only I could scoot my chair back without him noticing. Maybe I could lie and tell him my back hurt and I needed to get up and walk around. But did I really want to go down that rabbit hole? He would probably offer to buy a more ergonomically correct chair. I'd noticed how easily he threw around money. Like when I offered to have Henry eat with me and Chloe since he wasn't fond of the chef-prepared meals that Miles preferred, Miles offered to give me a weekly allowance for food on top of all the other perks of the job.

I tucked some hair behind my ear. "I appreciate that."

He tilted his head as if he could read me like a book and knew how uncomfortable I was around him. More like how uncomfortable I was because I wanted to be comfortable around him. "I do hope we will be friends."

I shifted in my chair. "I thought you wanted to keep a purely professional relationship between us."

"I do," he was quick to say. "But," he leaned in closer, "coworkers can be friends. Can they not?"

"You're my boss," I stammered.

"I do hate that term. I would much rather think of us as partners."

"Partners?" My voice hitched up a notch.

"You are helping me raise my nephew and run my business, which is why I wanted to talk to you."

"Great. What can I help you with?" I needed this meeting to end ASAP before I passed out from all the shallow breathing I was doing.

His demeanor said he knew he was having an effect on me. He was probably used to it. After all, women did hand him their panties. Not sure why that was a thing. I mean, were they handing him used underwear? That was plain gross. Or did they buy a spare pair? In that case, what a waste of money. Nice undies weren't cheap, which was one of the main reasons I switched to granny panties. They were economical and comfortable. Six in a pack, you couldn't beat that.

"We'll get there." He held out his hand. "Let us first agree to be partners and *friends*."

I stared at his hand, biting my lip. My head was saying proceed with caution, like, lots and lots of caution.

"Come now, what are you afraid of?" He extended his hand farther.

Him. Definitely him.

"Aspen," he whispered.

My eyes drifted up to meet his thoughtful gaze. He was studying me like a final exam. "I don't think it was by chance that we met."

"I don't either," flew out of my mouth before I even knew I thought it.

Miles liked my response very much based on the way he leaned in closer. "Perhaps we could start there then." He inched his hand forward.

My hand started creeping its way toward his. Miles tried not to stare at it, his eyes fixed on mine, begging me to trust him. I wasn't sure why it was so important to him. My hand did eventually land in his. But he didn't grasp it right away. It was as if he was giving me the chance to rescind if I wasn't ready. How he knew me so well, I wish I knew. When my hand remained, his gently but firmly enveloped mine.

It was no ordinary handshake; it was more like fusion—two things coming together to create a single entity. It caused massive stinging sensations, and worse, a clue to where the key to my heart was hidden. I wasn't sure I wanted to know where it was, so I pulled away.

Miles exhaled audibly. "Thank you."

"You're welcome," I responded though I wasn't sure what he was thanking me for.

He clapped his hands and rubbed them together. "Let's get down to business now, shall we?"

That sounded safer. "Yes."

"My publisher has informed me that I need to be more diligent about keeping up my social media presence and answering my electronic fan mail. I was hoping you could help me with both."

"Sure. Do you have a form letter you send out or do you respond personally?"

"I have a template you can use, but if the email is particularly touching, feel free to improvise."

"That could be dangerous."

He chuckled. "I trust you."

Again, that could be dangerous. "Do you have a site I can log in to?"

He reached over and retrieved a MacBook off his desk and a piece of paper. "You can use this for any business you conduct on my behalf." He held up the piece of paper. "I've listed all my logins and passwords."

I took both items. "Do you have any ideas about how you would like to present your brand online?"

"If it were up to me, I wouldn't be on social media. I find it trite and impersonal, but my publisher and adoring fans think otherwise, so any suggestions you have would be most welcome."

My first suggestion would be to stop thinking we were all adoring him, though it was probably true. "Can I think about it and do some research?"

"Of course. I would expect nothing less."

"Is that all?"

"For now."

I stood up and he followed.

"Good night, Miles."

"Good night, Aspen."

"I'll see you in the morning."

"I look forward to it."

Me too.

Chapter Ten

NANNY LIFE WAS the best kept secret. Never in all my years of working did I ever arrive at work with anyone as happy to see me as Henry was when I crept into his room early Tuesday morning. He had just woken up, but as soon as he saw me, he jumped out of bed and ran to me. "Nanny!"

I was becoming very fond of the title, and especially of his little arms around my neck. "Good morning. Did you sleep good?"

He nodded. "I need to go to the toilet."

It was funny to hear him say toilet instead of potty, but it was a British thing. I knew that from my love affair with the BBC. "Do you need help?"

"I'm a big boy." He untangled himself from me and ran to his own personal bathroom made for children. The toilet was tiny, and the sink and countertop were lowered so he could easily wash his hands. It also meant he could easily make a mess, which he had done yesterday. Water and soap were kid magnets. I listened intently while I picked out his clothes to make sure we didn't have a repeat of the bubble fest from yesterday. Another set of shorts with a collared shirt and sweater. I really needed to talk to Miles about getting him some pants and more casual clothes.

While listening to see if I needed to check on Henry, I heard something that caught me off guard. David Bowie's "Fame" blared from down the hall. As soon as Henry was out of the bathroom, I picked him up and followed the music to Miles's office. The door was cracked enough for me to see Miles in a whole new light. He was not only singing aloud at the top of his voice, which honestly wasn't half bad, but he was dancing. Like awful, white-guy dancing. Lanky arms and legs flying all over the place while he spun around. He even grabbed a pen and started singing into it like a microphone.

Henry started giggling, alerting Miles to our presence, but that didn't stop him. He only pointed at us with his pen and yelled, "Fame!" along with David Bowie. I probably should have turned around and left him to his party for one, but he mesmerized me. It was refreshing to see that the dashing Brit had a silly side. Henry wanted to join in, so I set him down and he toddled over to his uncle, who I was pleased to see picked him up and danced with him. Maybe he wasn't as inattentive as I thought. Unfortunately, he was getting more attractive with Henry in his arms. It made me wish I had my phone with me to snap a picture. Hmm. That gave me an idea to think about regarding his social media presence. For now, though, I enjoyed the scene.

Miles frequently flashed me his beautiful smile, making my body not only sting, but zing. My feelings were coming back. That couldn't be good. Yet I didn't want to look away. In fact, it had me wishing I could have given Chloe moments like this with a better man than I chose to be her father. She was turning out all right, I reminded myself.

As soon as the song was over, Miles flipped off his silly switch and set Henry down.

Henry wasn't pleased about it. "Dance more," he demanded.

"Not today. It's time for me to work." Miles looked my way. "This is part of my ritual."

"Ritual?"

"Yes, each day before I write, I read *The Telegraph* while I work out, then shower, dress, and dance."

"Do you dance to the same song every day?"

"It changes on my mood."

"How's your mood today?"

He grinned at me from behind his desk. "Quite well, thank you."

"I'll leave you to it. Come on, Henry, let's go see Chloe and eat breakfast."

Henry's mood remarkably improved with the mention of Chloe and food. "Co-ee!" He ran to me.

"Please shut the door and keep the noise to a minimum," Miles half barked.

That ruffled my feathers, but I chose not to mention it. My dad's advice for any of us kids starting a new job was to always get the lay of the land first to make sure you were seeing everything before you opened your mouth. It had mostly kept me out of trouble. Hopefully, this would be one of those times. I shut his door and started my own routine for the day.

This was a much different routine than I was used to, but I had to say I loved it. I got to make breakfast for two of the most beautiful children to grace the planet, and I got to drive Chloe to school. I hadn't ever been able to do that. It seemed like a simple thing, but it meant not only that I would see her off, but I would see her home. More time with her was the biggest perk of this job, and the adorable kid in his car seat in the back singing all the wrong words to "Fame" was a huge bonus.

Chloe was so excited to be going back to school in Carrington Cove, attending the same junior high where I met Emma, Jenna, and Brad and forged lifelong friendships with them. I wished the same for Chloe as I watched her walk in with her best friend, Brooke.

After we dropped Chloe off, Henry and I headed back to the guest house where, in between entertaining him and unpacking, I answered a few letters from Miles's *adoring* fans. Wow, were some of these women desperate. One even sent him her virtual panties. Unfortunately, she was still wearing them. She got the mundane form letter that basically said thanks for contacting him and have a nice day. I wanted to add, *P.S. Love yourself more. No man is worth your self-dignity.*

I only directly replied to one. It was a teenage girl who maybe loved Isabella Jones as much as I did. I made the letter sound as though

Miles was honored that she had written and praised her for understanding Isabella's complexities so well.

After that, Henry and I headed into town to have lunch with my friends. Another momentous event for me. I never had the time or expendable income to do such things during the day. We were meeting up at a new place near Shelby's boutique called Two Girls and a Guy. It was owned by three friends, two girls and one guy, like their namesake. Shelby highly recommended it. But Shelby pretty much loved all food now, so I wasn't sure how trustworthy her recommendation was.

When Henry and I walked into the restaurant, I immediately fell in love with the décor. It was decorated in movie posters. But not just any movies—love triangle movies. I wondered if that meant the two girls and a guy were in a love triangle. Awkward.

While admiring the *Sweet Home Alabama* poster, our favorite Southern Belle came walking in along with Emma, Jenna, and Jenna's baby boy, Elliott, in tow. He was getting so big. I couldn't believe he would be a year old in two months. Jenna said he took his first steps last week, but it scared him so bad he promptly sat down after.

Henry pointed at Elliot and said, "Baby." All my friends were enamored with his accent and oohed and aahed over him. Henry ate the attention right up.

We were seated right away even though the place was packed.

"This is fun, y'all. All of us together for lunch," Shelby commented as soon as she sat down.

"Yes." Jenna situated Elliot in his booster seat. "How goes your new situation?" she asked me. "Are you getting cozy up in the Bluffs?"

"Didn't you tell them?" Emma grabbed some of the complimentary bread, trying to stave off morning sickness. "He made her sign a contract agreeing to no romantic entanglements."

"What?" Jenna squinted.

Shelby placed her hand across her heart like someone had stabbed her there. "I hope you didn't sign it."

"Of course I did. I don't want to be romantically involved with anyone."

"She's lying," Emma batted her eyes at me. "Tell them what he said about you."

I picked up my triangle shaped menu and opened it. "He said, 'Aspen,'" I paused, baiting my friends.

They all leaned in eagerly.

I let out a fake sigh before saying, "'You missed a line. And make sure you initial the addendum.'" I smirked at all my friends, who were now glaring at me.

Jenna even threw one of the rolls at me. "You are such brat."

"I'm only telling the truth." I handed Henry the roll.

"Mmm," he said after his first bite. He was a kid after my own heart. I loved bread too.

"He also said she was fetching and if the circumstances were different, he would want to date her," Emma informed my friends.

"She's exaggerating. He said he would have invited me to dinner."

Shelby placed her perfectly manicured hand on my arm. "Miss Aspen, I saw the way that man looked at you on Friday night. He's smitten."

I patted her hand. "Can we talk about something else?"

"Not so fast." Jenna eyed me. "Enquiring minds want to know. What happens if you get entangled, which, by the way, sounds fantastic." She wagged her brows.

I ruffled Henry's hair. "Then I won't have a job."

There was a collective let down at the table.

"What if it's accidental?" Emma asked.

I narrowed my eyes at Emma. "How do you accidentally entangle yourself with someone?"

"Ooh, pick me." Jenna raised her hand. "I have lots of ideas. I can even draw you some pictures."

We all laughed at her.

Henry laughed too and said, "Draw me a picture."

Jenna pressed her lips together and looked at Henry. "Maybe I should tell you my ideas later."

"I think that would be for the best." We needed to protect the innocent ears at the table and, more importantly, make sure he didn't hear anything he shouldn't repeat to his uncle. "Or you can forget them altogether," I suggested.

"Uh, no." Jenna flashed me a devilish grin. "I'll text you."

I could hardly wait for those. Not. "Can we move on now?" I prayed the answer was yes.

Emma reached into her bag. "Well, I have some news."

We gave her all our attention.

"Sawyer and I went to the doctor this morning. We had our first ultrasound." Joy burst from her words. "And . . ." she pulled out an ultrasound picture, "we are having TWINS!"

The table erupted in excited cheers.

"Oh, Mylanta!" Shelby snatched the picture. She was obsessed with babies, being a former midwife and a general lover of babies. She and Ryder were planning on having five kids. Shelby carefully studied the picture of what looked like two peanuts. "Everything looks perfect. Now, you can still do an unmedicated birth with twins. I'll be there every step of the way." Shelby was also a big proponent of drug-free births. I wondered if she would change her tune on that after she herself had given birth. Though, Jenna did say Shelby was an amazing coach in the delivery room and made it possible for her to go natural with Elliott. Me, I was all for the epidural. And it wasn't like Leland was much help in the delivery room. He slept and watched sports most of the time.

Emma took back the picture and stared doe-eyed at it. "I can't believe it."

"What does Sawyer think?" I asked.

"He's over the moon," Emma gushed. "He cried when the doctor told us."

I was so happy for her. She never thought she would find love, but I always knew she would. She just needed the right man to be strong enough to not be intimidated by how confident and good she was. Sawyer was the lucky man. From day one it was plain to see he was in awe of her.

"Have you told your daddy yet?" Shelby asked.

Emma nodded. "He's so excited. He's already out buying two

rocking horses. And he's putting the word out that he'll be on the lookout for two ponies." Emma's dad, Dane, was an avid horseman. "Sawyer's dad was just as cute about it. He and Bridget are now talking about going to the courthouse to get married sooner rather than later. They are both questioning their decision to get married on the slopes this winter. They're worried I shouldn't be skiing in my condition. Personally, I think they just want to get married. And I think it will help Bridget feel justified being able to call herself grandma, which obviously to me she will be."

"Does that mean you haven't told Sawyer's mom yet?" I hesitated to ask. We all hated Josephine, especially Emma. No one could blame her after how awful Josephine was to her and her father. And there was the little issue of making Sawyer and Emma stepsiblings for a short period, which kept them from exploring their own romantic relationship. That would be a fun story to tell their kiddos—that they were stepbrother and stepsister when they got married.

Emma's face scrunched and her fists clenched any time her mother-in-law and ex-stepmother's name was brought up. "No, we haven't told her. We try to have as little contact with her as possible, though she has been calling Sawyer more often. He rarely answers. I'm not sure he will ever forgive her for trying to ruin our wedding."

"What about your sisters?" Jenna threw in quickly, trying to change the subject for Emma's sake.

Emma rolled her eyes. "I haven't told them yet either. I wanted to tell you guys first. They are both on my nerves anyway."

Shelby wrung her hands like she knew why. It wasn't surprising, considering Macey and Marlowe worked for her and Marlowe was dating Ryder's cousin Bobby Jay.

Jenna pulled a bib out of her diaper bag for Elliott. "What's up with the M&M twins?"

Emma gave Shelby a pointed look. "Well for starters, Macey keeps stringing along poor Jamie, and. . . Marlowe broke up with Bobby Jay."

"What? Is she an idiot?" Jenna asked.

We all nodded. Bobby Jay was a nice guy as far as I could tell, and funnier than anyone I had ever met. He also treated Marlowe like a queen.

Shelby bit her pouty pink lip. "He's pretty torn up about it."

Emma's shoulders sank. "I'm sorry. My sister has lost her mind."

"What was her reasoning?" I asked.

Emma let out a deep breath. "Honestly, I think she's scared."

"Well," Shelby cut in, "for as wonderful as he is, Bobby Jay can get in a hurry. I think he fell harder for her than he intended to, and he was ready for more than she was."

"I'm hoping she comes to her senses," Emma commented. "He was good for her."

"I hope so too." Shelby squeezed Emma's hand. "Sometimes we don't see the gift we've been given for what it is until it's gone."

All eyes turned toward me as if I should be taking Shelby's statement to heart.

I swallowed hard. "What are you all looking at?"

Jenna, never one to miss the opportunity to make a smart-aleck comment, answered, "Well duh, you better get to unwrapping that dashing Brit."

Not. Going. To. Happen.

Chapter Eleven

Not ONLY wasn't I going to be unwrapping my boss, I was thinking that maybe I wanted to exchange him. After another exhausting day of taking care of my young charge, soccer practice, homework, dinner, and doing some research for Miles, I finally got Henry to sleep. It only took five stories, two songs, a drink of water, and the promise of going to the park the next day. Not once had I seen Miles since that morning. I wasn't exactly sure how this nanny thing worked, but I was pretty sure the parent should have contact with the child more than once a day. Don't get me wrong, I hoped he was writing like crazy. I really needed that book. But it wasn't as important as Henry, who had broken my heart when I kissed him good night and he asked where his mummy and daddy were. All I could say while I choked back tears was that they were in a beautiful place watching over him and they loved him so much.

Poor baby fell asleep clutching his bear with his lip quivering. Miles really needed to be the one comforting him and tucking him in. Not that I didn't love doing it. I did, probably more than I should. I knew there would come a day when I would have to say goodbye to Henry, and I already couldn't stand that thought. I pushed it to the back of my mind when I made my way to Miles's office to hand off the monitor again.

It felt like déjà vu, me knocking on his door, him telling me to wait a minute while he hid his outline from me. Him answering his door looking worn but well in jeans and a tight knitted sweater. It didn't help that he looked happy to see me. My heart tingled more than stung this time. Definitely not a good sign.

I handed him the monitor, skipping any pleasantries. "Henry is asleep. Good night." I turned to go.

"Aspen, wait."

I stopped mid-turn.

"Please come in and tell me how your day was."

"Thank you, but I'm tired. I'll see you in the morning."

His lips downturned. "That is a shame. Perhaps tomorrow."

"Perhaps," I said, only because he was my boss and I felt like saying no wasn't the right course of action. But my plan was to prevent as much alone time with him as possible. I turned and walked away.

"Sleep well, lo . . . Aspen," he called.

Sleep sounded so wonderful, but as I walked between the main house and the guesthouse on the cobbled stone path in the chilly night air, I received a call that unfortunately woke me right up.

"Hello." There was no hiding the derision in my voice.

"Careful, I might think you don't want me to call you."

He was the last person I wanted to call me. "What do you want, Leland?" I took a seat on one of the cushioned wicker chairs on the front porch of the cottage, and tucked myself into a ball, wishing I had worn a jacket. I tried to never talk to Leland in front of Chloe in case things got ugly. Which was more likely than not.

"Same as always, to check on our daughter."

That wasn't always why he called. I used to get plenty of drunk calls from him a long time ago saying he was sorry and wanted me back. Then he'd sober up and call to tell me all the things I had done wrong in our relationship. I didn't dredge it up with him. Best just to get the call over with as soon as possible. "She's great."

"I want to talk to her."

"She's not ready to talk to you."

"She needs to get ready because I'm moving back to Colorado."

I almost dropped my phone. My heart certainly took a plunge. "When?" I breathed out, sick to my stomach.

"Soon. I'm tying up some loose ends here and then I'll be back. I'm taking a job at Mike Pratt's auto body shop in Edenvale, so I'll be close by."

Good old Mike Pratt. He and Leland were old cronies from our high school days and were both douche bags. At last count, Mike had three baby mamas and didn't support one of them.

"Chloe and I moved back to Carrington Cove."

"To live with your parents?" The thought obviously gave him pleasure.

"As a matter of fact, no. I took a position with Taron Taylor." I used Miles's pen name on the off-chance Leland recognized his name.

"Who's that?"

I figured it was a long shot. Leland only read the back of cereal boxes and his own lame songs. "He's a renowned author and international bestseller."

"So why did he hire *you*?"

"I'm going to forget you said that." If not, I was going to rip into him, and he wasn't worth the breath.

"You're so touchy. He must pay well if you can afford to live in Carrington Cove."

That was none of his business. "When will you and your family get here?"

He paused and paused some more. "It will only be me," he obviously hated to admit.

That was quick. I wondered what happened to the love of his life, the woman who showed him what real love was. And what about his baby daughter? "Trouble in paradise?" I couldn't help but ask.

"Don't worry about it. We're just taking a break."

Right.

"I want to see Chloe when I get back."

"I don't know if she wants to see you."

"Dammit, Aspen, you can't keep her from me."

"I never have. That's been all you. You left. Not me. So don't you dare blame me. And if you think you're coming back just to leave her again, then think again. I will not let you flit in and out of her life, breaking her heart over and over again."

"I want a relationship with her."

"Then prove it."

"I will. I'll be in touch." He hung up.

I dropped my phone and rubbed my arms only covered in a thin layer of fabric. Tears streamed down my cheeks. I hated that my daughter was paying for my mistakes. She deserved so much better. She deserved a dad like Sawyer, who cried during ultrasounds, or Ryder, who was already working on the nursery, or even Brad, who about threw up every time he changed a diaper, but he did it anyways because he loved Elliott and Jenna. I couldn't even trust Leland to watch her while I took a shower when she was a baby.

While I tried to compose myself to go in and face my daughter, a light switched on in the main house. I looked up to find Miles standing at the window in the great room looking out, drinking what was probably tea. He had an entire cupboard dedicated to it. Before I could look away, he caught me glancing up and wiping the tears from my cheeks. He cocked his head before he raised his hand and waved.

I ran inside. I didn't want him to notice me. I certainly didn't want to notice him.

The men in my life, past and present, were doing a good job of proving to me why I had sworn them off. Leland started my day off with a text. *I'll be there in two weeks. I expect to see Chloe.*

I expected a lot of things from him too, but not once had he delivered. And the thought of having to see him made me unable to eat breakfast. I wasn't even sure how or if I should tell Chloe about the possibility. Not only did I think there was a high probability of him flaking out, but Chloe truly didn't want to see him. She felt his abandonment acutely. Each and every broken promise of his shredded her tender heart. I needed to talk to my parents and get their advice. But first I had to get Henry up and then get Chloe to school.

Henry was already beginning to stir when I walked into his room. I loved sleepy little ones. And that smile of his when he saw me had me forgetting about Leland for a moment. I cuddled him for as long as he would let me. It soothed my heart.

After I got Henry dressed, he zipped down the hall, hoping for another dance party with his uncle. This time to Elton John's "Rocket Man." I was beginning to see a pattern here—1970s British rockers. Miles thankfully fulfilled Henry's wish and they danced around together. I hoped Miles would see how much Henry craved his attention, but like yesterday, as soon as the song was over, Miles set him down and went from fun uncle to brooding writer.

I took Henry into my own arms, trying to bite my tongue. *Get the lay of the land first*, I heard my dad say. It had only been a few days, I reminded myself. It also reminded me of some of the ideas I had come up with for his social media pages. I had stayed up late into the night, unable to sleep after my phone call with Leland, looking up different celebrities to get some ideas. I also read several marketing blogs about branding.

"Would you be amenable to me filming you each morning during your ritual dance and posting it on social media? I think it would be the kind of engaging content your publisher is hoping for. I also have some ideas for some contests we can run."

Miles gave it some thought. "Brilliant. We'll start tomorrow. Have a nice day," he dismissed me and Henry.

Yep, I still didn't like it.

I didn't like it even more that every day was the same thing. The only difference was the rest of the week, I used my phone to capture his ritual dance with Henry. It didn't matter which band, whether it was The Kinks or Queen he sang and danced along to, his fans were eating it up. The shares, comments, and reposts were through the roof. It was a tossup who people found more adorable, Miles or Henry.

I did take note of PWPhotography, whose comments were at the top of every post. That made sense since Miles followed her, and he followed very few people. She left comments like, "Looks like you're in need of some grown-up time" or "We miss you, darling." Out of curiosity, I clicked on her profile. I assumed the edgy yet ethereal creature with short, asymmetrical ebony hair and striking violet eyes was the same PW, short for Penelope Williams, who had given Miles the pictures that hung in the hall. I noted the similarities between the photos she posted on Instagram and the ones that Miles had longingly looked at. She had a gift. I wondered how well she and Miles knew each other. Were they lovers, maybe ex-lovers?

What did I care? I was annoyed with him and all the comments about him being the best uncle. I tried not to let them bother me. Maybe he really was. I'd known him all of a week. And I knew he didn't ask for this responsibility, but he had accepted it. I kept thinking maybe I should say something. Perhaps I should take him up on his invitation to talk to him one night. He seemed frustrated I was always declining. But how would he take some gentle parenting advice? I wasn't sure.

But on Sunday, when I should have had the day off and he asked me if I could take Henry anyway, I knew that I needed to say something. First, though, I needed to talk to my mommy.

Chapter Twelve

"HE'S DARLING," MOM commented while we watched Dad play with Chloe and Henry in the backyard after Sunday lunch. They were teaching Henry the fine art of American football. He had already mastered tackling. He giggled every time he got Chloe to fall. She was faking it all for him. Dad had even let the kids pile up on him. He was in heaven. My parents were still holding out hope for more grand-children.

I curled up tighter in the afghan I had brought out to sit on the porch swing. We were in the throes of Autumn. You could smell the crisp earthiness in the air. "He is sweet."

Mom patted my leg. "You seem a million miles away today. What's wrong?"

I sighed. "Leland is moving back." I kept my voice low.

Mom's penciled-in brows shot up to her graying hairline. "I take it Chloe doesn't know." She would have said something to my parents already had she known. She told them everything. Like anytime I swore in front of her, or once, when I accidentally set a hot pad on fire. She even tattled on me when I let her eat ice cream for breakfast. All my finest moments over the years.

"I don't know how to tell her. He's not exactly a man of his word."

Mom's face pinched enough to highlight all her creases. "Calling him a man is a disservice to his gender," Mom snarled.

"Agreed, but he's demanding to see Chloe."

"Then you demand that he pay you all the child support he owes you."

"Believe me, I'll be consulting a lawyer." Now that I could afford one. "But as far as I can tell from all my online research, I can't legally prevent him from seeing her."

"That is ridiculous."

"What do I do?" I leaned my head on her bony shoulder.

She smoothed my hair. "Tell her the truth. That's all you can do."

"What are my other options?" I teased, sort of.

She kissed my head. "That's a road you don't want to go down, my love."

"I know."

"So, tell me how this new job of yours is going. You're obviously taken with Henry, and the feeling seems to be mutual."

I thought back to how Henry sat on my lap during lunch and slathered me with kisses. I watched him and Chloe for a moment. Chloe was gently tossing the ball to him. He kept dropping it, but it didn't stop him from trying. "He's pretty much stolen my heart. Chloe's too."

"I see that." I heard the smile in Mom's voice.

"What about his uncle? Are you getting along?"

I thought about what to say. "When I see him, yes."

"Don't you live together?"

"No, Mom. I wouldn't move Chloe into a strange man's house."

"Only right next door."

"You met some of my neighbors in the apartment building. Miles is a dream compared to them."

"He's a dream now, is he?"

I sat up and ran a hand through my hair. "You're twisting my words."

"You're touchy today. I think there is a story there. Speaking of stories, I've been reading *Silent Stones.*"

I told her to start with that one. It was my favorite, after all. "What do you think?"

"It's very well written."

Cindy Parker was a tough critic, so that was a major compliment.

"But I do find it interesting that his heroine, Isabella, reminds me an awful lot of someone. It's almost uncanny how much."

I stared out into the distance, not really focusing on anything other than avoiding Mom's gaze. I knew who she was talking about.

Mom took my hand. "You have to see it too? It's like he took every part of you and created her, right down to your golden-brown hair, quiet intelligence, and closed-off nature."

I whipped my head toward her. "I'm not closed-off."

Mom squeezed my hand. "You didn't use to be, and for a chosen few I suppose you're not, but I think even for us who are closest to you, you hold part of yourself back. Like Isabella, you know you would have to feel again if you opened yourself up. It's why you avoid men."

I scowled at her, not liking the direction of this conversation at all. "I avoid men because they're idiots."

"See, you're doing it again. Deep down, you know that's not true. Granted, you married the biggest idiot of all, but he's not why you close yourself off. It's you. You can't forgive yourself for it."

Tears stung my eyes. Truth hurt.

Mom wiped a few escaped tears off my cheeks. "Honey, I didn't mean to upset you. I just worry that if you keep going down this road you might end up like Isabella, way over your head, alone, and scared."

"Since Dad isn't a serial killer, I think I'm safe," I said dryly.

Mom laughed. "He does know a lot about decomposition and where to bury a body."

"Mom."

"I'm kidding. Besides, I don't think Isabella's father is the real serial killer."

"I don't either."

"I think her father gets redeemed," Mom said wisely.

"Huh. That's interesting."

Mom tilted her head. "What?"

"It's just, Miles has some father issues."

"Care to share?" Mom put out her arm and, like a child, I

snuggled into her side and told her everything Miles had shared with me, right down to my own concerns about his ability to be the father Henry needed. Mom listened intently, never interrupting and even when I finished, she took a moment to comment. She rubbed my arm. "Sounds to me like he doesn't know how to be a father, never having one. And . . ."

"And, what?"

"You know how I feel about single men over thirty-five."

Yes, I did. She actually wrote a paper—not to get published, just to hand out to the family—highlighting what a threat single men over thirty-five were to society. I think the phrase she used was, "With a growing number of men never maturing beyond adolescence, we will begin to see a decline in stable family environments and more male youth and men incarcerated."

"But there is an antidote to their foolish, selfish behavior," she added.

"What's that?"

"A good woman."

My head popped up. "You think I need to find Miles a woman?"

"No, silly." She tapped my nose. "He already has one living with him."

"I just told you, we won't be having that type of relationship."

"I didn't say you needed to be his *lover*." She grinned.

"Don't use words like lover. Please," I begged.

"Fine," she placated me, "call it whatever you want. My point is, you are one of the best mothers I know."

"I am?" I always worried that my parents were so disappointed in my life choices that they secretly considered me a failure in every aspect of my life.

Mom placed her hands on my cheek. "Oh, honey, you are the best of the best. There is no one better to teach Miles how to be a good parent."

She had no idea what her compliment meant to me, but . . . "I'm not sure it's my place. He's my boss."

"Hmm." Mom thought, dropping her hands. "That may be true,

but after reading his book, I can't shake the feeling the two of you meeting was anything but a coincidence."

I swallowed hard. "He practically said the same thing."

"It must be like Isabella come to life for him."

"I don't know about that."

"That's the scared, closed-off you talking. It must be very uncomfortable for you being so close to someone who knows you so well."

I rubbed my heart. I was having more and more chest pains. I was also squirming inside. Mom was spot-on and I didn't like it one bit. "She's a character in a book."

"Like I said, it's uncanny how similar you two are. Miles must recognize that. Given that, and the way he so tenderly writes her, I have a feeling he will listen to you. But," she cautioned, "this will require that you open yourself up to him."

"Why?" I asked in a panic.

"Honey, you don't change people by telling them what to do. You have to show them and give them reason to." She took me in her arms and held me tight. "It might be time to take a chance," she whispered in my ear. "There's a little boy counting on you."

For the rest of the day, I thought about what my mom had said. Especially the part about Henry counting on me. Who else did he have? It didn't sound like Miles had any sort of real relationship with his father or living siblings, so I wasn't sure how much of an influence they could or wanted to have in Henry's life. And Kevin, Henry's father, had been an only child, and his parents had passed away several years ago.

With all that in mind, I was determined to at least broach the subject with Miles. So after dinner and doing soccer drills with Chloe in the backyard, which really turned into us trying to teach Henry how to dribble the ball because he didn't like to be ignored and he had us wrapped around his cute pudgy fingers, I took the little tyke back to the main house for a bath and bed. Henry was so worn out from playing hard all day he quickly drifted asleep halfway through the first bedtime story. It was then I made my nightly trek to Miles's office. This time, though, I walked a lot slower.

Before I knocked on Miles's door, I tried to think of some ways to casually bring up how he could do better as Henry's guardian. Not sure how casual that could be. I inhaled and exhaled, then knocked. The turning of the whiteboard could be heard, then his footsteps. His life was like one big ritual and he was sucking me into it.

He opened the door and like always, he hit me with his warm smile. "Aspen, it's good to see you."

I handed him the monitor. "Can I speak to you?" I held my hands behind my back wringing them.

"Would you like to come in?" he asked, hopeful.

"Yes."

His face brightened. "Splendid. Please take a seat."

I found myself in front of his desk with him right next to me. This time, though, I think he was even closer than the last time.

"How was your day?" he started off.

"It was nice. We spent most of it with my parents."

"I hope Henry wasn't too much trouble."

"Not at all. My parents were taken with him. He's a real charmer."

"He gets that from me." Miles winked.

I may have believed that if he actually spent real time with Henry.

Miles laughed when I didn't reply. "You find me arrogant."

I bit my lip. "Maybe."

Miles leaned back in his chair. "There is probably some truth there."

"Admitting you have a problem is the first step to recovery," I teased.

Miles placed his hands behind his head. "I do like you, Aspen."

I scanned his immaculately clean office, nervous, not knowing how to respond. I think I could like him. Maybe I already did. But there were some things I didn't like, and those needed to be addressed first.

Miles interrupted my train of thought. "I saw you playing football out back. You and your daughter are good."

My gaze locked with his. I had no idea he was watching us. "Were we being too loud?"

"Not at all. I was taking a break and noticed."

"You could have joined us. I think Henry would have liked that."

"I wouldn't have wanted to show you up," he said uncomfortably. "Besides, you Americans don't even call it by its proper name."

"That's not true."

Miles's brow cocked. "I think you are mistaken."

"I don't think so." I flashed him my best smirk. "The word *soccer* originated in Britain around two hundred years ago, but when it became too 'Americanized,' your people stopped using it."

"My people?" he barked out a laugh. "I'm going to have to fact-check you on this."

"Check away."

"You are cheeky."

"You have no idea."

"I think I do." The mood suddenly shifted in the room from playful to serious. "You are also brilliant. My publisher is raving about you. Your social media posts have sales up and me trending, so thank you."

"You're welcome." I folded my hands in my lap and began to wring them. With him happy about my job performance, I thought maybe this was a good time to bring up my concerns. I took a breath, and after one more good wring of my hands, I rested them on my legs and leaned forward. "Would you mind if we talked about Henry?"

"Not at all." His brow pinched. "Is he misbehaving?"

"No. He's a sweet boy. Rambunctious as all little boys are, but honestly, he's a doll. I love taking care of him."

"And you're marvelous at it."

"Thank you. But that's what I wanted to talk to you about."

Miles tilted his head.

"You see, as much as I love taking care of him, I shouldn't be the *only* person. He needs you."

Miles's ears pinked and his body became rigid.

"Henry is still hurting, as I know you are too, but you are his parent now, for all intents and purposes, and it's important for him and you to be together for the little moments, like bedtime, dinnertime, and playtime. Surely you don't need to work all day, every day." I ended with an apprehensive smile.

He didn't return it. In fact, his glare had me losing my smile in a hurry.

He cleared his throat before sitting up as straight as possible. "Here's the thing, love." The edge in his tone said he did not mean that as a term of endearment. "You don't know the kind of pressure I'm under, and you bloody well don't know what I've been through the last several weeks. I love my nephew and I hired you to be *his* nanny, not mine."

His curt response knocked the air right out of me. I sat stunned for several seconds, having an awful staring contest with him as he waited for my reply. When I could finally catch my breath, I stood on shaky legs, willing my lip not to quiver. "Thank you for clearing that up, Mr. Wickham. Good night." I marched out the door.

"Aspen, wait," he called after I was already down the hall.

He could keep on calling. I wouldn't be answering. But maybe one day I would thank him for reminding me exactly why I kept myself closed-off and for burying the key to my heart just a bit deeper.

Chapter Thirteen

"COME OUT AND show us how you look, darlin'," Shelby drawled.

I looked at myself one more time in the dressing room mirror. I loved the long, camel sweater with the white camisole and black leggings. I even liked the leopard print flats Shelby said would make the outfit. Not sure I loved the price, even with the discount Shelby was giving me. I never spent this much on clothes—I could never afford to.

I walked out to my audience, which consisted of Emma, who was holding Henry on her lap, and Shelby, who was standing there ready to pounce on me.

"Miss Aspen, these pieces were made for you. You look hotter than a firecracker on the Fourth of July."

Her Southern sayings killed me.

"Looks like a good kiss-and-make-up outfit," Emma wiggled her brows.

"Please, let's not talk about him anymore." I was still seething about last night. I didn't even bother to film his stupid dance ritual or say goodbye to him. I grabbed Henry, his clothes, and escaped to the cottage. After dropping Chloe off at school, I ran a few errands and then came straight to Shelby's boutique looking to blow off some steam.

"You pretty, Nanny." Henry melted my heart and reminded me why I wasn't quitting.

But that got me to thinking. "I better not buy anything new. What if he fires me?"

Emma waved off my concern. "He's not going to fire you."

Shelby hugged me and patted my back. "Of course he won't, sugar."

"I don't know; he was pretty livid."

"Yeah, well," Emma snuggled Henry closer, "no one likes to be told they are doing something wrong, especially when it's true. Besides, who's going to watch this cute kid for him?" She kissed Henry's cheeks repeatedly, making him giggle.

"I don't think he would have a hard time replacing me."

Shelby started taking off the sweater, wanting me to try on the other items she had picked out for me. "Don't you worry your pretty little head. He's going to come to his senses and beg you to forgive him."

"And if not, we'll order a cockroach in his honor." Emma laughed evilly.

Shelby squirmed. She still wasn't over us making her watch meerkats devour cockroaches named after the men who had done us wrong, namely Leland and Ryder at the time. The cockroach named Ryder, however, had escaped. I supposed that was fitting, seeing as Ryder and Shelby were married now and already procreating. Leland was getting a cockroach a week named after him now that I had some extra cash. Watching him die a painful death weekly would do me good.

"It's not a bad idea," I agreed with Emma.

"Y'all are just being silly." Shelby pushed me back in the dressing room. "I'm telling you, the man is taken with you. Now change. I want to take some pictures of you for my social media pages."

That reminded me of all the comments Miles was getting on his pages begging for a new song to be uploaded and for him to father hundreds of children. As pretty as those babies would be, they would all be neglected. Stupid man. I ripped off the camisole and leggings and threw on the skinny jeans and olive jacket Shelby picked out next for me. When I came out, Shelby tied a matching scarf around my neck and gave me some leather wedges to put on.

"Perfect," Shelby exclaimed. "Let me get my phone out. With you as my model, I'll be selling out of this jacket before I know it."

"I doubt it."

"Please, you're gorgeous," Emma quipped.

"I'm PMS bloated."

"You want to talk about bloated? I've lost fifteen pounds in the last few months and still can't eat or drink without puking—even Dr. Pepper—but despite all that, I couldn't zip my pants up this morning. How fair is that?" Emma complained. "And why do these babies hate my favorite drink? The thought of raising offspring who prefer water like their father is unthinkable." She faux frowned. "I still blame you, Shelby, for making me go on that sugar-free kick. My children were conceived without enough corn syrup running through their DNA."

We all had a good laugh.

Marlowe walked through the fabric curtains that separated the dressing room area from the rest of the boutique. She must have just gotten to work. She looked surprised to see us all there, especially young Henry. The normally poised and stand-offish Marlowe turned ashen when she noticed him and stammered, "I'll talk to you later, Shelby." She couldn't get out of there fast enough. In her haste, she got tangled up in the curtain.

Once she was out of hearing range, I whispered, "What was up with her?"

A look passed between Shelby and Emma that said they knew exactly what was up. Emma was the one to spill the beans on her sister. "We found out," she said quietly, "the real reason she broke up with Bobby Jay is because he wants kids."

"I thought he couldn't have children," I whispered back.

"He's always wanted to adopt." Shelby patted her heart. "I think now with Ryder having his own, he's itching to have himself a baby something fierce."

"And Marlowe doesn't?" I asked.

Emma squeezed Henry, who was starting to fidget before he jumped off her lap and busied himself with some of the trains I'd brought with us. "Marlowe is afraid. She and Macey have always been the babies. I don't think she would even know what to do with one."

"Maybe she'll come around," I offered.

Emma shrugged. "Who knows."

"I hope she does," Shelby sighed. "Bobby Jay is in a world of hurt." Shelby gave me an apprising sort of look. "You know, maybe if things don't work out with the dashing Brit, you and Bobby Jay could give it a go." She got a dreamy look in her eyes. "Oh my goodness, you would be the cutest couple, and Bobby Jay would make a great stepdaddy to Chloe."

I snorted. "I don't think so." Bobby Jay was a nice guy and, like me, he'd been through an ugly divorce, but I wasn't the least bit attracted to him. Which was probably my problem. Apparently, I was drawn to jerks, which was another good reason to avoid men altogether.

Unfortunately, I couldn't avoid my boss.

I tried my hardest to avoid him. I even contemplated having Henry stay with Chloe and me in the cottage that night, but I knew what havoc taking a kid out of their own environment could wreak. Then I had the smart idea to just take the monitor myself, but the thing didn't transmit that far. So I went with plan C.

After I put Henry to bed, I tiptoed down the hall and set the monitor in front of Miles's door. I knocked then, loud enough so he could hear, but not so loud to wake up Henry, I said, "I'm leaving the monitor in front of your door." Then I dashed down the hall. Not fast enough, though.

"Aspen, please wait."

Damn. I stopped near the stairs. I held onto the banister, not bothering to look at him.

That didn't deter him; he zipped down the hall. "Aspen." He landed right next to me. I was taken aback by how disheveled he looked. His curls were going every which way as if he'd run his hand through his hair a million times today, and his normally pressed clothes were wrinkled. Too bad it didn't make him look unattractive. The swooping sensation in my stomach was back.

"I've been hoping to talk to you today, but you didn't come by this morning."

"You could have found me if it was important." My snark came out. Probably not a good idea for job security purposes.

"It is important, but I've been busy."

"I've noticed."

He touched my arm, I think before he realized what he was doing. He removed it almost as soon as he made contact. "I apologize for snapping at you last night. There is mounting pressure for me to finish this book."

"You don't owe me an explanation." My eyes locked with his. "You made that clear last night."

He let out a heavy breath. "You are right, I don't owe you an explanation, but I want you to understand. I didn't ask for this."

I rubbed my chest, wishing I could massage the pain away. His statement brought back too many bad memories. "My ex-husband used to say the same thing," my voice cracked. "I am very sorry for your loss. I know how hard it is to find yourself alone and raising a child, but that's not Henry's fault, just like it wasn't Chloe's. And just like Chloe needed me to step up and put her first, Henry deserves the same from you."

Miles stood silently, but his eyes swirled with all the things he wanted to say to me. And by how brooding they appeared, I would say they weren't all pleasant. However, he said not a word.

"I didn't know your sister, but I know what it's like to be a mother. I can promise you this, she didn't want you locking yourself away every day from the most important thing in her life or placing him solely in my care. Not to say I don't love taking care of him; I do. But someday I won't be here." Like maybe any minute now, when he fired me for lecturing him. I wouldn't regret it. He needed to hear what I had to say. Henry was more important than my job.

Without a word, he strode off down the hall and locked himself back in his office.

I guessed I should probably start packing.

Chapter Fourteen

I SAT IN bed in the dark well after Chloe went to sleep with tears streaming down my cheeks, worried that I'd be disrupting Chloe's life again and moving back in with my parents.

I picked up my copy of *Silent Stones* from the nightstand, barely able to make out Miles's headshot on the back. Why did he have to be like every other man? I didn't know why I thought he might be different. Perhaps his beautiful words had seduced me. How could he write such emotion, but be so heartless? What was Sophie thinking, giving Henry to him? Her other family members must be awful. Obviously, their dad didn't have a lot of scruples, having an ongoing affair with the nanny. From the sound of it, Miles's mom wasn't the only one over the years. And it said a lot about Sophie's mom for putting up with it. Definitely not someone I would want to raise my child.

I wiped my cheeks and shoved his stupid book in the nightstand drawer. I was never reading it again. Or the sequel. It all felt like lies now. It made me feel ill that I related so much to Isabella. That I thought for one second, or maybe even two, that Miles might be a man for whom I would consider beginning the search for the key to my heart. *Ugh!* What was wrong with me? I threw the covers over my head. I knew better. Hadn't I learned anything from Leland? I blamed my friends for all having incredible relationships. False hope had crept in. Well, I was back on guard. No one was getting through ever again.

For most of the next day, Henry insisted on playing in his nursery. I had no reason to tell him *no,* other than it made me uncomfortable being so close to Miles, who was down the hall once again locked up in his office like some brooding master. I waited on pins and needles all day for him to come in and tell Henry to keep it down or, you know, fire me.

With that thought in mind, I got out my doodle pad with the intent of drawing a picture of Henry for me to keep as a memento. I intended it to only be of him, but I kept being drawn to the picture of Sophie and Kevin on the small table near Henry's toddler bed. I sat on Henry's bed and picked up the framed picture and ran my fingers across the glass. Sophie was beautiful, with sandy brown hair and the same enigmatic aqua blue eyes her brother had. More than that, she radiated goodness. I wished I could talk to her, understand her reasons for choosing Miles.

Tears filled my eyes when I set down the picture and saw the empty cloud-grey upholstered rocker. I could see Sophie rocking her son in it. How I ached for her and Henry. What had she seen in Miles to give him her baby?

I took my pencil out while Henry molded clay and crashed trains, and began to sketch Sophie rocking Henry on the chair. I knew it sounded crazy, but I felt like she wanted me to.

By the time afternoon rolled around and I still had a job, I decided to put away the sketch and do some work for Miles. I got out his laptop to answer fan mail while Henry stacked his large blocks as tall as he could before knocking them down. I kept waiting for Miles to come in and complain about the noise, but I never heard him stir. Did he even eat during the day? I knew his chef had come on Sunday to prepare him meals for the week. They were all neatly organized in the refrigerator downstairs that—get this—was a computer too. I could watch Netflix on it if I wanted to. Weird.

There were several emails to respond to when I logged in. His fans, mostly female, were rabid. I supposed I got the appeal. He was talented and gorgeous, but these desperate women had no idea what was behind his pretty exterior. Like this poor woman:

Dear Taron,

I just finished reading Silent Stones. It was bloody brilliant. I loved your use of allegory. The desolate castle was a beautiful way to symbolize Isabella and her journey. And those videos you've been posting with your nephew have me in heat. I would love to get together and discuss your works further. I live in Liverpool but do business in London all the time. After we've finished talking you can prove to me that smart men really do make better lovers and, from the looks of it, fathers. I'm happy to send a photo of myself. You won't be disappointed.

Patiently waiting,

Mary

I tried not to wretch. *You have me in heat.* Who said things like that? I was going to just send her the standard reply, but this woman needed some help and a dose of reality and self-respect.

Dear Mary,

Get yourself a fan or throw some ice down your shirt. Not only am I a bloody bastard, but I'm a selfish douche bag without the slightest idea of how to raise a child. You know what they say about selfish men in bed. It's all true, sweetheart. Stay away. Go find yourself a nice gentleman. Better yet, stay away from men all together. You'll be happier, I promise.

Sincerely,

Taron

P.S. You are spot on about the book.

"Nanny," Henry interrupted me before I could decide whether I should send the email. I mean, Miles was probably firing me anyway, right? And I was truly doing this woman a service. I set aside the laptop and career suicide to focus on my favorite part of my soon-to-be ex-job. Oh, how I would miss this little man who was tiredly rubbing his dark eyes he'd inherited from his daddy. I took him into my arms.

"Rock me," he sleepily pled.

I eyed the rocking chair. It felt like sacred territory. I wasn't sure if I should. Then I swore I heard Sophie say, *Do it for me.* With a lump in my throat, I carried Henry to the chair and reverently took a seat with him and his teddy, George. I held him tight for his mother and me while I kissed his sweet head. He snuggled into me. "Read me a story."

There was a basket near the chair filled with books. Sitting on top was *The Tiger Who Came for Tea.* It looked well-loved with tattered edges. I picked it up and began to read. Henry giggled softly against my chest, half asleep. I didn't even make it halfway through before he was sleeping soundly. I placed the book back in the basket and closed my own eyes for a minute, soaking in the moment. For Henry, I didn't want this job to end. I was beginning to love this little boy very much. I would even put up with his broody, boorish uncle if it meant I could take care of him.

I found my own eyelids becoming heavier and heavier the longer I rocked Henry. I hadn't slept well at all, worried about what today would bring.

I must have fallen asleep, because when I opened my eyes Miles sat on the bed staring intently at the sketch I had started of Sophie and Henry. *Crap.* I shut my eyes again. He'd caught me sleeping on the job. Worse, he sat closely to the open laptop I'd left on Henry's bed with that unsent email front and center. I prayed the screen timed out or maybe the computer went into sleep mode. He wouldn't check, would he? Maybe if I kept my eyes closed, he would go away.

I peeked my eyes open. He still stared at the sketch. His eyes were a bit misty. His show of emotion had me opening my eyes all the way. As if he knew I was staring at him, his head drifted up. Such a thoughtful gaze emanated from him. Much different from the one last night.

"Bloody hell, you are lovely," he whispered.

"I'm sorry." I don't know why I was apologizing, but it sounded like that was a problem for him.

"Don't be. I knew full well when I hired you how hard it would be to . . ."

"To what?"

"Never mind," he sighed. He held up the half-drawn picture on the doodle pad. "This is remarkable. Sophie would have loved it."

"I hope you don't mind that I—"

"Not at all. You captured her perfectly. She loved Henry more than the last breath she drew." His voice faltered.

I pulled Henry tighter against me. Tears stung my eyes.

"Aspen." He leaned forward and rested his hands on his legs. He looked like a giant sitting on the small toddler bed. "I apologize for being an arse."

That aptly described him.

He continued, "I wouldn't blame you, if you told me to piss off."

My lip twitched, making him half-smile.

"But I hope you don't. I can't stand the thought of you thinking ill of me. There are very few people who I care what they think about me. You have quickly become one. I've written nothing but drivel the last two days as your chastisement has filled my thoughts. You are right, Sophie expected better of me even though she knew what a selfish bastard I could be."

I bit my lip. Had he read the email? That's basically what I had called him.

He gave no indication that he had and continued. "Aspen." His eyes locked with mine. Those enigmatic things were back to making my heart sting and zing.

I held my breath waiting for him to speak. I told myself to breathe, I didn't hold my breath for men anymore. So why weren't my lungs filling up?

"I want to be a better man. Will you help me?"

My breath came out all at once. This wasn't what I expected at all. He wasn't what I expected. I thought I would be polishing my resume by now, instead I found myself nodding. I was doing it for Henry. Yes, yes. It had nothing to do with the dashing Brit who smiled at me.

Satisfied, Miles stood. "Thank you, Aspen." He held up the picture. "Can I keep this?"

"It's not finished."

"When you do finish it, I would be honored to have it."

"It's yours," I promised.

Pleased, he set the doodle pad back down. "Why don't we all have dinner tonight?"

I thought for a moment. "Okay. It will have to be after soccer practice."

"You mean football?" he teased.

"You still haven't fact-checked me."

"It's on my list of things to do. I will see you tonight?" There was a fair amount of hope and anticipation in his voice.

"Yes." Mine sounded timid.

"I look forward to it. By the way," he pointed at the laptop on the bed. "You were mostly correct, but I am a generous lover."

Oh holy mother of all that was good. My entire body was on fire. "I . . . uh . . ." What did I say?

"Good day." He didn't give me the chance to respond. He strode out chuckling.

I kissed the top of Henry's head. "Your uncle," I whispered, "might be my undoing."

Chapter Fifteen

WE ALL STARED at each other at the table, well, at least Chloe, Miles, and I did. Henry was chattering happily about balls and the snacks all the girls after soccer practice shared with him. He was very popular. Those of us over the age of three knew how different this was. It almost looked like we were a family.

Chloe sat extra close to me on our side of the square bar-height table in the kitchen nook that had a farmhouse style vibe to it. Chloe wasn't too thrilled with this arrangement. She didn't like to eat in front of strangers and mouth noises bothered her. After promising her that Miles chewed with his mouth closed, I bribed her with that new cell phone she'd been begging me to order. Suddenly she was very excited about dinner with Miles. Together she and I faced Miles and Henry. A steaming pot of beef stew and homemade whole wheat rolls separated us.

"I'm not sure what you like to eat," I said. All I knew was he liked to eat healthy, based on the perfectly proportioned food in his refrigerator.

"This looks and smells fantastic. I haven't had a home-cooked meal in ages, so thank you."

"Well, help yourself. Or perhaps Henry first." The tyke was already reaching for the rolls in his booster seat.

"Right." Miles jumped to it as if he should have thought to feed Henry first on his own. That was a good sign.

While Miles served Henry, I asked, "How is the writing going?"

Miles's shoulders raised and sank. "Not as well as I hoped. Actually, not well at all," he was reluctant to admit.

That was disappointing. Now that he wasn't a complete jerk, I could make a concession and read the book I'd been waiting forever for. "Anything I can do? I have some ideas," I joked, sort of. I did have some hopes for the where the book could go.

Miles's face lit up. "Actually, I was going to ask you for your help. Perhaps after *we* put Henry to bed tonight, we could discuss how you can help."

I held my stomach. It liked the way he said *we*. And I liked that he was planning on helping with bedtime. "Sure," I said nonchalantly.

Satisfied, Miles turned and finished serving Henry.

"Make sure to blow on his food to cool it down," I gently reminded Miles. I wasn't sure if he knew he should.

Miles squinted. "What?"

Chloe giggled while scooting over to the other side of the table to be near Henry. "It's easy." She picked up Henry's bowl and started blowing on it, stirring between every few blows.

Miles watched Chloe with interest. "I've never seen that technique." He laughed until Chloe handed him the bowl. "Your turn," Chloe dared him.

He took the bowl. "Cheeky. Like mother like daughter, I see."

"Cheeky? What does that mean?" Chloe wasn't sure whether she should be offended.

"In yours and your mother's case, I would say *bold*." He was no doubt referring to that email I had composed to Mary and never sent . . . yet. I was holding onto it in case Miles ended up disappointing me again.

Chloe shrugged. "I can live with that."

Miles laughed good naturedly while Chloe scooted back next to me. I squeezed her leg to let her know I approved of her actions, was even proud of them. I wished I had been bolder like her growing up. I was more daring, but if only I had stood up for myself more where her father was concerned. But then she wouldn't be here and that would be a tragedy.

When Miles was done cooling down Henry's food, he thoughtfully turned his attention back to Chloe. "Tell me, Chloe, are you enjoying school?"

Chloe tore off a piece of roll. "For the most part I love it, except math."

"Ah, arithmetic, the bane of my existence," Miles commiserated with her.

"It's a pain. I really don't care what x equals," Chloe commented. "I like creative writing, though, and PE."

"You're a writer?" Miles was very interested.

She tossed her head from side to side. "Not really. I've had to write some short stories for school, and in sixth grade my poem about the janitor won a contest."

I smiled thinking of that sweet poem. I had saved it along with the award. However, I had to say that sometimes the traits of Leland's that came out in Chloe worried me. Thankfully she wasn't writing angsty teen poems and songs yet. But she did have a knack for writing. She had even asked me if she could take guitar lessons. I told her no because we couldn't afford it, but that was only part of the reason. I didn't want her to be like Leland. Not even the few good parts he had to him.

"Your janitor?" Miles asked, surprised.

"Mr. Smith. He's the coolest. He's blind but he can see you. He even knew all our names."

Miles tilted his head. "How so?"

"He memorized our voices and how we walk. He said everyone has a different footstep. That's cool, right?" Chloe popped the piece of bread in her mouth.

"Very cool. I'd love to read this poem."

"I have a copy," I offered.

"I look forward to it." Miles took the ladle from me and dished his own plate. "So, do you like to read too?" he asked Chloe.

"I love the Harry Potter books." Her eyes brightened with a thought. "Do you know J.K. Rowling?"

"As a matter of fact, I do. Jo is a lovely woman."

Chloe sighed dreamily. "You're so lucky."

"That I am." Miles winked at me.

That wasn't a flirty wink, right? And he meant he was lucky because he knew the most famous author of our time? I'm sure that's what he meant because we were keeping this professional. I signed a contract and everything. Just to make sure I didn't draw attention to it or my internal fretting, I did what any woman would do when one of the most beautiful men alive possibly winked at you, I started shoveling food into my mouth.

"This is fantastic." Miles pointed at his stew with his spoon.

"Mmm," Henry agreed.

I swallowed down my rather large bite. "I'm glad you like it."

"We should do this more often," Miles suggested.

I looked at every face around the table. Two, I was more than fond of. One, I didn't want to be, but I had a feeling he was going to do his best to make that difficult. "I would like that." That was the truth. Besides, my mom said I would have to open up some to teach Miles how to be a good father.

"I'm happy to hear that." Miles turned from me and mussed Henry's hair before trying to wipe his messy face. He had no idea how happy that made me, and Sophie too.

After helping Chloe with homework and getting Henry bathed, I met Miles in Henry's room. Henry was looking adorable in his striped little man pajamas and combed back wet hair. Miles looked unsure about what he should do. It made me wonder what he had been doing before I entered the picture. I waved him over to the bed that Henry was now jumping on. I grabbed his cuteness midair and kissed his belly until he was giggling uncontrollably. I loved that sound. Selfishly, I wanted to keep on doing it, but I handed Henry over to Miles who was now sitting on the bed like me. "Uncle's turn."

Miles took Henry and held him out and away from him for a second, looking at him like he was a foreign object.

I cleared my throat and with my eyes and head gestures, I tried to tell him what he should do.

Henry helped him out and wrapped his arms around Miles's neck. Shelby would have called it a precious scene. I would have agreed with her. Miles relaxed and put his arms around Henry and held him close. He naturally rubbed his back. Miles looked over Henry's shoulder at me, his eyes asking if he was doing a good job.

I mouthed, "You're doing great."

That earned me his smoldering smile. The organs in my body certainly liked it. Heart was zinging more than stinging and my stomach was swishing. I reminded them both he was my boss and we all really needed to become immune to his charm.

I pulled the covers back on Henry's bed.

Miles kissed the top of Henry's head before laying him down.

I pulled up the covers and tucked him in tight with his teddy. "What should we read tonight?" I asked Henry.

"Caterpillar!" he shouted.

I noticed Miles winced but took a deep breath as if to remind himself he should get used to the noise. The sooner he got used to that the happier he would be. Kids tended to get louder the older they got. Thankfully, they did get better at controlling it.

I reached for *The Very Hungry Caterpillar* and handed it to Miles. Miles took the book, cracked it open and began reading in the most monotone voice known to mankind. Not even his sexy accent was saving him.

I pushed the book down and gave Miles a strained smile. "Perhaps you could put a little more life into it."

Miles gave me a quizzical look. "What do you mean?"

"You know, how the narrators for your books add inflection and emotion. Try that. Pretend like you're doing reader's theater."

Miles smirked and handed me the book. "Why don't you demonstrate?"

"You're only trying to get out of it."

"I assure you I'm not. I'm only trying to learn from the best."

"Fine." I snatched the book from him.

"Do the funny voice," Henry requested.

"Yes, do the funny voice," Miles taunted me.

I sat up straight, ready to rise to the challenge. I tapped Henry's nose before I used my "funny" voice, which was ridiculously high-pitched at times or deep and low depending on the page, but Henry loved it as we read about all the foods the silly caterpillar ate until he became a big fat caterpillar.

Miles too was highly amused, smirking at me through the entire book, holding back a laugh.

When I reached the end, Henry and Miles clapped. I bowed, taking in the applause.

"Again," Henry wished for an encore.

This time I let Miles have the honor, and this time he rose to the occasion. I might even admit he did a better job than me. Henry certainly enjoyed it and wanted to keep on enjoying it. He loved to stall during bedtime. Miles wasn't as big of a pushover as me, so after two readings of *The Very Hungry Caterpillar*, Miles told Henry it was time to go to sleep. Henry looked at me to save him, but I felt like I needed to let Miles call this shot. Henry whined, but Miles was firm with him. "I need to talk to Nanny and it's late. Time for little mates to be asleep."

Henry pouted but didn't argue.

I leaned down and kissed Henry's brow. "Sweet dreams."

"Sweet dreams, Nanny." Henry turned to his Uncle, waiting for him.

Miles patted his head. "Good night, Henry."

Henry blinked at him, waiting for more. At first Miles paused, not sure what to do, but then a dawning crept across his face. "I love you, Henry."

Henry snuggled deeper into his covers. "I love you, Uncle."

I was beginning to see why he did.

Chapter Sixteen

I STOPPED AND covered my eyes before I entered Miles's office. "Did you want to turn around your whiteboard?"

"No."

I dropped my hand and whipped my head toward him. "Really? Are you sure?" I could hardly contain my excitement.

He swallowed hard as if he wasn't sure, but his determined look and words said otherwise. "I'm sure. I've had to erase mostly everything on it. It's looking dismal at the moment. I'm hoping you can help."

You don't know how disappointed that made me. I thought for sure with all the time he spent in here, he was well into the story. "How can I help?"

"Isabella isn't speaking to me right now."

"Um . . . do you hear voices?"

He chuckled. "All the time, well, until the last couple of days. She seems to be giving me the silent treatment after she told me my outline was a load of bollocks."

"You talk about her like she's real."

"Because to me she is as real as you or I am." He cocked his head. "You think I'm crazy?"

"Not exactly. I guess I don't understand the writing process." And hello, I swore I heard his dead sister talking to me, so who was I to judge?

"Let me show you." He waved his arm out, inviting me into his office before shutting the door. I was beginning to learn he preferred closed doors.

I did my best not to run over to the white board and sit in front of it like a captivated schoolgirl. Well, what was left of it, at least. Instead, I glanced sideways at it, gleaning what I could until Miles laughed at me.

"You can look," he gave me permission.

I wasted no time and stood right in front of it, sad I couldn't bask in its glory liked I'd hoped, but happy to learn anything I could from what remained. Miles stood next to me to make sense of his notes for me. He pointed at the board. "It is separated into chapters, as you can see. The first grid under each chapter states the object, conflict, and emotion. After that are the characters and their connections. Then there are plot points, locations, phrases, and conversation prompts. Or at least there should be." He sounded discouraged.

Just seeing all the remnants of the words he had erased had me feeling sucker punched for him. "How long does it usually take you to outline?"

"Normally a few weeks, but this took months, and it was all for naught," he sighed.

"What happened?"

He longingly looked over the mostly empty board while he ran his hand over his head. "I've felt a bit paralyzed. The raging success of *Silent Stones* caught me off guard, as did Isabella. I think I've been so afraid to finish the next book for fear it won't live up to the first one, or to Isabella's expectations, that I've been playing it safe."

"Aren't you in charge of Isabella?"

"No, darling." He let the darling stand instead of correcting himself and changing it to Aspen. "She is very much in charge of her story. I am only her medium. And she let me know that she wasn't exactly happy with the direction I was going."

I finally took a good look at the board and absorbed what was left.

There were still several interesting bits of information, like how part of the story was going to take place in America in a Colorado mountain town, and there were more clues about her father's death and evidence that he didn't kill Lord and Lady Alexander. The most interesting plot point available was that Isabella's captor, Dexter, was also the hero. Her would-be lover. I began to wonder how Isabella would feel about that. So I asked, "Is Isabella ready to love someone, especially her captor?"

Miles studied me for a moment before he spoke. "Why am I not surprised you asked that question?"

I thought back to what my mother had said about how eerily similar Isabella and I were. "Do I remind you of her?" I carelessly asked. Immediately, I felt stupid and presumptuous. It showed in my burning cheeks.

He lifted his hand as if he wanted to smooth my red cheeks, but instead he made a fist and dropped it. "I can hardly get over how much you remind me of her."

After his admission, we stood locked in a gaze. I don't think either one of us knew what to do with the truth that hung between us. My heart beat rapidly, not sure whether it should hope or if it should reinforce the walls it had been building for so many years.

Miles did me a favor and broke the connection by turning his focus back to the board. "You will find that it is very much Isabella who is holding Dexter captive, not the other way around. And I do believe she wants to love him, but is afraid to. I don't blame her. The men in her past have shattered her trust. Like you, if you don't mind me saying." His ears pinked.

I don't know why, but I liked that the debonair man could get embarrassed. "It is a well-known fact that I distrust men in general." I kept my tone lighthearted.

"Can I ask you about your ex-husband?"

"What does he have to do with me helping you?"

"I believe getting to know you better will help," he stated unabashedly.

"Um . . ." I wasn't one for opening up, like my mother also pointed out.

A mischievous grin erupted on Miles face. "At least tell me whether you truly believe what you wrote to that woman. Are you better off without men?"

My cheeks were back to burning, along with the rest of my body. "I didn't send the email."

"I wouldn't have blamed you if you had, but you didn't the answer the question."

I shifted my feet, deciding if this was one of those moments to be more open. Miles's entreating stance convinced me. "It's easier for me to believe I am. Like Isabella, I have built a fortress around my heart. Not because of what Leland did, but because I was so foolish to allow him to. It's not men that I distrust, per se, it's me." That was enough of me being open. I shifted the focus off me. "I hope Dexter is a brave man willing to scale Isabella's walls and get back up and begin the climb again each time she makes him plunge to the ground."

"I believe he is." Miles looked at me with such tenderness. "Is that what you wish for? A man willing to take any risk to win your heart?"

Why couldn't he leave me out of it? He had to know how hard being open was for me. I shook my head, unsure. "I don't know. No. Maybe." I rubbed my neck. "I don't want to hurt anyone the way Leland hurt me. I scaled walls for him, every time I was pushed down, until I finally learned it was safer on the ground. How can I expect someone to scale walls for me when I'm not even sure I know how to love a man, or want to?"

"Isabella has asked the same question."

"What is the answer?" I begged to know.

"She's been waiting for me to figure that out. It's why I'm back to almost a blank board." Miles stepped closer to me. Close enough I could share in his warmth. Close enough to make my pulse race. "I have a feeling that maybe together we can find the answer . . . for her, of course," he stammered and took a step back.

I took a step away too. "I'm not sure I can help her or you. I can't even figure it out for myself."

"Perhaps if you look at it through someone else's eyes, you'll figure it out."

"How do I do that?"

"Well, for starters, I was hoping you would be willing to read what little I've written so far. What I've kept, that is."

"I accept," I said quickly, with probably too much exuberance.

Miles chuckled at me. "That is not all. I need to immerse myself in this town. Sophie always hoped I would use Carrington Cove as a location for one of my stories. The way she talked of it always intrigued me, but I need to feel it all for myself. I think it will help to get the creative juices flowing again. And who better to show me around than you?"

My entire face must have said what I was feeling. *Oh!* As in *oh*, what will people say if they see us together? And *oh*, was it safe for my heart?

"Is that a problem?" Miles responded to the question written on my face.

"What about Henry?" Yes, Henry was a great excuse.

"He would come with us," he said it like that solved everything.

What did I use for an excuse now? "Well . . ." I rubbed my lips together. "I suppose I could."

He clapped his hands. "Brilliant. We'll start tomorrow, after a dance video. My publisher is begging we put more up. After that, we'll hit the town together."

I nodded, not sure what to say. I was stunned at this turn of events.

Even more stunned when Miles said, "I knew from the moment we met, you would be good for me."

But are you good for me, Miles?

Chapter Seventeen

I CAN'T SAY how odd it felt to have all four of us in the car dropping off Chloe for school. Not only were we doing it in style in Miles's Range Rover, but it felt familial. Miles asked Chloe about what her day had in store for her while Henry happily pointed out everything from horses in a nearby pasture to the blinking school zone lights. Meanwhile, I uploaded a video of Miles and Henry dancing to Pink Floyd's "Learning to Fly." It seemed *apropos*. I couldn't help but smile, remembering them both with stretched out arms as if they were flying, circling around the room. I captioned the video, "Cutest Copilot Ever." Henry certainly was.

I tucked my phone away when I was done and reveled in the conversation. Chloe and Miles were talking about soccer, though Miles kept insisting on calling it football.

"Do you run the blind shot drill?" Miles asked Chloe.

"No. What's that?"

"It helps with reaction speed. As the name indicates, you are blind to where the ball is coming from. You stand at the goal line facing away from your partner who yells right before she takes the shot, giving you time to turn, react, and adjust."

"Ooh. I like that. Can we run that drill tonight at practice, Mom?"

"Sure." I was loving being able to coach with Emma.

"I played for my University's Football club. I would be happy to give pointers, if welcome," Miles offered.

"Only if you admit the word soccer originated in the UK," I teased him.

His laughter filled the car. "Remind me to google that."

"Maybe you could come to one of my games?" Chloe asked. "We're undefeated so far this season."

"I would be honored. If that is all right with your mum." Miles glanced my way.

"If you have the time, yes, you are more than welcome to come," I responded. It wasn't often Chloe took to people so easily. For her sake, I didn't want to push him away. That was a good story. One I was sticking to.

"Excellent." Miles turned into her school. "I'll plan on it."

Once we dropped Chloe off, Miles turned to me. "So where to?"

"Why don't you tell me what you are looking for?"

Miles turned out of the school parking lot. "Will it ruin it for you if I give you a brief synopsis of the book?"

Uh, no. I had been hoping last night for a copy of what little he had already written of his unfinished manuscript to start devouring it, but he said he wanted to go through it one more time before he shared it with me. "Honestly, I like to know what I'm getting into. I'm the worst movie goer; I always look up spoilers. And I admit to sometimes reading the ending of a book if I'm really worried how it will turn out."

"Ugh!" He slapped his chest. "Direct blow to the heart. That's an awful crime against humanity."

"If I'm too nervous I can't enjoy it," I defended myself.

"Now I'm debating whether I should tell you or not. Your reading etiquette is atrocious."

"Fine, don't tell me, but just so you know . . . not once did I peek at the end of *Silent Stones*. I was too engrossed in the story," I admitted.

Miles glanced at me when he stopped at a stop sign. "I'll take that as a compliment. Thank you." He focused back on the road. "I suppose for that I'll share with you. But you must promise me you'll correct your wicked behavior."

"Write another fascinating book and we won't have to worry about it."

A rumble of deep laughter escaped. "You are cheeky. I'll do my best. Well then, the book."

"Wait. What's the title?"

"That is an excellent question. It's one my publisher and I can't agree on. They are dead set on calling it *Whispering Stones*, but I don't feel like when it is all said and done that it will encompass the story, and since my contract states the title must be approved by me, we are at a standstill."

"What do you want it to be called?"

He pressed his lips together and thought for a moment. "I think I will keep that to myself for now. After you've read what I've written, perhaps you'll have some suggestions."

"I wouldn't count on it. I'm not very good at that sort of thing."

"I don't believe it. Are you ready for the synopsis?"

I nodded eagerly while Henry shouted, "Yes!" though he had no idea what for. It made Miles and me laugh.

Miles pulled off to the side in one of the nearby neighborhoods, put the car in park, and turned toward me. His eyes shone with excitement, like he couldn't wait to share. I wasn't sure I had ever known a man to be so passionate. Leland liked to pretend to be, but it never lived in his eyes, the way Miles's love for his work lived in his. It was kind of endearing.

"I'll try not to give too much away. I don't want to spoil it for you, but a little information will help, assuming I am able to finish."

"I believe in you." I covered my mouth with my hand. I couldn't believe I blurted that out. I didn't like feeling so comfortable around him. It made me feel too vulnerable.

Miles pressed his lips together, holding back a bigger reaction to my slip of the tongue. "Thank you, Aspen. That means the world to me." He moved on from it, knowing that's exactly what I would want. And he gave me something to take my mind off it. "As you know, at the end of *Silent Stones*, Isabella has disappeared," Miles began. "And Dexter, who you think is the villain, is actually her savior. The wrong person has found out that Isabella possesses her father's journal and it has put her life in danger."

This was good. I sat on the edge of my seat, waiting to hear more.

"Dexter," Miles continued, "has been keeping an eye on Isabella for many years unbeknownst to her, afraid something like this might happen. He knows he must act to protect her, but he doesn't have time to gain her trust. So, for lack of a better term, he kidnaps her, but he makes it look as if she left of her own accord."

"I bet she isn't too happy about that," I interrupted.

"Quite right," Miles confirmed, "but she does come to trust him enough, or at least enough to begin to wonder if what he's telling her is true. Her father didn't kill the Alexanders."

"I knew it," I couldn't contain myself.

Miles smiled, amused. "You are very clever. Can I proceed or would you like a moment?"

"I'll gloat later; please continue." I held my hands together, anxious to learn more.

"After some, let us call them unfortunate events that almost get Isabella killed, Dexter convinces her they need to come to America for her safety. He chooses 'River Cove', as I'll be calling it, because of a trip he had taken here once as a boy with his parents. Not even Dexter knows how significant that is until they arrive."

I wanted him to go into more detail but also didn't want him to so I could savor the words he had written and would write.

"Dexter and Isabella pose as a couple on holiday in hopes of not drawing any attention to themselves. So, I need you to help me blend in, become a local. Help me see and feel what Isabella needs me to."

I let out the breath I'd been holding during his captivating synopsis. "That's all you're going to tell me?"

"For now." He tapped on the steering wheel. "What do you think so far?"

"I'm hooked."

"Music to my ears. So where to?" He faced forward.

"It's still early; not much is open except places to eat, doctor's offices, and banks."

"Where would Isabella eat?"

"Well," I thought for a moment. "She does love tea and out-of-the-way quiet places." *Just like me*. "There is a little bakery that's only open in the mornings in the older part of Carrington Cove. My dad used to take me there sometimes on Saturday mornings. The woman who owns it uses old family recipes and, you will be happy to hear, tea leaves, not bags." Miles had complained that he couldn't find "real" tea in the grocery store here. Except he called it the supermarket.

"I must meet this woman. Lead the way."

"Take a left at the next light."

Bernadette's had a fair number of customers. Mostly locals who only came in to grab a sweet roll or two and a cup of coffee or tea before they headed off to work. She did have a cute nook filled with an entire bookcase of classics, with limited seating for those who didn't need to rush off. It was weird how I could picture Isabella and Dexter sitting there making notes or casting furtive glances at each other across the table. Kind of like how Miles and I were doing while we picked at our blueberry scones and he jotted down notes for his book in his leather-bound notepad.

Henry gobbled down his raised donut. It looked as if he had dipped his mouth in a sugar jar.

Miles reveled in his Darjeeling tea with milk. "I may love America after all."

"You didn't think you would?"

He set his tea down with a longing sigh. "No. I miss misty mornings and old things. Everything here is so new. Even this place."

I looked around at the old place that had seen better days and probably hadn't been updated since the eighties, with linoleum floors and burgundy curtains. To me this was old, but when you lived around architecture and buildings that had survived for several centuries, I could see his point. "New can have a certain charm."

"That is true, but we Brits love traditions, even ones that don't make sense, like putting young Henry in shorts every day."

"I've been meaning to ask you if he has any pants. It's only going to get chillier here."

"You mean trousers, darling."

"No, I mean pants." I pushed back, playfully.

He ran his finger along the rim of his china teacup. "Sophie would have liked you. She loved to contradict me. Nudged me to be better."

"Is that what I'm doing?"

"I believe so."

I had to turn from his smoldering look. Holy mother did he do that well. I picked Henry up and set him on my lap almost like a security blanket. "So, tell me why this little man only owns shorts."

"For the aristocracy, it is a tradition that goes back several centuries, when young lads would be dressed in gowns until they were 'breeched' and put into shorts. They didn't wear trousers until around eight years old. As much as Sophie didn't like the rules of growing up titled and wealthy, she did appreciate tradition."

"Would she be upset if Henry wore pants?"

Miles's brow crinkled. "Hmm. That is a very good question. What do you think, Henry? Would you like some trousers?"

He puffed out his chest. "I'm a big boy." He must have known on some level that getting trousers was a rite of passage. "Daddy wears trousers."

Oh, my heart. I kissed Henry's head.

"Would you like some trousers like Daddy?" Miles asked.

Henry nodded vigorously.

"Trousers it is." Miles glanced up at me. "Does Carrington Cove have a children's boutique?"

"They do."

"Let's add it to the list of places to visit today. Now, where to next?"

An unexpected tiny thrill ran down me with the thought we would be spending even more time together today. "I've been thinking about where Isabella and Dexter might stay, and I think I know just the spot."

Chapter Eighteen

MILES LOOKED AROUND Carrington Ranch with wide-eyed wonder as he got Henry out of the car. I knew it was the right choice as soon as we turned into the entrance and drove far enough in to see some of the cabins that were available to rent in the summer. Miles had pulled over to the side of the road and jotted down several notes, not saying a word, but his furious scribbles said it all. I wondered if that mean Isabella was speaking to him again.

"Your friend Emma grew up here?" Miles set Henry down and took his hand.

"She still lives here." I pointed down the gravel road. "She and Sawyer are staying in her late mother's cabin while their new cabin is being finished."

"Her mum's cabin? What about her father?"

I met him around the car. "There's a story there. Her biological father and mother lived there, but he died when Emma was a baby. Mr. Carrington, who was best friends with Anders, the biological father, stepped in to help take care of Emma and Mrs. Carrington," I choked. Did I ever miss that woman. She was like a second mother to me, to all of Emma's friends. "From there, their love blossomed, and they married."

"When did she pass away?" Miles asked concerned.

"Just over two years ago."

"You were fond of her."

"Yes, and of this place. There are a lot of good memories here. Emma, Jenna, Brad, and I used to run all over the ranch and up the mountain trails, especially in the summer. There's a lake and a stable full of horses."

"Is that so?" Miles's eyes darted around looking for the stables.

I figured he might be interested in that. I had seen pictures of him online playing polo or at polo tournaments.

"Horsey!" Henry was excited too.

Mr. Carrington walked out of his grand log cabin with Mrs. Carrington's mark still on it. Her big pink wreath adorned the door no matter the time of year now. Mrs. Carrington loved pink everything.

"Did I hear someone say horsey?" He set his sights on Henry. Mr. Carrington was a well-known horseman and a sucker for cute kids. Chloe had been known for getting the distinguished cowboy to take her on many "horsey" rides and to even be the horsey on occasion. He was going to make an excellent grandpa.

"Hi, Mr. Carrington, thank you for letting us tour the place today."

Mr. Carrington was to me in no time, wrapping his big, strong arms around me. "Anytime, honey, it's good to see you. How's your girl?"

"She's great." I gave him one more big squeeze before letting go. "I'd like you to meet Miles Wickham, my boss, and his adorable nephew, Henry."

Miles cringed when I referred to him as my boss. I'm not sure why.

"It is a pleasure to meet you, Mr. Carrington." Miles extended his hand to shake Mr. Carrington's.

Mr. Carrington took his hand. "Nice to meet you as well. Please, call me Dane." He gave me a pointed look. "That goes for you too, young lady. All you kids still calling me Mr. Carrington makes me feel old."

I wasn't sure I could call him Dane. "I'll try," I promised him.

Satisfied with my answer, Mr. Carrington—Dane—knelt so he was almost eye level with Henry who had suddenly become shy and hid behind Miles. That didn't deter Dane. "How would you like to see my horses?"

Henry's dark eyes widened, along with his cute grin.

Dane held out his calloused hand. He may have owned half the town and was the wealthiest person I knew, but his hands told how hard he worked for the Ranch. This was his wife's dream, after all, and he wanted to keep it that way. "How about you come with me and we'll give some of those horses a treat."

Henry liked the sound of that. His little hand made its way into Dane's. Dane stood and took the lead with Henry, who was dressed like a little gentleman. Thankfully, the sunshine was abundant even though it was still cool and crisp. Henry's wool socks and sweater seemed to keep him warm enough for now.

I pulled my long cardigan sweater, the one Shelby had convinced me to buy—more like practically gave to me for free—tight around me as we made our way to the stables.

"Would you like my jacket?" Miles asked me.

I looked over at him. He was dressed smartly, like Henry, in a midnight blue wool blazer. I wished he wasn't so handsome. And that cologne of his, mixed with the earthy scent playing in the light breeze, was ridiculously intoxicating. "I'm fine, thank you." I faced forward, enjoying seeing Henry warm up to Dane and get excited about a couple of squirrels playing in the golden-leaved trees.

Miles apparently had no regard for my senses. He sidled up to me and in a low voice said, "I wish you wouldn't call me your boss."

I scrunched my face. "Why?"

"I thought we agreed we were friends."

"Actually, we didn't. I think we agreed it wasn't by chance we met."

"Your memory doesn't serve me well."

Our hands accidentally brushed. Lots of zings coursed through my body. It startled me so much I took a step away from him.

He clasped his hands together as if he felt it too.

Why did I feel like we were flirting with danger? I decided to change the subject. "What do you think of this place?"

"It's lovely." He sounded grateful for the change of subject. "It has the creative juices flowing."

"I'm glad. I need that book." I almost nudged him but stopped before I made that fatal mistake. No more touching, accidental or otherwise.

"If I haven't said it before, I am deeply honored that you love my work."

"Well . . . not all of it . . ."

He pounded his fist against his heart. "Please don't tell me you read *Murder River.*"

"I'm sorry to say I did," I sing-songed. "But at least now I know that a group of crows is called a murder. However, I will be forever creeped out by that knowledge every time I see one." I got the shivers thinking about the gruesome details of the book and the chopped off crows' heads left in the protagonist's bed.

"I've learned a lot since that first book."

"Agreed, but a lot of people did love that book, and your publisher must have, so I wouldn't beat yourself up over it."

He shoved his hands in his pockets. "But I do. I worry that if I can write such drivel and get it published, what if the same thing happens with this book?"

"It won't."

He stopped and peered at me. "How do you know?"

"Because . . ." I stammered, "because . . . I won't let that happen. And neither will Isabella." I walked off, not giving him a chance to respond. I caught up with Henry and Dane. I took Henry's other hand to calm my racing heart. I wasn't sure I liked being open. Or maybe I just wasn't used to it. I'm not sure I ever would be. Or was it that I would never allow myself to be? It's not what I wanted. Truly.

Dane grinned between me and Miles, who had quickly caught up to me. Dane's grin said he wondered if there was something between us. There was—a contract. A contract that protected both of us.

"What breeds do you have?" Miles asked.

"Quarter Horse, Palomino, Paint, and Thoroughbred."

"I own a Thoroughbred myself," Miles responded.

"You're from London, correct?" Dane asked. "Do you own a stable there?"

"I'm a city dweller by nature. I board my pony at the polo club where I'm a member."

"You're a polo man. Sorry to say we don't have any clubs around here. My horses are used mostly for trail rides and working. But if you ever want to take a ride, I do have some English and dressage saddles available."

"Very kind of you," Miles replied. I could hear the longing in his voice. He missed his home.

I couldn't blame him, seeing as I was obsessed with the UK. I knew it wasn't all garden parties and handsome men with delicious accents and large fortunes. One of the reasons I enjoyed watching the BBC was the realness of it. American television was so stylized, and everyone was glamourous. In the UK, it was gritty. In their crime shows you didn't get DNA back immediately and the men and women stars were for the most part average-looking people. It was refreshing. Miles was an exception. There was nothing average about him.

I loved Carrington Ranch's stable. The gray stone and wood structure had a storybook feel to the outside, and inside it was like a deluxe hotel for horses. Several of the horses were out in the nearby pasture, but Henry was enthralled with the few that were in their stalls. Dane picked him up and showed him how and where to stroke the horses. Henry was particularly delighted with the foal born just this past summer and her mother. The duo was named Dolly and Madison. Dolly, the Palomino mare, was a favorite of Shelby's. She was a beautiful, gentle creature. Henry thought so too, by the way he loved on her head. Her foal, Madison, made Henry giggle when Henry fed her a carrot and she tickled his fingers with her mouth.

Miles stood back and took pictures with his phone of everything from the high-beamed ceilings to the tack room and, of course, Henry. His eyes swirling with all the possibilities. Personally, I could picture Isabella here talking to the horses, trying to sort out the mess in her life. More than anything, probably trying to come to terms with her feelings for Dexter. Miles was going to have to write that relationship carefully. Isabella would put up a fight; I knew her battle well. I fought on the front lines with her. Once she fell for Dexter, I would miss my sister in arms in this war I started for myself, but now it felt like I was fighting more and more against myself. How did I ever forgive myself and call a truce?

I wanted Miles to be right. If I looked at it through Isabella's perspective, maybe I could figure it out.

"Nanny," Henry called, drawing me out of my own head. "The horsey likes me."

I took Henry out of Dane's arms and kissed his cheek. "That's because you're so cute."

Henry reached out again to pet the horse.

"I wish I could spend more time with you," Dane said to me, "but we have some fences that need repairing before winter hits. Feel free to go anywhere on the property. You know it as good as anyone. Make sure you drop by the house and say hi to Frankie. She said something about making some chocolate chip cookies." Frankie was their cook and a character. She probably fed us as much as our own parents had in high school.

"I can't say no to Frankie's cookies. Thank you for everything."

Dane kissed my cheek. "Always a pleasure to see you. Bring Chloe by soon, and this kiddo." Dane mussed Henry's hair.

"I will."

Dane turned toward Miles. "I hope this old place makes for some good story material."

"It most certainly will. Thank you for allowing me to tour your beautiful property."

"You picked the right tour guide."

"That I did." Miles gave me a thoughtful smile.

"May I suggest a walk around the lake?" A mischievous grin lit up Dane's weather-lined face. "My wife always said there was nothing better than a romantic walk around the lake."

"Mr. Carrington, I mean Dane," I spluttered. "Miles is my—"

"Friend," Miles interrupted. "A walk around the lake sounds lovely."

Mr. Carrington patted Miles on the arm. "That's a good man. Have fun." He walked off chuckling to himself.

That left me standing there holding Henry, staring at my *boss* while my cheeks burned hotter than the sun. "I'm sorry for that."

"Don't be. If circumstances were different, if I were different . . ."

I peered into his conflicted eyes. What did he mean by *if he were different?*

In haste, he took Henry from me. "Let's go take a *friendly* walk around the lake. Shall we?"

I nodded and led the way, not sure what to say. Tension hung between us. Not the angry kind, but the kind when things were left unsaid, or when too much was said. I felt like I was back in high school, walking down the hall after one of my guy friends admitted to having feelings for me and I couldn't say it back. But this was worse because I did have some feelings, but they scared me and needed to remain unspoken.

The only sounds that could be heard was Henry pointing out every bird and squirrel he saw and the crunch of the gravel beneath our feet. Our trek had us passing several vacant cabins and the empty volleyball courts down to the lake. The Ranch was a quiet place this time of year, as it only had guests during the summer months. It was more of a hobby and a legacy to Mrs. Carrington now. The Carringtons didn't need the money, but Emma loved walking in her mother's footsteps and hosting guests who had become more like family.

I hated awkward silence, so I did something about it. "Is Isabella speaking to you again?"

Miles set Henry down so he could do some exploring under our watchful care. By exploring, I meant picking up every rock and stick he could and throwing them or showing them to us if he found them interesting. He may have looked like a little gentleman, but he was all boy.

Miles didn't answer right away. Instead, he took his blazer off and draped it around my shoulders. "You keep rubbing your arms."

It was the cruelest, nicest thing a man had done for me in a long time. Holy heaven his spicy smell was driving me mad with desire. Not to mention his thoughtfulness. I had to remind myself that my cerebral cortex was fully attached now and I was no longer an impulsive eighteen or nineteen-year-old who got tattoos because I was dared to by an attractive smelling man, or who slept with her ex-boyfriend because he promised he would love her forever. Neither of those men were thoughtful. They never would have offered me their jackets. Neither offered me anything but lies.

"Thank you," I whispered and, against my better judgment, I wrapped the warm jacket around me tighter. His scent engulfed me. I held my breath. Then a long ago thought hit me. In the psychology course I had taken in college I remembered reading in one of my textbooks, that if you wanted to do better and heal, you couldn't avoid triggers. You needed to face them head on and deal with them. I staggered as if I'd tripped on a rock. Miles reached out to steady me. If that wasn't poetic. I took a deep, deep breath. In that breath, I had an epiphany. It was so strong I had to stop and take a moment. That was my problem. I needed to stop avoiding men. I could never learn to trust myself again until I did. Wow. I so didn't want to hear that.

"Are you all right, Aspen?"

I blinked a few times, trying to come out of my truth bomb. "I just had a thought about Isabella," I stuttered. Yeah. That was good. Use the fictional character to deal with real life. Seriously, I needed help.

"I've been thinking a lot about her as well. She's very pleased with this place."

"I'm happy to hear that."

"But tell me your thoughts," he encouraged.

I started walking again to keep up with Henry because I knew as soon as he could see the lake, one of us would need to grab him before he took a very cold bath.

Miles followed, eager to hear what I had to say.

"It just dawned on me that you have to make Isabella face what she's been avoiding, namely her father's secrets, her ex's betrayal, and emotional intimacy. But she has to come to that conclusion on her own. She'll never heal if she doesn't, and if she doesn't heal, she won't believe there are any reasons to not only trust Dexter, but to trust herself with Dexter." Suddenly I was on a roll. "And . . . she needs to understand that she's never known what emotional intimacy really is, because if she realizes that, then maybe she won't be so afraid of it."

Oh crap, my brain was saying. *Ding, ding, ding. We have a winner. Did you just hear what you said? For the love of all that is good, listen to it.* This was all very unwelcome news. I rubbed my heart furiously. At least it made someone happy.

Miles beamed at me. "You are brilliant, love."

But would I listen to myself?

Chapter Nineteen

THE LAST STOP on the tour was the amphitheater. It had special meaning to me because of the pergola that sat front and center. I had watched the three best friends I ever had get married under it. It looked a little sad this time of year with dying leaves clinging to the vines. In the summer, it was covered in pink crawling roses, Mrs. Carrington's favorite.

"Mr. Carrington and Mrs. Carrington were married under the pergola," I told Miles while he took pictures of it. I stood close by, but far enough away to not be in any of his shots. "It used to be at the country club where they got married, but for their first anniversary, he brought it here."

Miles lowered his phone. "He's a romantic."

"He is."

"I will have to use that bit of knowledge for my story." He waved me toward the pergola. "You and Henry get under the pergola, so I can take a picture of you."

I froze in place. "I can't stand under it." And why did he need a picture of me?

Miles rubbed his lips together, confused. "Why not?"

"Because the pergola is kind of like a town legend. Anyone who has ever married under it has never gotten divorced. I don't want to ruin that kind of mojo."

Miles walked closer to me and Henry, who had been zipping all over the open space, crawling over and under all the wooden benches that lined the rows of the amphitheater. His fancy clothes had attracted a lot of dirt and his shoes were muddy because, yep, he had to check out the lake. Boy could that kid run fast. Miles barely caught him before it wasn't only his shoes that had gotten wet.

Miles lightly touched the pergola. "Truly no one has ever been divorced that has married here?"

"It's true. I know several personally, including Emma, Jenna, and Shelby."

"But you don't think you're as worthy as them to stand under it." He said it as a statement, not a question, and, wow, it felt like punch to the gut.

I placed my hand on my stomach. "Maybe. They each did it the right way. They got their education and grew up before they decided to raise a baby. And they picked good men." I absent-mindedly picked one of the dying leaves off the vine. "I could have gotten married here. Mrs. Carrington offered it to me, but I instinctively knew even then it wasn't going to last. Yet I did it anyway," my voice cracked. I blew out a heavy breath to stave off unwanted emotion. "Anyway, do you want to head up to the main house and get some cookies?" I needed to eat my feelings.

"Aspen, wait." Miles grabbed the lapels of his jacket I was still wearing and pulled me closer to him.

Whoa. I knew I needed to quit running away from men and emotional intimacy—more like discover what emotional intimacy even was. It would probably be best, though, to do that with someone who I hadn't signed a contract with agreeing not to get entangled. But when I peered up into his eyes, I wanted to stay right where I was. No one had ever looked at me so tenderly.

"Aspen," he repeated. My name never sounded so beautiful. He leaned in as if he wanted to do more than whisper my name. In his eyes, there was a battle raging. His lips parted and acted as if they were unsure what they should do, touch my own or speak. I held my breath, not certain which I hoped for.

With great reluctance he pulled away, yet he kept ahold of his jacket, keeping me close enough to stir long forgotten desires.

"I don't know the ins and outs of your life," he spoke low. "I hope someday we will become good enough *friends* that you trust me enough to tell me. But this I know; I've never met a lovelier woman. You deserve as much as anyone to stand under the pergola. I hope someday you find a man worthy of the honor and you." He let go of me as abruptly as he had pulled me to him and strode off, leaving me to stare at him and rub my heart he had pricked in the most pleasant way.

Tuckered out from his adventures on the Ranch, Henry fell asleep in the car on the way back into town where we would be stopping at a local children's boutique for his first pair of trousers. I glanced in the rearview mirror while I drove to catch a glimpse of my young charge with cookie crumbs on his sweater. His full lips and rosy cheeks made him look like an angel.

Miles sat in the passenger seat. He'd asked if I could drive so he could make notes in his notepad And I think he hated driving on the wrong side of the road, as he called it. He was writing furiously next to me. I was happy the tour was as meaningful for him as it had been for me. I wasn't sure what to do with my epiphany, but I knew something had to be done. I mean, how do you go about discovering, or perhaps creating is a better word, emotional intimacy with the opposite sex? Obviously, it would mean I would have to choose someone to try it with. But how would I know who to choose? I wasn't good at picking men. Then there was the question of if an emotionally intimate relationship had to involve a physical one? Could I perhaps be emotionally intimate with a friend? My boss? That was probably a bad idea, right?

"What do you think of Isabella and Dexter staying at the cabin in Shannon's Meadow?" Miles asked out of the blue. "Obviously, I would have to think of a different name, but I like the privacy of it, and the pond and meadow would make for some good love scenes, don't you think?"

According to Emma and Shelby, the meadow had seen plenty of love scenes, but that was talk amongst girlfriends, not for Miles's ears. I wondered, though, if I should mention to Miles that while he was an amazing writer, his love scenes were lackluster. It wasn't like I was looking for them to be erotic, but he could add more sizzle, or at least more tension. I decided to hold off since he was just coming out of a funk. Instead, I agreed with him. "I like that. I can picture Isabella walking among the tall grass and wildflowers that bloom abundantly in the summer."

Miles tapped his pen against the notepad. "Me as well. I think it would remind her of home."

"And her father," I added.

"Yes. Perhaps it would be cathartic for her."

"I think so," I agreed. It was so weird to be talking about Isabella like she was a real person.

"I will also use the small cemetery as a way to introduce clues about Dexter's family and involvement."

"And what would those be?" I asked nonchalantly.

Miles wasn't falling for it. "You will have to read those. I'm not going to spoil everything for you."

"I could just read them on the whiteboard," I goaded him.

Miles held up his leather-bound pad. "This will be my outline this time. Isabella reminded me today that I know her story and I should trust my instincts. And . . . that she believes in me. Thank you for that reminder."

I turned onto Main Street in downtown Carrington Cove. "I'm glad I could help. Now hurry up and finish this book."

His laughter filled the car. "It does take time, even when the story wants to write itself."

"Okay, fine. Let's go get Henry in touch with his American side and buy him some *pants*."

"Trousers, darling."

I pulled into the only empty spot in front of Tykes and Dolls, a place I could have never afforded to buy Chloe clothes when she was younger, but my mom had bought several things here for her that I adored. "Fine, trousers," I conceded.

"I'll have you speaking properly before you know it." Miles exited the car, gloating.

I met him around the back to get Henry's stroller out. Little man was still napping.

Miles had no sooner opened the hatch when the most unpleasant sight hit me from across the street. Leland was walking out of Two Girls and a Guy with Kylie Robison. She went to high school with us and was a girl Leland frequently chose over me even after we were married. I grabbed onto Miles's arm, hardly able to breathe, shaking where I stood. What was Leland doing back so soon, and wasn't he married? Not like that ever mattered to him, but I had hoped he'd matured for Chloe's sake.

Miles wasn't sure what to make of my physical contact. The apprehension on his face was apparent.

"My ex-husband," I whispered, "is across the street." I put Miles's mind at ease that I wasn't trying to romantically entangle myself with him. I only needed the support before my knees buckled and I collapsed. I couldn't believe Leland had actually come back. And there he was once again being himself, rubbing in my face that Kylie was worth coming back for, but never me or his daughter.

Miles looked in the direction my eyes were dead fixed on. "The man in the denim jacket?"

I nodded. That was him all right, dressing as if he had never grown up. Still wearing his Brad Pitt do from 2003 with spiked hair on the top, cut short on the sides.

Miles placed his hand over mine gripping his arm like a vice. "I thought he didn't live here."

Tears welled up in my eyes. "He called me last week to say he was moving back to Colorado, but I didn't believe him."

Miles and I watched as Kylie stood on her tiptoes and whispered in his ear before she kissed him. And like the douche bag he was, he kissed her back. My heart broke for his wife and baby daughter, for my daughter who had such a father.

"Who's the woman?" Miles asked.

"A girl we went to high school together with. His favorite bimbo. The jerk is married to another woman."

"Let's go home, love," Miles suggested, but it was too late. Leland saw me. Not only Leland, but Kylie, who wasted no time taking off. She always did anytime she saw me. We didn't run into each other often as she had gotten married and moved away several years ago, but her parents still lived here. Was she still married too?

Leland, with no shame at all, crossed the street and headed our way.

I wiped my eyes with one hand and gripped Miles's arm tighter with the other.

"Steady, love," Miles whispered. "Do you want me to tell the wanker to sod off?"

The thought gave me some pleasure. "I'll let you know."

Miles gently caressed my hand. If I wasn't so upset, I probably would have pulled away, it felt so nice. Like a nice I had never known before. Like the kind of nice you shouldn't have with your boss.

Leland, unfortunately, made it across the street. I was hoping he would have gotten hit by a car. If only I was so lucky.

He strutted up to us like he was still the most popular boy in school. To my delight, he was paunchy around the middle and his tight jawline was looking a little saggy. All that drinking finally caught up to him. Leland's confidence took a plunge when he got nearer and came face to face with Miles, who, on the other hand, took great care of himself and looked fabulous at forty.

Leland sized him up before zeroing in on the iron grip I had on my boss. "Aspen, I didn't expect to see you."

"I could say the same. I thought you weren't coming until next week." Or ever.

"Change of plans," he said ever so smugly.

Probably more like his wife kicked his butt out, or Kylie called and he came running.

"Who's this?" Leland flicked his head toward Miles. He had no manners at all. "I didn't know you were with anyone."

"I'm—"

"The name is Miles Wickham," Miles interrupted me before I could tell Leland that he was my boss. Though we didn't really look professional at the moment.

"English," Leland sneered. "Why am I not surprised?"

"Careful," Miles warned.

Leland, who was a bit shorter than Miles, looked up at Miles with his cocky attitude that said *what are you going to do about it?*

Miles wasn't intimidated at all. "Aspen and I have places to be, so state your business and move on."

Leland wasn't used to being pushed back. I reveled in watching his face redden and him taking a step back. Unfortunately, that meant his sights were back on me. "I want to see Chloe."

"Where's your wife and daughter?" I asked.

"That's none of your business."

"Actually, it is. How long are you going to be in town?"

"For a while, so get used to it. I'm crashing at Mike's in Edenvale."

"Chloe will never be allowed to go there." My skin crawled at the thought.

"You can't keep me from her."

"Probably not forever, but until you can prove to me that you aren't the same man who left her and didn't bother to contact her for years, I will do just that." I shook my head, disgusted at him. "But I don't see that happening. After all this time, you're still sneaking around with Kylie and cheating on your wife and little girl," I choked out.

"What the hell do you know?" Leland spat.

Miles stepped in between Leland and me. "It's time for you to go."

Leland's fists clenched, but they remained by his sides. "I'll be calling you, Aspen," he hissed my name. "You can't hide behind your boyfriend forever."

I stepped around Miles and faced the jerk. "I've never been the one to run and hide. That's your job. And not that it's any of your business, but Miles isn't my boyfriend." I turned toward Miles who was taking a protective stance. "He's my b—"

Miles's eyes pleaded with me not to say boss. I wasn't sure why it was so important to him, but this weird sensation came over me and I found myself not wanting to disappoint him. "Friend," I whispered at first. I stood a little taller and owned it. "I mean, friend."

JENNIFER PEEL

For that I got a warm smile from Miles.

"Right," Leland sneered. "I'll leave you to your *friend.*"

As soon as Leland walked off, the adrenaline coursing through me drained out of me. I was back to shaking and tears. This time, though, I found myself in my friend's arms. Miles wrapped me up so quickly I didn't have time to react or reject the gesture. I stood stunned for several seconds. I hadn't been in a man's arms other than my father's or Brad's in a long, long time.

Miles wasn't deterred by my stiff posture. He ran his hand down my hair. "I'm here for you," he whispered.

I believed him and sank into him. Um . . . oh . . . wow, did it ever feel nice.

Chapter Twenty

"CAN I ASK you something?" Miles whispered across the bed from Henry who was out like a light after only one bedtime story. I should take the kid to the Ranch every day.

"Sure?" I whispered back.

"Why did you feel the need to tell your wanker ex we weren't a couple? We could have had some fun with that. Used it to your advantage."

I sank down on my knees and thought about what to say. As far as Leland knew, I worked for Taron Taylor, not Miles Wickham. For a split second, the abandoned young woman in me wanted Leland to think I had moved on to much greener pastures. I wanted Leland to think I was wanted. But I didn't want to be ruled by that abandoned girl anymore. "I don't ever want another pretend relationship. I felt like that was all my marriage was. If I decide to be in a relationship again, I want it to be all real."

Miles lowered his head. "You deserve that and more," he sounded melancholy.

"I'm not even sure I'm brave enough to attempt one again."

Miles lifted his head. "But you're open to the idea?"

I stood up and tiptoed toward the door. "I don't know about that. Right now, all I can think about is that I have to go tell my daughter that her sperm donor is back in town."

Miles met me at the door. "I don't envy you that task."

We stood at the door together, staring at one another awkwardly like we had just been on a first date and were saying goodbye, like we wanted to keep the conversation going but didn't know what else to say.

"Well . . . good night." I stared down at my black ballet flats. "I hope you get in some good writing."

"Aspen."

I tilted my head up and met his gorgeous eyes.

"Thank you for today. And I apologize if I made you feel uncomfortable leading your ex to think we were more than we can be. I was out of my head. I haven't been that riled in a long time."

I noted his language, *more than we can be.* "I appreciate what you tried to do. And I enjoyed helping you today."

"I look forward to many more days like it."

"Will we be going on more field trips?" I hoped the answer was yes.

"Count on it, love. Good night."

"Good night." I watched him walk down the hall. Something felt different. Maybe it was me.

On my way downstairs, my phone buzzed. I answered when I entered the mud room that had an exterior door which allowed easy access to the path that led to the cottage.

"Hey, Emma."

"Hey there yourself. How was your day?" She was fishing for some juicy details. She knew full well I was at the Ranch with Miles. I'd called her first to see if her dad would mind.

"It was interesting."

"Oh, come on, I heard it was more than that. My dad said the two of you were awfully cozy together and he could sense a spark between you."

My first instinct was to say there wasn't, but that wasn't true. "Even if there was, nothing is going to happen."

"So you are admitting to sparks between you two?"

"We're friends."

"I used to say that about Sawyer and me, remember?"

I sat down on the upholstered bench and kept my voice down. "Yeah, well you didn't sign a contract agreeing to no romantic entanglements, and we all tried to tell you Sawyer was into you."

"True, but contracts can be amended."

"That's not going to happen. Miles has made that very clear. Besides I had this weird epiphany thing happen to me today and I'm not really sure what to do about it."

"What is it? Are you okay?"

"I think so, but I'm not going to lie, I'm a little freaked about it."

"Do you want to talk?"

"It's kind of embarrassing and I don't even know how to say it."

"It's me, Aspen, you've seen me in panda pajamas and burping the alphabet. And let's not forget half naked in a vat of slime singing to the Spice Girls. It doesn't get more embarrassing than that."

She had me laughing, remembering some good times. "All right. While we were doing some research on the Ranch today—which, by the way, this book is going to be killer good, but I can't tell you about it. Anyway, it struck me today that I've never been emotionally intimate with someone of the opposite sex. And worse, I don't think I know how."

Emma was awfully silent on her end, which had me pulling up my knees, feeling stupid for sharing so much of myself.

"I'm just being dumb," I tried to play it off.

"Not at all. I'm just trying to figure what to say. I think you may be on to something regarding the first thing you said, but I do think you know how to, you're just too afraid to try because everyone is afraid of the unknown. The question is, do you *want* to try?"

I rested my head on my knees. "Maybe."

"With Miles?"

"Can you be emotionally intimate with a man and remain only friends?"

"I suppose it's possible, but . . ."

"But what?"

"If there is a spark there, I can imagine that will get difficult. What brought about this change? I thought you were upset with him?"

"I was, but he apologized, like sincerely apologized. What's more, he's trying to be better. And he cares about what I think. Maybe it won't last and I'm just being foolish like always where men are concerned."

"Aspen, you can't think like that. If you want to be emotionally intimate with someone, you have to trust them until they give you reasons not to. Maybe Miles is the real deal. As your boss, he had no reason to apologize to you."

"He's the first boss who has treated me like an equal. Actually, he treats me like I'm better than he is."

"That's because you are."

"Thanks, friend. How are you feeling?"

"Like I'm pregnant with twins, but the doctor told me to take B6 and Unisom at night and it's given me some relief. At least I'm down to puking only a couple of times a day."

"I'm sorry this has been so rough on you."

"It's worth it. It's kind of like your situation. You have to go through all the pukey stuff knowing eventually you are going to get what you always hoped for. In my case, two beautiful babies. In yours, you will finally get to know the joy of real love. Whether that is with Miles or someone else. But if you feel like it's Miles and you're supposed to give it a chance, don't let that stupid piece of paper get in your way."

"It's a very important piece of paper and my livelihood. And it's more than the paper; he said he wished the circumstances were different and he was different."

"What does that mean?"

"It means we will be staying friends. Which is good. You can never have enough good friends."

"You're lying. The Brit is getting to you."

"I hardly know him."

"It doesn't take long. When you know, you know. All it took for me was one phone call with Sawyer."

I remembered her gushing about him after the said phone call and about their date that never came to be because the unthinkable happened when her mom died and Sawyer, in a weird twist, became her stepbrother. We watched Sawyer and Emma for a year as they tiptoed around their feelings all while becoming "best friends." She never said it, but we all knew Emma preferred him over any of us. No one could blame her. He instinctively knew how to take care of her. He knew her. Kind of like how Miles seemed to know me. Or was that Isabella? I wasn't sure.

Maybe now was a good time to tell Emma about Miles's family. "I'm happy for you, Em. But Miles didn't have me sign that contract just for the fun of it. His mother," I whispered, "was the nanny to his older brother."

"So?" Emma questioned, but then it dawned on her. "Ohhhh. Was his dad married to another woman?"

"Yes, and Miles's mother ran away, so Miles's father never knew about him until he was in his late teens."

"Holy crap! Talk about a soap opera."

"Exactly, which is why Miles doesn't want a scandal with his nanny."

Emma thought for a second. "Yeah, but neither of you are married. Unless he is. Is he?"

"No, but you don't need to be married for scandals to occur and . . ."

"And what?"

"Well, there's this woman, Penelope Williams, who he's *friends* with. She's constantly posting on his social media and he has several of the photographs she's taken hanging up around the house. You should look her up. She's based out of London and extremely successful and talented, not to mention striking. Not like gorgeous, but I could see why Miles would be attracted to her. I get the feeling there is unfinished business between them."

"Hmm. Are you sure?"

"It's the vibe I get from her comments and the way he looks longingly at the photos. At first, I thought it was only because he missed London, but I think it's more than that. I think he misses her." A tinge of jealousy coursed through me.

"You can miss a friend."

"Right." I laughed. "I better go. I have to go inform my daughter that her scumbag father is in town."

"WHAT! Why didn't you say anything?"

"Because I just found out today when I ran into him with guess who?"

"Kylie," Emma growled. "I had heard rumors she was back in town and getting divorced. I wondered if Leland was why but didn't say anything, hoping it was a coincidence."

"It never is with those two."

"I'm sorry, Aspen. I can't imagine that was easy on you."

"It felt like a punch to the gut, but . . . Miles was with me and he was . . ." I didn't want to tell her about how Miles tried to protect me or the amazing hug that lasted for a few minutes, "nice." I went with.

"Nice?" she snorted. "There is a story there, but you can tell me when you're ready."

I loved her. "I will. Wish me luck."

"Good luck. Call me if you need anything."

If she could get me a better father for my daughter, I would be forever grateful.

Chapter Twenty-One

EVERY TIME I walked into the cottage, I had to remind myself this wasn't mine to keep. It was going to be hard to leave the cozy home with shiplap walls, stone hearth, and sweet little window nooks with built-in benches for reading or drinking morning coffee. The designer furniture was dreamy as well. So was the girl who sat on the couch in her PJs doing her homework. For a moment, I reasoned I shouldn't tell her while she was studying. I knew she wanted to do well on her math test tomorrow. But what if we ran into Leland again? I knew I couldn't keep this from her, as much as I wanted to.

I sat next to her on the couch and brushed back her wet hair with my hand. "You were looking fierce this evening on the field at practice."

She set her pencil down, relieved to have an excuse not to study. "That new drill Miles showed me was awesome."

I thought back to an earlier scene today in the backyard after school and before Chloe, Henry, and I headed to soccer practice. Miles skillfully showed Chloe the blind shot drill. He didn't go easy on her, but he was kind and he worked with her until she was blocking everything he sent her way. My favorite part was when she got a few shots past him. My next favorite part was seeing Miles in athletic wear playing the sport I loved.

"I think you're ready for the game on Saturday."

"Do you think Miles can come?"

"Um . . . we can ask him if he's available." I was finding myself conflicted about him coming, especially given what I had to tell her. I didn't want another man to disappoint her. *Maybe he won't*, Emma seemed to whisper to me. That scared me.

"I'm going to ask him tomorrow."

I nodded, giving her my approval.

She picked her pencil up and went back to staring at her textbook. I placed my hand on her book. "Baby girl, I need to talk to you."

Her cute button nose wrinkled. "Did you forget to order my new phone?"

I wished that was all it was. "No. That should be here on Friday."

"Yes," she squealed.

Great, now I got to crush her in her moment of joy. I took her hands, remembering how they were once tiny and kissable. I didn't think she would appreciate me kissing them now. Instead, I held onto them tight. "Honey, there is no easy way for me to say this, so I'm just going to say it," I rushed my words. "I saw your dad today," I half mumbled.

Her trembling chin said she'd heard me loud and clear.

"He's moved back to Colorado," I added.

Her eyes began to water, making mine do the same. I pulled her to me and stroked her damp hair. I could feel her tears wet my shoulder.

"Do I have to see him?"

"Not if you don't want to."

"Does he want to see me?" her voice quivered.

"Yes," I said quickly to soothe her aching heart.

Her shoulders relaxed against me. "But I can choose?" she needed me to reiterate.

"Yes, baby girl."

She nestled into me like she was little. I loved it, but my heart ached for her.

"Why did he come back?" she begged to know.

I so badly wanted to tell her it was because of her, but I wasn't sure. I hated Leland more than ever, but I knew I could never let her know that. Despite how awful he was, my little girl was half of him. I couldn't tell her I despised part of her. But I knew I had to tell her the truth because odds were Leland would hurt and disappoint her again. And the higher her hopes got, the harder they would fall.

"He got a job with an old friend of his." That was the truth. There was some other truth I needed to let her know too. "You should also know that you have a baby half-sister."

She pulled away from me. Her red eyes were blinking rapidly, trying to process this unexpected piece of news. I felt guilty that I hadn't told her sooner, but the way Leland told me had crushed me. He basically told me he loved his new wife and daughter more than he ever loved Chloe and me. But he lied. He loved no one but himself. Now my heart profoundly broke for his other victims.

"Is she here too?"

"I think she lives in Texas with her mom."

Chloe's eyebrows squished together. "How come?"

I struggled a bit to find the right words because all the words that kept coming to me were riddled with four-letter words. "Your dad didn't say."

"Oh." She looked down at her lap.

"Honey, tell me what you're feeling."

She fiddled with her hands that were graced with multiple shades of bright fingernail polish, a different color for each fingernail. "Why did he leave me and his new baby?" It wasn't the first time she'd asked this question.

I took her fidgeting hands in my own and held onto them for dear life. "Look at me, Chloe."

Her wet eyes drifted up. I peered as deeply into them as I could, hoping she would believe what I was going to say. "He didn't leave because of you. He didn't leave because of me." I needed to believe that more than anyone. "He didn't leave his new wife and daughter because of them either. His choices are his own. I don't know why your dad does the things he does. But I know that despite his choices, we can be happy. You are the most wonderful thing that has ever happened to me and I'm so happy you're mine." I kissed her forehead and lingered for a moment.

She wrapped her thin arms around me. "I love you."

"I love you more." I held her as tight as I could.

"Can I meet my sister?"

Oh. I wasn't ready for that one. I leaned back. "I don't know," I responded, dazed. "Maybe?"

"I think I would like that." She gave me a small smile.

"Then I'll see what I can do." I swallowed hard. "You should get back to studying. Do you need any help?"

"I'm good, but . . . Mom?" She paused. "You won't make me see him, right?"

"Not until you're ready," I promised.

"I want to think about it."

"Take as much time as you want."

She nodded, relieved.

I was glad if one of us got to be relieved it was her, but what had I gotten myself into? Even if I did find Leland's current wife, how did I go about approaching her? Send her a welcome letter to the douche bag's exes club? More like a congratulations. I wondered if she even knew about me or Chloe. I supposed I would have to try and find out. Chloe deserved at least one parent who kept their word.

I set my phone on the table in the nook and focused on Henry, who was shirtless, eating spaghetti for lunch. This kid loved anything with tomato sauce. While I smiled at Henry and his saucy grin, I thought about the direct message Miles just received on Instagram from Penelope. He had never told me whether to respond to those. I felt this one deserved his attention. She wondered why he wasn't returning her calls. And she was coming to the states next month along with some of their other mates and they were hoping to come here for a few days. They all missed him terribly. Especially her.

"Mmm," Henry shoved as many noodles as he could in his

mouth. Several dropped down his bare chest. After he was done eating, I would be giving him a bath and mopping the floor. Miles's housekeeper only came once a week, which was not near enough to keep up with the cutest tornado ever. I think that was hard for Miles. He seemed to live a very ordered, freakishly clean life.

Speaking of the clean freak, he came strolling down the stairs looking like the weight of the world had been lifted off him. I also noted how impeccably dressed he was. He worked all day from home, yet there he was, looking like a million dollars in slacks and a pressed black button-up.

"You look happy," I commented.

He smiled at me before grimacing at the noodles on the floor and the sauce dripping on the table and in Henry's hair.

"Don't worry, I'll clean him and the kitchen up."

Miles's brow furrowed. "I apologize. My reaction was not a judgment against you. I'm just used to . . . well . . ."

"Life how you like it," I helped him out.

"Yes," he conceded. "But," he grinned between me and Henry, "there are many aspects I like about my new arrangement."

I tucked some hair behind my ear. "Henry is adorable."

"So is his Nanny, especially when she blushes." He headed for the fridge.

I took a drink of my water, trying to get the blush out of my cheeks. "How's the book coming?" I changed the subject.

He popped his head out of the fridge. "Incredible."

"That good, huh? Does that mean I get to read part of it soon?"

"Soon, love. I promise." He held up one of his preprepared meals. "It's back to the grind for me."

"Do you have couple of minutes?"

He tensed but immediately recognized his reaction and took a deep breath. "Yes," he said, strained.

"It can wait."

He set his food on the counter. "Please, what would you like to discuss?"

"Chloe wants to invite you to her soccer game during dinner

tonight, so I wanted to give you a heads-up so that if you don't want to or can't make it, you can think of a good excuse so she's not let down."

His brows knitted together. "I would never deceive her or you."

"I'm not saying you would," I stammered. "It's just she's in a vulnerable state right now after I told her about her father."

"I can relate to that. But please believe me, I am a lot of things, but I always tell the truth. And I would love to come."

"Thank you," I whispered.

"Is that all?"

"One more thing. I wasn't sure if you wanted me to monitor your direct messages on Instagram, but a Penelope Williams—"

Miles's face flooded red.

"—would like you to contact her. She's coming to visit."

Miles cleared his throat and hastily picked up his food. "Thank you for letting me know." He darted off up the stairs.

Interesting. Very interesting.

Chapter Twenty-Two

"PLEASE DON'T EMBARRASS me," I pled with my parents as they were double-timing it toward the soccer field. I had to intercept them before they made it to Miles and Henry, who had arrived earlier with Chloe and me. Miles thought it didn't make sense for us to take two vehicles this morning. The stares and wicked grins I had received from Emma and Sawyer and even Gwendolyn when we arrived this morning were more than obvious. I think Gwendolyn was considering husband number four or five by the way she kept ogling Miles.

With all that said, I didn't need my parents giving him the third degree. They were intrigued that Miles and I had a close enough relationship already to where he was coming to Chloe's game. Not only that, Mom was eager to give him her book report of *Silent Stones*. I so badly wanted to yank that spiral-bound report out of her hands. She must have known, as she had a killer grip on it.

Mom patted my cheek. "Honey, we would never embarrass you on purpose."

"It's the accidental embarrassment I'm worried about."

Dad chuckled.

Mom waved at Emma, who was doing warmups with the girls. They would need it this morning. It was cool enough to see your breath.

"Is she feeling better?" Mom asked me.

"She seems to be this morning."

Mom set her sights on Miles and Henry at the park near the soccer field and picked up her pace.

Miles was letting Henry run around the park, hoping to get some of his wiggles out before the game started. Even in his "trousers," Henry looked too proper. Miles insisted that Henry needed slacks, not denim. He said Sophie would roll over in her grave if he went from breeches to denim. Henry's short double-breasted wool coat made him look like a fifty-year-old man. But the cutest fifty-year-old.

As we approached, Henry saw us and ran to me as fast as his little legs would go. Gosh, I loved that kid. Miles followed him, looking like he was walking at a fashion show in his own wool jacket with a scarf around his neck. His dark curls rustled in the light breeze.

"Wow," Mom commented next to me. "He's something."

Dad, who was still a handsome guy even though he definitely had the dad body and thinning gray hair going on, gave Mom a pointed stare.

Mom gave Dad a side hug. "Russ, we've been married for almost forty years, I was only making an observation."

"I would appreciate if you only observed me from now on," Dad replied, making Mom and me laugh.

I bent down to pick up the boy who owned my heart.

"I slided and swinged," Henry reported.

I kissed his nose, pink from the cold. "Are you ready to watch Chloe play soccer?"

"Yes!" He threw a fist up in the air. "GO CO-EE!"

Miles was upon us. He grinned at me before standing right next to me. I told him my parents were eager to meet him and to prepare himself for anything. I never knew what to expect when it came to my mom. I mean, the woman had taken the time to write what looked like at least a twenty-page book report. She seriously needed a job or some more hobbies.

The way Miles and I were facing my parents had a meet-the-boyfriend vibe going on. My first instinct was to step away from him, but I knew that would hurt his feelings, which was the last thing I wanted to do. Day after day, Miles was chipping away my defenses. This morning was the perfect example. He'd made Chloe what he called his game-day protein shake. Then, on the drive in, he went over strategy with her. He had no idea how much that meant to me, especially considering her father was in town and hadn't bothered to try and make contact again. But I did hear from Emma that he was spotted with Kylie at a local bar in Carrington Cove. I swore, if Chloe and I ran into them together and that was his first contact with her in years, the gloves might come off. I'd done my best over the years not to bad-mouth him in front of her, but in that case, I might not be able to restrain myself. Enough ruminating over my ex, it was time to make awkward introductions.

"Mom and Dad, this is Miles Wickham. Miles these are my parents, Russ and Cindy Parker."

"I'm Henry." Henry didn't want to be left out even though my parents were already well acquainted with him.

We all chuckled at Henry before Miles shook my parents' hands. "It is a pleasure to meet you both."

Mom wasted no time and handed him her report before she looped her arm through his. "I read *Silent Stones*. Beautiful job, but I made some notes you may want to consider for the sequel."

I wanted to do a face-palm. "Mom."

"What, honey?" she asked innocently.

"You should really find some seats in the bleachers before all the good spots are taken," I forcefully recommended.

"Good thinking," Mom responded. "Miles you can sit next to me and we can discuss your intriguing book."

"I'd be delighted." Miles winked at me. "Let me just wish Chloe a good game. Save me a seat, Cindy."

My mother blushed. My father narrowed his eyes at his wife before taking her hand and pulling her toward the bleachers. "Take your time," he told Miles.

Miles walked with me and Henry toward the field.

"Are you trying to break up my parents?" I teased.

"As lovely as your mother is, she is a bit old for my taste."

"I wouldn't mention that to her. And let me apologize for any critiques she throws your way."

Miles looked down at the report he had in his hand. Mom had gone as far as making a cover with fancy lettering and his book cover front and center on it. "I look forward to reading her analysis."

"Sure you do."

"I'm in earnest."

Henry saw Chloe and he jumped out of my arms and ran straight for her. All her teammates immediately stopped whatever they were doing and fawned over the little man yelling, "CO-EE! CO-EE! Come slide with me."

Chloe picked him up and spun him around.

Miles and I both beamed at the scene.

Miles moved closer to me. "Sophie would have adored you and Chloe."

Yep, that scent of his was still intoxicating the crap out of me. I had to compose myself before I answered. "I wish we had gotten to know her." The more I worked on the picture of her and Henry, the more I felt connected to her. In an odd way, I felt like she was my champion, beckoning me on with Henry and Miles.

"Me too," Miles replied.

It was then I noticed Shelby, Ryder, Jenna, Brad, and Elliott all walking toward the bleachers. My mom was already waving them over. I cringed. It wasn't that they had never come to a game before, but I knew they were coming because I told them Miles would be here.

"Um . . ." I hated switching the conversation's direction, but he had to be warned. "All my friends just showed up and they're sitting with my parents. Please let me apologize again for anything ridiculous any of them might say. Especially watch out for Shelby. The Southern Belle believes everyone deserves a Disney fairytale ending, so she might . . . you know, never mind." I just realized I was implying that I talked to my friends about him, which obviously I did, but he didn't need to know that.

"She thinks we deserve one." Miles correctly guessed.

"Yes." I tugged on my ponytail. "But don't worry. I've told them all that it isn't going to happen." I felt like I was digging myself in deeper. This was probably why I was never emotionally intimate with someone. I was a blustering idiot. "I need to go help Emma," I said, flustered.

"Aspen." He tugged on the sleeve of my jacket.

I looked up and faced him eye-to-eye, which wasn't my brightest idea. Between his cologne and the soft expression in his eyes, my heart was zinging all over the place. Why after all these years of rebuffing men did my heart come alive for the one man it should have remained dormant for?

Miles leaned in. "Please don't apologize. It is natural for people to assume that I would have a hard time resisting the beautiful nanny. And they would be right."

I was suddenly feeling lightheaded and flushed. "They are? I mean, you think I'm beautiful?" I closed my eyes and cringed. "I mean I'm not beautiful. Seriously, I need to go."

"Aspen, please look at me."

I peeked one eye open like a child to see a bemused smile on Miles's face.

"I wish you wouldn't be embarrassed around me."

Both my eyes popped open. "I don't see that happening."

"Well, in that case," he leaned down and whispered in my ear, "you are beautiful, but for your own good, I will resist you." He walked away to wish Chloe luck and take Henry from her before I could respond.

My body was in shock from the massive shivers Miles just sent down my spine. When my body and mind came to, all they could think about was what did he mean by *for my own good*?

Emma was to me in no time, shaking her head, stunned. "What was that all about? A good luck kiss?"

"Will you keep your voice down? He didn't kiss me. Is that what it looked like?" I looked up into the bleachers to find all my friends and my parents gawking at me with expressions varying from disbelief to downright awe. Shelby even had her hands to her mouth like she was keeping herself from bursting into a song. *Crap! That's exactly what that probably looked like.* I didn't have time to dispel any misconceptions before Miles got to them. All I could do was turn back and face Emma.

"Looks like you'll be amending that contract after all." She wagged her brows.

"You're wrong. He was just telling me that's exactly what won't be happening."

Emma's forehead scrunched. "You're lying. Both of your bodies were screaming, 'Forget the contract!'"

"I'm not lying." I jogged over to our bench to grab my clipboard. It was almost time for the game to start. Time for me to focus on anything but my boss.

Emma was going to make that difficult. She followed me, slowly. Growing twins was no easy task. She took the clipboard from me and tilted her head to study me. "What is going on between you two? And don't say nothing, because the heat between you is palpable."

"I know," I whispered.

Emma's eyes popped at my admission. "If you know, then what's the issue?"

"Em, we have kids and we work together. That makes any situation complicated. Besides, I don't even know my own heart right now. It's experiencing some difficult growing pains. And I'm pretty sure he left a girlfriend in London."

"Well, I would hate to be his girlfriend. No man should look at another woman the way he looks at you if he's taken."

"I don't know if they are still together, but I get the feeling that they're not done, if that makes sense."

Emma's lips pursed. "I suppose it does, but that doesn't mean something won't happen between the two of you."

I rested my hand on Emma's arm. "Em, he's promised me it won't, and so far, he's been a man of his word." I'd finally gotten what I'd always hoped for, a man of his word. Why then, did I hope he would go against it?

Chapter Twenty-Three

"HE FITS IN well," Mom whispered in my ear during lunch at Sage's Café in Edenvale.

I thought the same thing all through the game as I caught glimpses of him talking to my friends and parents when he wasn't cheering loudly for Chloe. I can't say how attractive that was. He and Henry were also the first ones to congratulate her on the team's win. It brought a tear to my eye when Chloe hugged him and thanked him for helping her. She credited her final spectacular save to his advice. He'd come down at halftime to tell Chloe to watch number seven on the opposing team. She always looked the opposite way of where she kicked the ball. He was right, and had he not mentioned it to Chloe, they might have tied the game up in the last thirty seconds. Instead, it was a sweet victory.

I smiled across the table at Miles and my dad talking about all the geological wonders in the UK. Dad was particularly fascinated with the Seven Sisters in Sussex.

"Did you know those majestic chalk cliffs began forming around 87 million years ago," my dad informed an attentive Miles. "Back then, Great Britain was entirely under water." Dad was a geological encyclopedia.

"I've been there. I have a friend who owns a holiday home in one of the hamlets nearby. It is quite the sight to see," Miles graciously replied.

Henry caught my attention next. He had been passed around the table. More like the three tables the restaurant staff had pulled together to accommodate our large group. He was now sitting on Shelby's lap. Henry had just said, "Mylanta," forever securing the love of our dearest Southern Belle.

The men, Sawyer, Ryder, Brad, and Bobby Jay, who had joined us for lunch since he lived close by the café were in a heated discussion about who would win tomorrow's football game. Sawyer and Brad were team Broncos and Ryder and Bobby Jay, sons of Georgia, were of course rooting for the Atlanta Falcons. Bobby Jay was the loudest of the bunch.

"Y'all can claim home field advantage all you want, but your boys are going down. Ever since your boy Peyton Manning left, you've been a hot mess."

"You don't know what a Mile High crowd can do," Brad countered.

"If y'all win tomorrow, you can butter my butt and call me a biscuit," Bobby Jay replied. He had several of us laughing at the table.

If everyone in the South talked and acted like Bobby Jay and Shelby, I really needed to visit.

Jenna was next to grab Miles's attention while bouncing Elliott, who was more than ready to be home and napping by the way he was rubbing his eyes, on her lap. "Miles, did Aspen tell you that Brad and I own a comedy club here in Edenvale?"

"She has mentioned that." Miles swirled his ice water.

Jenna, who was sitting next to me, nudged me with her leg under the table. "You should come with Aspen one night. Maybe you could use it in your book. It could be a research trip." She nudged me again.

I nudged her leg back, indicating she should be quiet now.

"That's a great idea. I can babysit the kids," Mom offered.

I craned my neck toward my mom and tried to convey with my eyes she should also refrain from speaking anymore on the subject.

She didn't heed the warning in my eyes. "We can even keep them overnight if you want to make a late night of it."

I rubbed my forehead and grimaced. Before I could say a word, Emma voiced her thoughts.

"That would be a lot of fun. We could all make a night of it together and do dinner afterward."

"Ooh, yes," Shelby agreed.

"Miles is busy, and Henry might not feel comfortable spending the night with people he hardly knows," I hurried to say before anyone else got a word in.

Several fits of laughter erupted as most eyes turned toward Henry, who had no issue with being passed around from person to person enthralling them with his cuteness. Not once had he complained about being with anyone he didn't know all that well, even burly Bobby Jay. It was a lame excuse, but Miles and I weren't a couple. We didn't need to get babysitters to watch our children because there was nothing *ours* about it.

To top it off, my daughter betrayed me too. "I could always watch him at home." Did she grin mischievously at me? I was beginning to smell a conspiracy.

"Aspen," Miles directed my attention to him.

I had been trying hard since our odd conversation on the soccer field to avoid long periods of direct eye contact. But Miles had forced my hand. To be polite I faced him, once again embarrassed because my family and friends were imagining things that would never be.

Miles gave me a warm smile, trying to put me at ease. "Do you think the comedy club is a place Isabella would enjoy?" That was a totally unfair question. By the playfulness in his tone he knew it.

I could feel everyone staring at me. I wanted to lie, but that lie would hurt one of my best friends. Jenna prided herself on her club. As she should. It had been one of my only sources of entertainment since I always got in for free. I didn't only love it for that. The place had honestly given me a reprieve from the difficult circumstances of my life. Laughing really was medicine for the soul. I believed it would do the same for Isabella. You know, if she were real.

Mom squeezed my leg after what I was sure she considered too long of a pause.

"Yes," I blurted, "she would."

Miles looked between my parents. "Cindy and Russ, we would love to take you up on your offer. I'll let Aspen choose when."

"We?" Jenna said not so quietly under her breath.

I would have smacked her arm if Miles wasn't still staring at me, drumming his fingers against the table, knowing exactly what he had just done. The question was why? Why was he willing to let everyone believe we were more than we would ever be? Why did he want to push the bounds of our friendship? Or was this how friends of the opposite sex behaved? Maybe he treated all his female friends this way.

All the blood drained out of Chloe's face. "Mom," she yelped, transfixed on the entrance.

I whipped my head in that direction and my worst nightmare walked in with his douche bag friend and supposed new boss, Mike.

I jumped up, not sure what I was going to do, but knowing I needed to act. "Chloe, stay here, honey."

My parents' heads darted toward the entrance too. Red anger flooded each of their faces.

Miles too was alerted and stood immediately.

Chloe, who was sitting next to my dad, buried her head into his chest. My dad securely wrapped her up in his arms.

By now, everyone at our table saw Leland. For those who didn't know who he was, Brad filled them in.

I knew I had to go talk to him, intercept him from causing further damage to our daughter, but my feet didn't want to move.

"Do you want me to go with you, love?" Miles asked.

If I was being honest the answer was yes, I wanted him to hold my hand through this, but I knew that would make the situation worse. If Leland felt threatened, he would retaliate.

"I've got this." Sort of. "Stay on standby."

"I'll be watching." Miles lasered in on my jerk ex-husband.

Mom squeezed my hand before I walked away while all my friends gave me sympathetic looks. Brad, though, was on his feet and ready to join Miles if he needed to. Not sure what they would do, maybe brawl by the looks of it.

Thankfully, Leland didn't notice me until I was almost to the hostess desk. It was the first time I was glad there was an attractive female around to distract him. Leland and Mike looked as if they had come from his auto body shop. They were in blue coveralls, each with a smudge or two of grease on their hands. Mike the slick, as we used to call him on account of his slicked back brown hair that he was still wearing, saw me first. He tapped Leland and pointed my way.

Leland stopped trying to impress the much younger woman and sneered my way.

I didn't let his dirty looks stop me. "Can I speak to you outside?" I needed to get him as far away from Chloe as I could.

"Looking good, Aspen." Mike eyed me up and down. "Still single?" He licked his lips.

I didn't even bother to respond to him other than wrinkling my nose. I walked toward the door hoping Leland would follow. He did, which might very well be the first thing he had ever done right by me. We stood outside the café in the cool autumn air, the sun bearing down on us to keep away the shivers.

Leland stood there with his left hip cocked and arms folded. "What do you want?" he growled.

So many things, but it could all be summed up in one sentence. "I want you to be a good person."

His nostrils flared. "How do you know I'm not?"

"For starters, you're cheating on your wife . . . again."

"What do you know about it? We're separated."

"Right. Let me guess, because you were cheating on her?"

"Get to your point, Aspen," he snapped.

"My point is, our daughter is in the café—"

His head jerked in the direction of the café window. What we both found there warmed my heart. Miles and Brad stood in menacing poses watching over me.

"You brought your boyfriend and that pansy Brad with you, I see."

"Brad is more of a man than you'll ever be, so lay off him." He was never very nice to him growing up. That should have said something to me. Sure, Brad was somewhat of a nerd, but he was our nerd

164

and I loved him. I should have been better at showing that. "And Miles isn't my boyfriend."

"So why is he with you?"

"Not that it's any of your business, but I work for him and he came to see Chloe's game today."

Leland faced me and smirked. "You're sleeping with your boss? Didn't know you had it in you. But I thought you said his name is Taron."

I was surprised he remembered that tidbit. "It's his pen name and we're not sleeping together."

"Since it's you, I believe you. Always so uptight," he said, trying to rattle me.

It was working. I know a lot of people thought Leland and I were having sex in high school. After all, Leland had a reputation, so it was no surprise to them when I turned up pregnant my freshman year of college. But we got pregnant my first time. He'd begged me at least a dozen times before that, but I'd always said no. I stupidly thought if I finally gave him what he wanted, he would give me what I always wanted, his whole heart.

I hated that I ever gave him the honor. That he made it something so cheap. That I was so easy to discard. Most of all, I hated that I never knew what it was like to be cherished. For a man to love me soul and body. Someone to be gentle with me and never compare me. I clasped my hands together and breathed. I refused to be the abandoned girl anymore.

"Leland, keep talking like that and you will never see Chloe. I'll hire the best lawyer money can buy. That's a promise, not a threat."

That wiped the smirk off his face. "I just want to see our daughter."

"Why?"

He stared at me blankly like I'd asked him a difficult question.

"Is this just to spite me?" I finally asked when he couldn't answer.

He shoved his hands in his pockets. "I know I screwed up. I wasn't ready to be a dad when we had Chloe. I didn't want to marry you, but my dad told me that's what a real man would do."

I grabbed my heart and held back tears. I wasn't under some delusion that deep down Leland had wanted to marry me, but his words still cut because the girl inside me wanted to believe that he loved me in his way, and that she was at least wanted by the boy she gave everything to. "You can quit reminding me that you didn't want me. I got the message loud and clear."

"I did want you," he scoffed, "but not the way you wanted me to. I wanted to have fun and you always had expectations. Like my wife," he said quietly.

"I thought she was *the one*," I mocked him.

He ran his hands through his hair and paced. "She doesn't have any idea, just like you didn't, about the pressure."

"What pressure?"

"To provide for a family. I didn't get to finish college, so it's hard to find good paying jobs." He cast me an accusatory look.

I found it rich he didn't think I knew how hard it was to provide for a family. What did he think I had been doing for the past twelve years in his absence? "Don't blame me for that decision. Your dad offered to pay for you to keep going and I supported that. I even offered to work two jobs so you could finish. You're the one who dropped out, insisting it was a waste of time."

He threw his hands up in the air because he knew I was right.

"Leland, I don't know what's going on between you and your wife, but think about this before you decide if you really want to see Chloe. She has expectations of you. Those include you being all the way in. So, if you're not ready to be present and involved, don't continue to hurt her. She doesn't deserve it." I pointed toward the café. "She's in there right now scared to see you because she so badly wants you to love her," I choked out, "but she's afraid you won't."

"I do love her." It was the first time I ever heard any real emotion in his voice.

"Then prove it to her. Even if that means leaving her alone."

He stared at me with bulging eyes. His lips parted several times to speak but he never did. He eventually walked off without another word.

I bent over and tried to catch my breath.

Miles came rushing out. "Are you all right?"

I stood up and inhaled and exhaled deeply. "I think I'm going to be."

Miles opened his arms.

All I had to do was nod my acknowledgment and acceptance of what he was silently offering, and like oppositely charged magnets, the force drawing us together was too hard to fight. I found I didn't want to. In his arms, I felt empowered and safe.

I sank into him, letting go of all the tension in my body. "You're the best boss ever," I laughed against his chest.

He didn't laugh with me. Instead, he rested his chin on my head. "We may need to do something about that."

Chapter Twenty-Four

I FELT LIKE there was a weird tension between Miles and me all week after what transpired on Saturday. He wasn't avoiding me, but our interactions were short and to the point, including dinner and bedtime. He would eat, help clean up Henry, and then go back to work. At bedtime, he would meet me in Henry's room, read him a story, tuck him in, take the monitor, and say goodnight. He was never curt, always kind to me, but professional. It was as it should be.

Why did I feel so empty, then?

I was going to contemplate that question while I drank a glass of wine and binged *Broadchurch,* a British crime drama I had been meaning to watch on Netflix. Chloe was spending the night at my parents', so it was a good night to unwind and watch a show I wouldn't allow her to see. Her soccer game had been canceled due to all the cold rain we had received the last week and chances were high it was going to snow tonight. Hello, October.

Before I headed for the cottage, I wanted to give Miles the drawing I had completed of Henry and Sophie. I was kind of thinking it could be a 'thank you' for being so kind to Chloe and me last week. It meant the world to her that he had come to her soccer game and taken interest in her. Especially in light of Leland failing miserably. He hadn't contacted me again. I supposed that was his answer. I wasn't sure if I should be relieved or devastated. Or pensive. Leland had a way of surprising me in the most unpleasant ways imaginable. For all I knew, he would show up with Kylie one of these days.

I pulled the newly framed sketch out of my bag while I watched Henry sleep. I should have just given it to Miles before he walked out the door after tucking Henry in, but embarrassment had won out. Maybe I should keep it. Except I had promised Miles I would give it to him.

I skimmed the glass with my fingers. "What do you think, Sophie?" I whispered to no one but me. I gazed at her sleeping angel. Henry was holding onto George, his teddy, and every once in a while, he smiled in his sleep. Oh, how I loved him. "I hope you don't mind how much I love your son," I spoke to Sophie again.

I stood up, half convinced to go home and put the framed photo in my room, but I swore I heard Sophie say, "*They* need you." I froze in place. I never heard voices until I took this job. It was probably all in my head, maybe even wishful thinking. I didn't want to admit how many times I had thought about the embraces Miles and I had shared last week. The connection I felt with him was both disconcerting and wonderful. I think he felt it too and it was why he was staying away from me. It was the right and smart thing to do. That settled it. I was going to the cottage.

I kissed Henry's smooth brow before heading for the door. I was startled when it opened.

Miles's hand flew to his chest. Apparently, I'd startled him too. "I didn't realize you were still here," he whispered.

"I'm sorry, I was just leaving." I nonchalantly shoved the frame in my bag. As hard as I tried to be sneaky, it hadn't gone unnoticed.

Miles stared at my bag. "Is that what I think it is?"

"Um . . ." I stared at him in the glow of the hall and Henry's night light. "What do you think it is?" Maybe in the semi-dark, he hadn't gotten a good look.

He bent his head as if to wonder if I'd lost my mind. The answer was yes, I had. Working for him had been my undoing.

"My picture," he responded.

"I'm not sure it's complete."

His mouth twitched up. "Then why did you frame it?"

"To see how it would look," I said as if it were obvious.

He held out his hand. "I'd be happy to offer my opinion."

I wasn't ready to give in yet. "What are you doing here, anyway?"

His left brow raised. "I could ask you the same question."

He got me there, but I was ready to respond. "I love to watch Henry sleep. It reminds me that there's good in this world."

Miles rested his hand on the door frame, drawing himself closer to me. "Sophie used to say the same thing. And as crazy as it sounds, I'm here because of her. I swore I heard her tell me to check on Henry. I must be going bonkers."

Him and me both. "I think it's sweet. Well, I'll leave you to it. Good night."

He gently grabbed my arm. "Not so fast."

Yep, his touch still made my body zing.

His gaze held mine. "You still didn't give me my picture."

I supposed I hadn't. I resigned myself by reaching into my bag and slowly pulling out the driftwood frame that I thought would go well in his office.

Miles took it from me, probably afraid I would change my mind and shove it back in my bag. He let go of me and cradled the sketch of his sister rocking her little boy who eternally slumbered in her arms. Miles ran his fingers repeatedly over the glass. "It's lovely," there was a hitch in his breath.

He had me tearing up. "I'm happy you like it. I also wanted to say thank you for being so kind to Chloe and me."

His head lifted. "Why would you think you need to thank me for that?"

I pressed my lips together, not sure what to say. "I don't know," I answered, flustered when nothing came to mind. "I'm going to go."

"Aspen, please don't." He stepped closer, too close. "You don't need to thank me for treating you how you deserve to be treated. It is I that should be thanking you. Not only for the picture, but for how well you take care of Henry and me."

JENNIFER PEEL

"You're welcome," I whispered. "Good night." I had to leave before I got lost in his eyes. Before I suggested he embrace me to show his thanks. Yes, that's how much I missed being in his arms.

"Good night," he sighed.

I sidestepped him and walked out the door. Before I made it to the stairs he came after me.

"Chloe is at your parents' tonight, correct?"

"Yes, why?"

"What are your plans?" he rushed to say.

"Wine and Netflix," I admitted.

"Would you like some company?" He shifted his feet.

The honest answer was yes, but was it the wise answer?

"I have a bottle of *Sauvignon Blanc* begging to be enjoyed," he tried to convince me. His white wine was a lot more expensive than the fifteen-dollar bottle I'd been saving for a "special" occasion. "I'll let you pick the film," he said, sweetening the deal.

"I thought you were writing tonight."

"I could do with a break." His gleaming eyes were imploring me to agree to this unexpected plan.

I was torn. I wanted him to write because I needed that book and he promised me once he was a hundred pages in, I could read it. But admittedly, I'd missed him this week and I was tired of spending Friday nights alone or as the seventh wheel.

"Okay, but I get to control the remote," I playfully replied before I realized how flirtatious that sounded.

Miles walked past me. "Believe me, darling, you are in control."

He hadn't called me darling or love all week. And what did he mean by I was in control? I followed him down the stairs. He headed straight for the kitchen. He stopped and propped the picture up on the island, taking a few seconds to admire it again before he headed to the built-in wine refrigerator.

"Have a seat." He pointed at the couch in the great room. "I'll grab the wine and a couple of glasses. The remote is in the coffee table's drawer."

I stared between the comfortable gray linen couch and the stiff

171

looking cream chair, wondering if I should take the seat for one even though it meant not seeing the TV as well and a sore butt. Sitting on the couch felt more like this was a date. I went with the very end of the couch, like, I was seriously hugging the armrest with a hairy white throw pillow on my lap. Safe and secure.

Miles chuckled at me when he walked in carrying the wine glasses in one hand and the chilled, uncorked wine in the other. He sat directly in the middle of the couch. While he poured, I pulled up the show on the massive screen above the fireplace. Miles poured a generous amount into each of the larger-than-average wine glasses. Afterward, he jumped up and turned on the gas fireplace before turning down the lights. The firelight flickered and danced in the floor to ceiling windows and wouldn't you know it, it started to snow. The gentle flecks of white added a hint of magic. In an instant, the room changed from a friendly atmosphere to one inviting romantic entanglements.

I gripped the pillow tighter, reminding myself I had signed a contract and I'd made Chloe an appointment with an orthodontist. Getting fired wasn't an option for me.

Miles sat back down, looking pleased with himself. "That's better."

Better for who?

Miles handed me a glass. "Relax."

I wasn't sure I should. I took the glass, and deeply partook of the liquid gold. A crisp flavor burst hit me. I had never had anything like it. "Mmm. That's delicious. Thank you."

He held up the bottle. "There's plenty more."

Note to self, do not refill your glass. That's how tattoos and babies happen. I set my glass on the coffee table and pulled up the show.

"So, what are we watching?" Miles sat back and sipped his wine as if he hadn't a care in the world.

"Well, I was going to watch *Broadchurch*, but I hear it's pretty gritty, and the first season is eight episodes long, so we can pick something else."

"*Broadchurch* was an ITV show. It was quite the obsession when it came out. Sophie loved it."

"Have you seen it?"

"Not much of a telly watcher."

"I can go to the cottage."

Miles leaned over, took the remote from me, and clicked play. "I'm yours for the night."

I liked the sound of that, but I shouldn't. I took another sip of my wine before hugging my side of the couch tighter. Miles had inched closer.

"Ah, Clevedon," Miles commented on the town setting.

"You've been there?"

"Yes."

"It looks quaint."

Miles rolled his head my direction. "Do you watch a lot of British shows?"

"Define a lot."

"That many?" He tugged the pillow from me. "Why are you so nervous around me tonight?"

"I'm not."

"Liar." He batted me with the pillow.

I tried relaxing, meaning I wasn't white knuckling the arm rest. Instead I was gently resting my arm on it. "I've never watched a movie with my boss before," I admitted.

"Don't remind me," he growled.

I shifted my body in his direction. "Why don't you like being called my boss?"

"Please, let's not talk about it. Tonight, we're friends." He hugged the pillow.

Well, okay. I turned back to watch the show. It wasted no time getting to the gut-wrenching scenes. I stole the pillow from Miles, needing some comfort. I might need a tissue too. The tears were real.

"Do you want my hand?" Miles held out his.

Yes, please. "Nope. Nope, I'm good." The poor pillow was getting the life squeezed out of it.

Miles kept his hand available in case I changed my mind. So not happening. If I held his hand, I was sure I would want to be entangled.

"How's Chloe?" he randomly asked. "Other than her phone case dilemma?"

I exchanged a knowing look with him. Chloe had been in a tizzy two nights ago at dinner because the wrong phone case was delivered with her phone and it was taking forever, in her opinion, for the right one to be delivered. I wouldn't let her take her phone to school until it was properly protected. She must have begged me for thirty minutes. She'd even tried to get Miles on her side, which she did. I still didn't budge.

"The correct case came today and she's with my parents, so she's as happy as can be, well, mostly. She's bummed because she has to ask my dad to be her date for the daddy-daughter dance next week. I think every year it's her secret wish that her own dad, if you can call him that, will take her. And with him being in town, I think it hurts more."

Even in the dark I could see Miles's face redden. "The bloke is an arse. I hope he stays the hell away from you and Chloe. He owes you that at least."

"I told him he either needed to be all in or all out. Sadly, I don't know if he's capable of the first option. Or if he just doesn't want to try."

Miles shifted uncomfortably. "Every man should own up to his limitations and bloody well have the courtesy not to commit to someone if he can't follow through. And he sure as hell shouldn't father a child with her."

I paused and took a moment to study him before I replied. His response felt more like a self-indictment. Or maybe he was angry about his own father. Or both? "Leland set his own limitations and has used it as an excuse. He wants all the perks without any of the work it takes to make a relationship work. Whether that's a romantic relationship or a parent-child one. But people can change if they want to. Even me."

Miles drummed his fingers against his legs. I had come to recognize that as his way of releasing tension. "What are you trying to change?"

I curled my legs under me. "I don't want to be the woman Leland left. I'm trying to forgive her. Maybe in the process, I can figure out what a real relationship is."

Miles's finger ceased drumming. His gaze intensified. "Are you looking for a relationship?"

"Let's just say I'm not swearing them off anymore. But I still reserve my right to think most men are douche bags." I grinned.

"You'd be right." He sat up and took a long sip of his wine.

We each turned our attention back to the show. We watched for several minutes in silence, but I could tell Miles was restless. He kept inching closer and looking my way. No wonder he never watched TV; he couldn't sit still and enjoy it. I finally paused the show and turned toward him. "Would you rather talk?"

"I thought you would never ask." He scooted closer.

I had nowhere else to go so I shifted the pillow to be between us. This didn't go unnoticed. His eyes were laughing at me.

"Do you have something on your mind?" I asked.

He nodded slowly and deliberately. Yeah, that was kind of sexy. We really needed to turn a light on. Or maybe Henry could wake up and need me. Anything to save me from entangling.

"Your mother said something in her report about *Silent Stones* that bothered me."

Great. I knew I should have wrestled that thing away from her. "What did she say?" I grimaced.

"She said my kissing scenes were pathetic."

I rubbed my lips together, trying not to smile. "Well . . ."

He sat up straight with his jaw dropped. "You agree with her, don't you? My biggest fan thinks I can't write a bloody kissing scene."

"When did I become your biggest fan?"

"Don't try and change the subject," he teased. "Tell me why you think that? Better yet, tell me how to fix it."

"I don't know that I'm qualified to do that. You're the writer." And surely the man had more experience than me in that department. By his own admission, he was a generous lover. I believed him.

"I write thrillers, darling, not romance."

"Given my life situation, I haven't read a lot of romance novels either. And the only romance I've experienced in the last several years has come from watching every period romance the BBC and Masterpiece Theater has ever produced."

He ripped the pillow away from me. "That's excellent material. Show me what you've learned."

"What?" I spluttered.

"Show me what I'm doing wrong."

"Don't you mean *tell* you?"

"No, Aspen." He moistened his lips.

My palms got sweaty and I began to shake. "I can't. We can't." I reached for the remote. "Let's watch one."

Miles took the remote from me. "I'm a hands-on learner, and writers are supposed to show, not tell." He leaned in, evaporating the little space that was between us. "Besides I don't want to plagiarize another person's work. I need to know what Isabella would want, and who better to show me than you? Think of it as research." Seductive undertones ran through his words.

My heart was in a panic. Half of it was beating erratically, wanting desperately for me to agree. It was tired of being locked up. The other half beat double-time, begging me not to unearth the key it had worked so hard to bury, especially for a man I couldn't have.

"Research?" I swallowed hard.

"Nothing more. Nothing less." He made it sound so easy and sterile.

"I haven't kissed anyone in years," I confessed.

His brows hit his hairline. "Are you in earnest?"

"Yes. I'm sure I would be awful at it."

"I highly doubt that." He brushed some hair away from my face. "But I don't want you to do anything that makes you feel uncomfortable."

"Thank you. You are probably the first man who I've ever believed when he said that."

"Aspen." He took my hand.

Yep, just as I feared—a fierce connection. One I didn't want to lose.

"You have to stop thanking me or any man who is treating you with decency. You deserve it and more. Will you please believe that? Get that bastard ex out of your beautiful head."

I squeezed his hand before reluctantly letting go. "I'm trying."

He patted my leg. "Try harder." He grabbed the remote. "Let's watch your show."

I lowered his hand before he could press play. "Miles . . . I'll help you."

Chapter Twenty-Five

WHAT HAD I agreed to? *Why* might have been the better question. But when I gazed into his beautiful eyes, I knew exactly why. He got me. It was as if he could see into my soul, and as broken as it was, in each piece all he saw was me. The whole me. How did he do that?

"Are you sure about this?" he asked.

No, I wasn't. Don't get me wrong, I wanted to kiss him like I wanted to take my next breath, but I thought about Addendum A in my employment contract. While it didn't enumerate romantic acts, I felt like kissing definitely qualified as one. "Does this qualify as a firing offense?"

He let out a long, drawn-out breath. "I would never fire you."

If I wasn't mistaken, I swore I heard a hint of regret in there. Did he want to fire me? "Do you think I'm doing a good job?"

He hesitantly reached up and ran the back of his hand down my cheek, leaving a trail of heavenly sparks. "You have been more than I ever hoped for."

"Um . . ." I stammered. "That right there is a good way to start a kissing scene."

"You think so?" He inched closer. Our legs were now touching.

"Yes," I whispered, hardly believing this was happening. "I think what's missing in your books' kissing scenes is the build-up."

"What would you like to see?"

"Well," I bit my lip. "For Isabella, she needs someone who will take his time. Someone who will seduce her with his words and gentle touches."

"How should Dexter touch Isabella?"

All over. No. Not going there. Holy mother what was I doing? I let my legs relax and turned more toward him. I took a deep breath and reminded myself this was only research. "I liked the way . . . I mean Isabella would probably enjoy having her cheeks caressed."

Miles leaned in with a hungry look and rested his warm hand on my cheek. His thumb stroked my blushing cheek. "Like that?" he asked.

I nodded through heart palpitations.

"What next?"

"He would whisper her name like it was a secret that he wanted to keep to himself."

He drew close enough that I could feel his breath on my face. "Aspen," he groaned low.

Wow, did he follow directions well. The butterflies in my stomach gave him an A+.

"What is Isabella thinking?" he breathed into my ear.

"She wants him, but she's afraid."

"How does Dexter help her?"

"He tells her the truth."

Miles leaned back with a tentative gaze. He was lost in his thoughts for a moment before he was back, and we were sharing the same breaths. "The truth is that you are like a dream come to life. In every second we share together, you captivate me and scare the bloody hell out of me all at once. I know I will never be the man you deserve."

Oh. That was beautiful.

His thumb outlined my lips.

I closed my eyes, wanting to better savor his touch.

"Aspen." His lips brushed my ear, making me shiver. Next, he pressed a gentle kiss to my neck. There he lingered, breathing me in, driving me mad until my hands ran through his thick hair. That ignited something in him. He pulled my legs across his lap, drawing me closer to him. His hand ran down my silky hair. "You are beautiful."

"Thank you."

"Don't thank me for telling the truth," he spoke against my lips. There he teased my own, so close but never touching. The anticipation brewed to the point of bubbling over. It was torture waiting and breathing in his sweet breath. Just like I had imagined it would be in my dreams. But now that it was happening in real life, I didn't want to wake up before I tasted him. I didn't want to miss out anymore.

My lips captured his. His twitched against mine, surprised. Believe me, no one was more surprised than me. It was the first time in my life I felt comfortable enough to be vulnerable. That's what Isabella and I really wanted. A man who protected our vulnerability, who never used it to his own advantage.

Miles's tongue slid across my lips, slow and wonderful as if he wanted to taste every part. His soft, sensual lips tasted like the wine, zesty with a hint of lime. His steady hands inched down my back, beckoning me closer, making me feel wanted. As did the way his tongue danced around my mouth. He wasn't racing to the finish line or coaxing me to do more. He was content with me. Just me, in the moment. I basked in each minute, and there were many.

But then, Miles abruptly ceased. He leaned away with a terrified look in his eyes.

I bit my lip, worried. "Was it awful?" I knew I was out of practice, but we seemed so in sync. Had I read it all wrong?

"You were perfect. Too perfect." He pushed my legs off him and stood up. He paced in front of me, running his hand through his hair. The fire cast a foreboding shadow of him. "Bloody hell," he repeated to himself over and over again.

"Are you all right?" More like was I all right? I wasn't sure I would ever be the same after that kiss. And his agitation and the way he pushed me away only added to the perplexity of it all.

He stopped and stared at me. "I won't hurt you."

"What does that mean?" I responded, confused.

He paused and paused some more until finally he said, "I'm going back to write." He rushed toward the stairs.

"Miles?"

"Thanks for the research," he called as he took the stairs two at a time.

I sat back against the couch and let out a heavy breath. That's right. Research. It was only research for him. But was it? I touched my lips where he had left a lasting imprint. It felt real. Whether it was or not, that bit of research led to discovery, as research often does. My findings were anything but simple. Miles was the key to unlocking my heart.

Shelby waved her hand in front of my face. "You're a million miles away today, darlin'."

I shook myself out of my Miles stupor. I needed to be present in this moment for Chloe, who was trying on the tenth dress in Shelby's boutique for the daddy-daughter dance in five days. She was so excited she could finally get the exact dress she wanted, brought to her by my new paycheck. The one I was putting in jeopardy because of the feelings I had for my boss. My boss, who was acting like that kiss never happened. It was business as usual for him. He happily took Henry today for some man time while I shopped with Chloe. He even offered to make dinner tonight. A proper English dinner, he'd called it. Meanwhile, I couldn't stop thinking about that kiss. The kiss to end all kisses. No one had or ever would compare.

"Sorry," I answered Shelby. "I have a lot on my mind."

She rubbed my back. "Anything you want to talk about?"

I looked at the dressing room door my daughter was behind and thought it best to keep all that had transpired Friday night to myself. It was probably best to keep it from my friends too. No need for everyone to know what an idiot I was. I honestly thought when Miles told me he found me captivating he was talking to me, but he was talking about Isabella. I'd gotten lost in the moment. Lost in him.

"How are you feeling?" I redirected the conversation.

Shelby was no fool. Her pressed lips said she knew exactly what I was doing, but she was a good enough friend not to call me on it. "I'm feeling fabulous. Our little bun in the oven has been an angel to his momma."

"His?"

"We don't know for sure yet if it's a boy or a girl, but Ryder swears it's a boy. He's already planning on coaching peewee football."

"What's he going to do if it's a girl?"

Shelby placed her hand across her chest. "Mylanta, he's going to be in heaven. That little girl will have her daddy wrapped around her finger. He's always said he wants a little girl just like me. Isn't that the sweetest thing?"

It really was. I was happy to know that men like him existed. Sure, it made me jealous. I mean, Shelby left Ryder without saying a word while they were engaged the first time around, and yet he still came chasing after her. As in he started a company and moved it across the country for her.

Me? I have men so desperate to *not* want to get involved with me they make me sign a contract. In all fairness, I agreed to it and thought it was a good idea. And maybe it was. Maybe all relationships should start that way, with clear-cut boundaries. Each one of mine would start with *Aspen, you are not worth the hassle of a meaningful relationship.*

I lost it. And I never lost it. Tears started spouting out of my eyes.

Shelby jumped into action and put her arms around me, smashing my head against her voluptuous chest. "Miss Aspen, sugar, what's wrong? Did I say something?"

It wasn't her. It was me. All me. I didn't like feelings. This is why I had buried them. I wanted to go back to naming cockroaches after men and watching them die agonizing deaths. Look what I had been reduced to, bawling into my friend's breasts.

Poor Chloe came out of the dressing room looking as lovely as could be in a black dress covered in floral embroidered tulle expecting her mom to be oohing and aahing over her, but all she found was her wreck of a mother.

"Mom, did something happen?"

I sat up and wiped away my tears so I could look at my girl. My beautiful, beautiful girl who was looking too grown up. I stood and wrapped her in my arms. "You happened." I kissed her head. "You are the most wonderful thing on this planet, and you look gorgeous."

She looked up at me with skeptical eyes. "Why are you crying?"

I tipped her chin up. "Promise me something. Promise me you will always remember your worth."

Her nose and brows scrunched. "Um, okay."

"I mean it," I sniffled. "Don't settle for anything less than being someone's priority."

"Mom, are you feeling all right?"

Shelby's stare asked the same thing.

Before I could answer, I had some insult added to my injury. At least it was a good life lesson for my daughter. Bobby Jay sounded like he appeared out of thin air. All we heard was, "Marlowe, girl, get out here."

Shelby, Chloe, and I all looked at each other before we rushed out into the main storefront area to see what was going on. There we found Bobby Jay in the middle of the boutique, dressed in his Sunday finest, a button-up shirt, jeans, and his cowboy boots, standing there like he meant business. All the patrons were staring at him wondering if perhaps they should be dialing 911. Macey darted toward the offices in the back. I assumed that's where Marlowe was.

Shelby approached Bobby Jay. "My lands, Bobby Jay, what are you doing, disrupting my store?"

Bobby Jay's eyes stay fixed on the backroom door. "I'm here for my girl, and I'm not leaving until she comes with me."

Shelby beamed up at the determined man.

"Marlowe, I know you're here, darlin'. I'll stand here all day if I have to," Bobby Jay hollered.

Still no Marlowe.

Bobby Jay upped his game and started singing some out-of-tune country song I'd never heard at the top of his lungs. It had something to do with him crossing his heart and true love. Chloe was giggling so hard next to me it was hard to focus on the words. Several patrons were now recording him with their phones.

Finally, Marlowe came out in a blaze of glory, her ebony hair whipping behind her, wearing a skintight dress that drove her curves like a Maserati and a stone-cold look that said she was dressed to kill.

That didn't deter Bobby Jay. He wore a grin a mile wide. "It's about dang time, woman."

"I don't want to talk to you," Marlowe spewed.

"The heck you don't." Bobby Jay moved forward.

Marlowe marched closer to him, hands on her hips. "Don't tell me what I want."

"Well, I'll tell you what I want. I want you. Just you."

Marlowe's arms dropped, along with her defenses. "No, you want children and a white picket fence." Her voice shook with emotion.

Bobby Jay stepped near enough to take her reluctant hand. "Baby, I don't care where we live or if we ever have children, I love you. You're the one for me."

Marlowe rolled her gorgeous ice blue eyes at the man. Bobby Jay must have found it endearing. He pulled her to him and wrapped her up in his big burly arms. He whispered something in her ear that made her playfully smack him. Then before we knew it, he picked her up and slung her over his shoulder. "Shelby, Marlowe's shift is over, we have some making up to do."

Several women in the store started clapping as he carried her off like a Neanderthal.

I wrapped my arm around Chloe. "Don't settle for anything less than that."

Chapter Twenty-Six

"DID YOU FIND a dress, Chloe?" Miles asked while we all sat down to a traditional English roast beef dinner, complete with roasted potatoes and Yorkshire pudding. What Miles meant when he offered to make dinner was that his chef would be preparing the feast before us that smelled divine.

Chloe poked her Yorkshire pudding, trying to figure out why pudding looked like a puffed piece of bread. "I did. It's so pretty."

It really was. She ended up picking out a handcrafted lace dress in deep rose.

"Mom even let me get some heels."

It was a rite of passage for every girl. One I had been hoping to hold off on. Heels meant she wasn't my little girl anymore.

Miles gave me a knowing grin that I didn't return. Why did he have to know me well enough to know how hard it was for me to watch Chloe take another step into womanhood? And why did I want to cry on his shoulder about it? He was my boss and I needed to treat him that way. I was going to forget that his kiss had disintegrated the barriers protecting my heart, leaving me feeling emotionally raw. It wasn't real. I don't think I was meant for real.

Miles narrowed his eyes when I didn't return his look in kind. I wanted to, but I focused on Chloe and Henry. More than anything, I needed to keep it professional for their sakes. Chloe needed me to have this job and maybe it was a grand delusion, but I thought Henry needed me too. My sweet Henry, who was purposefully not eating his peas but licking the gravy off his hand until he got every last drop. If I could have gotten away with it, I would have dunked my hands in the gravy bowl and licked them off too. I wanted to know what that chef laced it with. Whatever it was, I was going to get a bottle and do shots with it.

"Miles," Chloe tucked some hair behind her ear, "do you think you could help me with my research paper about War of the Roses? I read that one of the books you wrote was a modern-day retelling of it."

Miles looked absolutely delighted.

Me, not so much. We couldn't afford entangling ourselves further with the man. I couldn't have more reasons to want to give him my heart. Though *A Rose for Every Season* was a brilliant book—it was probably my second favorite of his—we didn't need his insights. "Honey, Miles is very busy right now. I can help you," I answered before Miles could get a word in.

Miles dropped his fork and knife but recovered them quickly.

Chloe sighed. "Oh, okay. It's just, I told my teacher I wanted that topic because we were friends with you, and she thought that was really neat because she's read all your books."

"Your mum has been misinformed." Miles gave me a closed-lipped smile. "It's actually she who will be busy. I need her to go over my manuscript before I continue. While she does that, I would be honored to help you."

Oh. He. Was. Good. He knew how bad I wanted to get my hands on that manuscript.

Miles's eyes said, what else do you got?

Chloe clapped her hands together. "Thank you! Thank you! You're the best."

Crap. What could I say after that? Not a thing. At least not then.

After dinner and putting Henry to bed, I met Miles in his office while Chloe was setting up our laptop and her notes downstairs. He had printed out a copy of his manuscript because he didn't want digital copies of it floating around. That and I think he wanted a moment alone to talk.

I waited by his door, leaning against the frame.

He stared at me from his desk.

I tried keeping my eyes on my bare feet. Note to self, get some moisturizer on them stat and paint the toenails.

"Aspen, have I done something to upset you?"

Was he kidding? Yes, he had done something. He woke up the freaking giant living in my soul and she was confused. She didn't know whether she should be seeking emotional intimacy or burying herself under the hundred different defense mechanisms she had created over the years.

I tipped my head up and dared to look at him. "I just feel it's better if we keep things more professional between us."

His shoulders slumped. "You are wiser than me."

I wasn't sure about that. All I wanted to do was push him in his chair, crawl onto his lap, and have a repeat of Friday night.

He grabbed a black folder on his desk and walked it over to me. When he handed it to me, he kept ahold of it and my gaze. A palpable heat simmered between us. His eyes shifted to my lips. Did he ache to kiss me again? Maybe the words he'd spoken were for me, not Isabella. I was surprised how much my heart wanted it to be so. I almost asked him if that kiss was more than research for him.

"I wish for us to remain friends," he pled, answering my unspoken question.

Friends. "Why is that so important to you?"

A soft expression washed over his face. "Because you've quickly become irreplaceable, one of the voices in my head, and friendship is all I can offer you without fear of hurting you." He let go of the folder, leaving it in my eager hands. He took a step back. His face was a shade of pink as if he had said too much. "Speaking of friends, I have a few mates visiting this week. They will be staying here. I look forward to you meeting them."

Why was he so afraid he would hurt me? *Perhaps* . . . "Is it Penelope?"

Miles cleared his throat. "She is one of them." He rubbed the back of his neck. "Oscar and Molly will be joining her. We've all known each other since our university days. They have a photo shoot in LA, and they are stopping by on their way over. Penelope is a renowned photographer and Oscar and Molly are part of her team. Oscar does amazing things with hair and Molly is an award-winning stylist."

I held his manuscript to my chest. So many long forgotten and repressed emotions ran through me. Jealousy being the main one. "If you need us to, Chloe and I can stay at my parents so your friends can have the cottage."

"Nonsense. There is plenty of room for them to stay here."

There were only two guest rooms. Did that mean Penelope would be sharing his room? I would like to have said I didn't care where she slept, but that would have been a lie. Maybe she was what kept Miles from being able to offer more than friendship. Maybe he wished for them to be more, or perhaps they already were. Surely, he wouldn't have kissed me if they were, right? He would have waited to do "research" with her. *Please don't let him be a cheater.* Even if that kiss meant nothing to him, it wouldn't have been right if he was committed to someone.

I held up the folder. "I look forward to reading this."

"Please be honest in your feedback."

"You have my word."

"You don't know what that means to me."

Did I have his? Had he been honest with me?

I sank into his couch, the same one where Miles had rocked my world, and stared at the folder, wondering if I was being that naïve girl who had trusted Leland. I stopped and thought about that. I had never trusted Leland. It was worse, I thought I could change him and make him see I was the only girl he needed. That would never be me again. I would never try and change someone's mind about me. If they didn't want me, I would believe them right from the start. I needed to believe Miles. He had the power to hurt me. I wouldn't let that happen.

I opened the folder with great anticipation. I couldn't believe I was getting a sneak peek of the sequel before anyone else. He hadn't even sent it to his editor yet, and she was salivating for it. His publisher wanted to start doing promos and teasers, but they needed excerpts.

Before I could begin reading, I was drawn to the scene playing out at the kitchen island. There Miles and Chloe sat. He was looking over her outline. "You are well organized like your mum. And opinionated too, I see. You don't seem to like Henry VI."

Chloe sat up straight to make her case. That was my girl. "He was the King, but he did what everyone else said."

"There may be a bit of truth there, but if you are going to do research, you must be unbiased. Look at his life from all angles. For instance, he was nine months old when he became king. Too young to even comprehend his responsibilities. He was also someone who valued peace, so perhaps he wasn't weak willed, but shaped by his life experience."

Chloe scrunched her nose and thought for a moment. "That make sense. But Shakespeare didn't like him either."

Miles chuckled. "No, he did not, but Henry VI did found Oxford, so he can't be that bad of a chap. And just remember, dear Chloe, history turns on little hinges. Sometimes we make decisions that in the moment may seem insignificant, but when we look back, we see how monumental they were. As we study this ugly bit of British history, let us keep that in mind."

It was interesting to watch Chloe think about what he said, to see the respect she had for Miles in her eyes. "You're really smart," she commented.

"You think so?"

"Well, it could be your accent," she teased.

Miles laughed loudly. "Cheeky girl."

"Thank you, Miles," she said sincerely. "I can see why my mom likes you."

I dropped his manuscript. Why would she say that? Didn't she know I could hear her?

Miles's head jerked up; our eyes locked from across the room. "How can you tell that she does?" he asked her, still very much staring at me.

She shrugged. "She's different around you. I think it's because she's not so lonely." Chloe faced me now too and gave me a half smile. "I'm glad she doesn't have to do everything alone now."

My heart broke a little. I thought I'd been a better actor, but my daughter had seen through my brave front. It appeared she knew me better than I knew myself. My heart ached, wondering if she thought she wasn't enough for me, because there was nothing further from the truth. But there was something nice about having someone around to share responsibilities with. Until tonight, never had anyone said, *go read a book while I help Chloe with her homework.* Even at her last game, Miles picked up on something I missed as her mom and coach. Had he not, the game could have turned out completely different. Because of him, Chloe was the hero. The man brought laughter to our dinner table and car rides. Henry too had added a dimension I hadn't realized how badly I was missing. The need to mother more little people. I never thought I would have the chance again, so I'd buried that desire like I had so many others. Miles and Henry had both awoken something in me.

Maybe that's what Chloe was seeing when she said I was different. She was seeing a mother who allowed herself to feel and possibly even hope for the true desires of her heart. But that couldn't be with Miles, even if I was different around him. Even if, like Chloe said, I did like him. I liked him very much. How could I not? There he sat with my daughter giving her priceless wisdom along with his time. He valued my opinions and treated me with respect. He even endured my criticisms of him and tried to change. He was different than any man I had ever known. But he was my boss. And that's all he would ever be.

Chapter Twenty-Seven

I NESTLED INTO my pillows, ready to finally dig into the manuscript. I'd tried while Miles was helping Chloe, but the two of them were more compelling than his book, and that was saying something. From the snippets I had gotten in, I knew it was going to be good, but watching Miles help Chloe had a profound effect on me. Not only did I wish for someone like that for her, but it made me realize Henry was in good hands. Miles had the makings of a great father. He was patient but he knew when to push, like when Chloe just wanted him to tell her how and why Henry VI came to be the king of England and France. He nudged her to look it up, telling her she would retain the information better if she read it for herself. He even had her make notes to further commit it to memory. I smiled when I thought of the great introductory line they came up with together. *Henry VI, well intentioned fool or whimpering ninny?*

Before Chloe went to bed, she reiterated some of the same sentiments she had so boldly declared to Miles, but this time she asked me directly if I liked him. I told her I did like him, that he was a good friend to us. She wrinkled her brow at the word friend. She expressed herself how much she liked him and liked living here.

I hadn't counted on that. I mean, I knew she would like to live back in Carrington Cove, but I didn't expect either of us to feel so comfortable basically living with Miles and Henry. Yet while that was true, I had also never been more uncomfortable. At least with myself, that was. I didn't know who or what I should be anymore. I didn't want to be that lonely woman my daughter saw. But how did I change that without Miles? Why couldn't it be Miles?

Ugh. I sank farther into my pillows. I couldn't think like that. I needed to read. Do my job and read his book. Right. Job. This was my job. I needed this job.

I opened the folder to read his glorious words only to have my phone ring. It was a Texas number. One I didn't recognize, but it was the same area code as Leland's number, so I decided to answer even though it was late.

"Hello?"

It was quiet on the other end, so I was about to hang up, but then I heard a quiet voice with a hint of a drawl. Not Shelby Southern drawl, but definitely a bit of twang to her tone. "Is this Aspen?"

"Who's asking?" I kind of already knew and my defenses were up.

"This is Faith. I'm . . . well . . . I suppose I'm Leland's wife."

Once upon a time I supposed myself the same thing. I wasn't sure what to say.

"You are probably wondering why I'm calling."

Yes. Yes, I was.

"I feel like I owe you an apology."

I wasn't expecting that. "Why?"

She was sniffling on the other end. "When I met Leland at the beginning of last year, I thought he was everything I'd ever wished for. Handsome, charming, loyal."

I coughed. Loyal was a laughable word in relation to him.

"I know," she commented on my less than tactful interruption. "I used to think you were an awful person, keeping his daughter away from him and kicking him out just because he talked to an ex-girl-friend."

I held back my derisive laugh. "Is that what he told you?"

"Yes, and I believed him for a while. Then I got pregnant and we got married."

I knew how this story went.

"Things were good until Ruby, that's my baby," she sniffled, "was a few months old. He couldn't keep a job, which meant I had to go back to work even though he promised me he would take care of us. I left a really good job as an account manager for a tech firm here in Austin. Thankfully, they let me come back. But when I would come home at night, I'd find that Ruby had practically spent all day in her swing. He wasn't feeding her and changing her like he should. Then . . ." she choked, "I found some messages on his phone from—"

"Kylie," I interrupted.

"Do you know her?" Her voice hitched.

"We all went to high school together. I hate to tell you this, but . . . I saw them together." She needed to know the truth for her sake and her daughter's. My daughter's sister. What a weird thought that was.

"I figured," she cried. "I'm so sorry I ever belittled you and forced Leland to get back in contact with you. I thought I was doing a good thing for your daughter. I wanted my baby to know her."

I could hardly blame her. I knew the kind of lies Leland was capable of telling. "Please don't apologize, you had no idea."

"Oh, I don't know. I think I did, deep down. My daddy warned me about smooth talking men, but I didn't listen."

"I've been there. I still beat myself up over him. I'm sorry for the pain you are going through."

"He talks a good talk for a while, doesn't he?"

I pulled my blanket up and snuggled under it. "That's all he is."

"Well, I'm done talking to him," her tears seemed to cease. "Unless it's through my lawyer. Unfortunately, my lawyer can't seem to get ahold of him; he's disconnected his phone."

That was news to me.

"I hate to ask, but do you know how I can find him?" she asked.

"Have you tried Mike's Auto Body shop in Edenvale, Colorado? He said he was working there, but I haven't seen him in over a week when I told him he had to be all in our all out. Sounds like he made his choice." How was I going to tell my daughter? I hated him even more.

Coward.

"We are all better off without him," she had some fire to her. I liked it.

"I agree."

"I'm sorry for calling so late. I just needed to clear my conscience. I'm sorry I judged you without knowing your side of the story. My own story now."

"I hope your story has a happy ending."

"It will because it ends with Ruby."

"You know, my daughter would love to meet her sister."

She thought for a second. "I'd like that. I'll text you a few pictures you can show her in the meantime."

"Chloe will be tickled. I wish you all the best. If you ever want to talk, I'd be happy to listen."

"Thank you, Aspen. I might take you up on that. I'll be in touch."

I stared down at my phone. My life was full of twists and turns lately. While I was contemplating all the unexpected events in my life, a little ginger baby popped up on my phone. Ruby looked all of six months old and was as cute as a button. She and Chloe had the same mouth and chin. I hoped with all my heart the sweet smiley girl would never feel the hurt my own little girl had felt and would continue to feel once I told her that her dad had once again disappeared. At least I assumed he had. I should probably call that sleaze ball Mike myself to find out.

That could wait until tomorrow. For now, I was going to be carried away into the world Miles had created. It only took a second for me to be hooked.

It started with Isabella trying to escape from Dexter, who Miles led you to believe at the beginning wasn't a good guy, except he tries to keep Isabella comfortable and he never touches her. But she's being held against her will, so that didn't engender any warm and fuzzy feelings between them. In fact, the insults she lobbed at him were fantastic, like, *You pikey pillock.* Why did everything sound better in a British accent? Dexter, for his part, took them all in stride and never retaliated, not even when she told him his mother must have been a slag. Yikes.

The only time Dexter exerted any force was when he came in to bring her food and she used her feminine charm on him. Poor Dexter was stupid enough to believe it might be real. Wishful thinking on his part. Except when Isabella did get close to him, she felt a little something and it startled her. I could relate to her. She kneed him in the groin anyway and ran away. Dexter recovered quickly enough to catch her. That's when he started sleeping in her room to make sure she didn't escape. And that was when things started to get interesting. Isabella meant to lure him into believing she was interested in him to gain his trust, but the more she got to know him, the more she can't help but like him.

I read their exchanges as they talked late into every night, with him on the floor and her on the bed, asking all sorts of questions from his family to how he felt about politics. I began to see how much of Miles was in Dexter. Each man possessed a calm reassurance about himself and a deep understanding of people and situations. It made them both wise.

Poor Isabella thought she was getting the upper hand in all of this, but it didn't take her long to realize she was losing ground. She began looking forward to their nights spent talking and sometimes playing Stop the Bus, a card game she used to play with her father. Dexter began using these moments to gain her trust, to start telling her the truth of her situation. It was enough that when they were discovered by two men clad in black who claimed to be there to rescue Isabella, she chose to flee with Dexter after some kick-butt fight scenes.

Dexter was kind of yummy. I wondered if Miles knew some martial arts. I decided not to ask. I didn't need more reasons to be attracted to my boss. He probably had defined abs like Dexter too. Nope. Not thinking about it. Yes, I was totally thinking about it. And that kiss.

Focus on the book.

Isabella and Dexter fled to France. They almost kind of had a moment there. Isabella was furious with him because she felt like he was hiding something from her. She goes to slap him, but he grabs her hand before she can make contact. The unspoken words and emotion between them were totally hot. You thought he was going to kiss her, and so did she. She found herself yearning for it and she hated herself for it. *Oh, Isabella, I totally understand you girl.*

While in Paris, Isabella discovered a clue in her father's journal that led them to Colorado. It had to do with a town legend involving a tree where lovers carved their names. It was said any pair to carve their name into the Aspen tree would only be parted by death. I loved that he used an Aspen tree. That was where they began to see how intertwined their lives were. Dexter's mother's name and Isabella's father's name were carved together into the tree long before either of them was born, but Isabella's father's name was crossed out.

At first, I was grossed out thinking that they might be siblings, but Dexter was ten years older than Isabella, and his mother died before Isabella was born. But their parents were lovers. Interesting. And who crossed out the father's name and why?

While they tried to figure out who might have crossed out Isabella's father's name, Isabella and Dexter started dancing on the edge of their feelings. Miles made the cabin they were staying in at the Ranch one room, not just one bedroom. A large, single room with only a bathroom for any privacy. Inch by inch, the sexual tension between them grew. Little touches here and there. But more than that, there was an emotional connection. Isabella began to let down her guard. She owned how afraid she was that her life had been a lie. But on the flipside, she had this desperate hope her father was innocent. More than that, she longed to be able to trust someone, but she didn't know how.

I started tearing up when she wrote in her journal how broken she felt.

These last few days, I've woken up before the light of morning to see Dexter inches from me, his breaths steady and deep as he slumbers by my side. He has been true to his word and not once touched me. At least, not physically. Emotionally, he pricks me, making me feel as if I'm bleeding drops of self-doubt. How can I truly trust him if I don't even trust myself? I ache to reach out and touch his bare skin, to feel the rise and fall of his chest beneath my hand. To have his strong arms enfold me and keep me as emotionally safe as he has kept me from physical harm. Is that even possible?

I wiped my tears. It was like reading an autobiography, except I wasn't on the run with a handsome yet mysterious man who knew everything about me. But I was working for one who emotionally and physically touched me. Who wrote words that came straight out of a chapter of my heart. How did he do that? Did it mean anything?

Chapter Twenty-Eight

I NOTICED A light on in Miles's office before I went in to wake up Henry for the day. We had a big day planned that started with story time at the library with my meddling friends who were all worried about me and decided to crash toddler time. Then I was taking him to the early works museum we had in town.

All good activities that didn't involve being around his uncle. His uncle, who kept me up late into the night mesmerized with his words. Not only did I devour the entire manuscript, but I went back to re-read several parts. Especially those that involved Isabella and Dexter almost kissing, or some of their fights. They were delicious scenes. Miles had upped his game, especially the sexual tension. I guess he took my mom's words to heart. I held his manuscript to me as I would my child. It was better than I'd hoped. I wanted to kiss him for it, and I didn't mean that figuratively. But I wouldn't.

I decided to creep down the hall and give him back his manuscript. He said he was waiting to write more until I got it back to him. Which made me curious as to why he was already in his office. There was no singing going on, so he wasn't following his rituals, unless I'd missed that. But surely that would have woken up Henry.

I lightly rapped on his door. "Miles?"

"Come in," he called right away.

I walked in to find him looking a little harried, sitting at his desk, eyes fixed on the sketch I had given him. And OH, HOLY MOTHER, he was shirtless, wearing only pajama pants. That answered that question. He, like Dexter, had a nicely defined chest with the perfect amount of dark hair, with some sexy gray strands playing among them. So sexy you wanted to nestle your head on his chest and run your hands across it repeatedly.

Stop. Stop, Aspen. Avert your eyes, woman! My head went overboard and looked straight up at the ceiling. I. Was. An. Idiot.

Miles stood and looked up at the tray ceiling. "Something amiss, love?"

Uh, yeah. You're shirtless and I want to pet you. My head lowered to normal levels as did his. Our eyes met in the middle. In his, I saw distress. "Are you all right?" I asked.

He swallowed hard. "I have a lot on my mind."

"Anything I can help with?"

"Hmm. That is a good question. Not one I have an answer for at this time."

"Will you let me know when you do?" Oh, my gosh. That came out way too flirty. I was supposed to be professional.

He ran his hands through his mussed hair. "You will be the first to know." His eyes drifted toward the folder I was clutching in my arms. "How far did you get?" He was anxious to know.

Against my better judgment, I approached his desk. Seriously, I should have kept a ten-foot barrier between us at all times, but as always, I kept finding myself drawn to him. I handed him the folder. "I finished it."

His tired eyes came to life. "And?" He took the folder from me.

"It was amazing. I can't wait to see where you go with it."

Relief washed over him as he sank into his chair.

"I did make a few notes, but it was mostly typos and a few clarifi-cations. I also," I bit my lip, "made a title suggestion."

He started furiously flipping through the pages. "Don't leave me in suspense; where is it?"

"I'll let you discover it. I'll bring Henry by soon for a dance party.

You might want to throw on a shirt before I record it, or your publisher will get inundated with panties or knickers as you would call them."

He laughed into his manuscript, still searching for my suggestion. "We wouldn't want that."

No, *I* wouldn't. I headed for the door.

"Aspen," Miles called.

I turned to find him looking even more troubled.

He held up the folder. "Thank you. As always, I'm honored. Your opinion means a great deal to me."

"You're welcome. I'm anxious to see Isabella and Dexter come together. And to figure out what Dexter's hang ups are. I thought Isabella would be the only one keeping them apart. It's almost as if it's more Dexter than her."

He lowered the folder, slow and steady. "He's afraid he will never be good enough for her."

"I got that vibe, but Isabella has felt thrown away and abandoned for most of her adult life. She can't be with someone who is hesitant with her. It will only make her doubt herself more. She's not asking for perfection; she only wants someone who will make her a priority and keep trying." I realized how I was pouring my own heart out to him. "I mean, that's how I see it, but you're the author." I pointed at the door. "I better go get Henry up."

"Aspen, is that how you feel?"

I twisted a loose strand of hair that had escaped my messy bun. "I'm trying not to feel right now because it scares me." I was too honest with him. He brought that out in me.

"Because you figured it out?"

I tilted my head. "Figured out what?"

"That you're ready to scale walls again, as is Isabella, for the man who isn't afraid to give her his all."

I stood stunned. The conversation we had in this very room came back to me. The one about if Isabella and I would know not only who we would scale walls for but if we even remembered how or wanted to. I stared blankly at him for several moments trying to process what he said, more like trying to truthfully deny it, but he was right. I would scale walls for a man who would give me his all and climb side by side with me, reach for me when I faltered. Throw me over his back and carry me if need be. For that man, I would try.

"I suppose we are," I answered for Isabella and myself.

"What if the man in question wants to, but he himself is afraid?"

"Then he should own up to it and be honest with me, I mean, Isabella. She, better than anyone, would understand."

"Would she?"

"Yes." With all my heart, yes.

I could only imagine how ridiculous my friends and I looked sitting in the children's section of the library on the beanbags talking about my unexpected life and watching the two most adorable boys ever pretend to read books. Well, Henry pretended and we had to keep Elliott from shredding the pages. Henry did know several letters. We had been working on those and he loved to point out the ones he recognized. It was mainly the ones that made up his name.

"I can't believe his wife called you," Jenna commented. We were hashing out the Leland saga first.

I was surprised too. I pulled out my phone and showed them pictures of Ruby. Chloe was half in love with her already. She was begging for me to take her to Texas to meet her. On the other hand, she was crushed her dad left. I called Mike and confirmed it. At first, the douche bag tried to cover for his friend and not give me a direct answer, but I was relentless until he caved. It wasn't that Chloe was ready to see Leland, but she wanted him to choose her.

I offered to let her stay home from school today and we would eat ice cream for lunch, but she put on a brave front and soldiered on. It might have had something to do with her helping with the daddy-daughter dance decorations after school today with her BFF Brooke. I prayed she didn't feel less because her dad wasn't taking her. Her grandfather was so honored to have the privilege. He called this morning to see what color of corsage he should order. I loved that man.

Emma shifted in her beanbag chair, trying to get comfortable. "I did hear a rumor that Kylie left town with someone. No need to guess who with."

"They deserve each other." I handed Henry a pop-up book.

"You know he'll eventually cheat on her too," Shelby commented.

"Probably. I never understood why they didn't end up together in the first place. Why bother with me, when she's who he really wanted?"

Jenna and Emma gave me pointed looks.

"You never got it, did you?" Emma asked.

"What do you mean?"

Jenna saved yet another book from her son in the nick of time. "You were steak and Kylie was a hamburger."

"You're saying I was a piece of meat?" I joked, making everyone laugh.

Emma smacked my arm. "First of all, I could totally go for some red meat. But most importantly, you were and are the 'it' girl. You just never saw it. You still don't."

I ruffled Henry's hair. I couldn't get enough of the kid's curls. "I'm definitely not. I mean, look at me." I waved a hand over my go-to outfit of a cardigan and ankle pants. "I've turned into Mrs. Brady from the Brady Bunch, minus the five extra kids. And even Mrs. Brady wore shorter skirts than me. She probably wore skimpy panties too. How do you think she got all those kids?"

"Half of them were her stepchildren," Shelby snickered.

"True, but my point is that I'm a boring mom and nanny who wears grandma panties. And I'm fine with that."

Henry looked up when I said nanny and gave me the cheesiest grin. I loved him.

Jenna pulled out her phone and pulled up an article. "I've been meaning to share this with you. Look at this, it says the new celebrity trend is grandma panties."

I took the phone from her to see if she was joking. She wasn't. "Wow. Those are some expensive, ugly panties. They could seriously get a six pack of those for half the price of the one pair." I handed Jenna back her phone. "Listen to how boring I sound."

Emma sat up and turned toward me and shook my shoulders. "Aspen, you're gorgeous. You've always been put together. Your look is classic, and it comes off as confident. Of course Leland went running, because he knew he was never worthy of the steak. He's a ground beef guy. And you are anything but boring. Not only are you singlehandedly raising a preteen girl, but you work for one of the most popular authors in the world right now, not to mention the most attractive."

"Ooo la la." Jenna fanned herself. "Seriously, how do you keep your hands off him?"

"Well . . ." I bit my lip. "I don't, exactly."

"What!!!" they all yelled in unison. The librarian came over and gave us a stern look. We all hung our heads in shame for a moment. But it didn't take long until I had three sets of eyes begging me to give them some details.

I wasn't sure I should, but I guess I had already let the cat out of the bag. And honestly, the cat needed some advice. I set Henry on my lap and covered his ears for a second. He thought it was a game, but I didn't want him accidentally repeating anything. "So, we kissed Friday night."

They each faux screamed into their hands, lest we should have to wear the cone of shame from the librarian again.

I removed my hands from Henry's ears and kissed his head.

Shelby took my hand. "Is that why you were crying on Sunday?"

"It's part of it," I responded.

"Did he say something about the K-I-S-S?" Jenna spelled out to protect Henry.

"He said it was perfect, but it only happened because my mom told him his kissing scenes were pathetic and he wanted to know how to fix them."

"And you volunteered?" Emma wagged her brows.

"In a manner of speaking." I grinned.

Jenna rolled her eyes. "He was totally looking for an excuse to make out with you."

"I don't know. He kind of freaked out afterward and left."

Shelby kicked her legs like a child. "You got to him. And I think he's gotten to you."

"So why were you crying?" Emma rubbed my leg.

"Because," I sighed, "I felt something. I felt him. But I signed that stupid contract and he's always going on about how we need to stay friends because he doesn't want to hurt me. To top it off, his 'friends' are coming to visit on Thursday and staying through the weekend. One of them is that woman, Penelope, I told you all about. And honestly," I choked up, "I'm confused and scared. I don't know what's happened to me."

Henry turned around and smooshed my cheeks. "Don't cry. I love you, Nanny." It was the first time he had ever said that.

"I love you." I wrapped my arms around him and snuggled him for as long as he would let me while my friends watched half in adoration and half in awe. Henry would only cuddle for so long, before he climbed out of my lap and toddled over to Elliott, who was playing with some toy cars now. Jenna gave Henry some to play with as well.

Shelby patted my leg. "Sugar, I know what's happening to you. It is as I expected all along; you're falling for your boss."

"The Brit got to you." Emma wiggled her brows.

"Forget all that. You never said if he was a good K-I-S-S-E-R." Jenna was back to spelling.

"Of course, he was," Emma said. "Look at her, she still has the afterglow."

They all looked at me to confirm.

"It was amazing," I sighed. "But . . . it will never happen again."

Each of their shoulders sagged.

"Do you think this Penelope woman has something to do with it?" Shelby asked.

I shrugged my shoulders. "I think so, maybe. And his no dating the nanny rule. Please just tell me, though, if I'm one of those women?"

"The hot kind that most women would chew their foot off to become?" Emma asked. "Yes, that's you."

I reached over and nudged Emma. "That's not what I mean. I don't want to be the woman who is constantly picking the wrong guy.

Or the unobtainable one. Or worse, the one who always wants some-one else more than her."

Emma pushed herself out of her beanbag chair with some effort. She knelt in front of me and got right in my face. "Listen here, I've been waiting for years for this to happen to you. Does this mean Miles is the one? I don't know. But I know you're intelligent and you're not a teenager anymore. You of all people wouldn't let just anyone in. The fact you've let him in at all is a miracle. So there must be something about him."

There was something about him.

She smooshed my cheeks too, but harder than Henry. "If he's not smart enough to see what he has in you, then let him have Penelope. But," she smirked, "I've seen you two together, and if Penelope is coming here hoping to rekindle something or keep something alive, she's going to need a really big match."

Chapter Twenty-Nine

"HOW QUAINT THIS is." Penelope ran her hand along Miles's back before she took a seat next to him at the table. Her tone indicated she thought our "family" dinners were anything but quaint.

I wasn't sure why Miles insisted we keep our usual routine with his friends in town. I thought for sure when they arrived a couple hours ago Miles would want to go out to dinner like Penelope suggested. After an elongated hug, I might add. I wouldn't be surprised if Miles had claw marks on his back where she'd marked her territory with her sharp black nails.

She'd immediately marked me as her enemy. Her violet eyes had been shooting daggers at me since the moment Miles introduced us. What did she say? "You are not matronly at all." She squeezed my hand like she was hoping I would bleed. "Miles's description of you did not do you justice."

Miles had given me an uneasy smile and responded, "I said she was motherly."

What the heck did that mean? I was under the impression he thought I was beautiful. But who knew? He'd been acting odd ever since his friends arrived. He was following me around everywhere and insisted on helping me make dinner. His friends found this to be entertaining. They all perched around the island while Miles and I made rosemary chicken and roasted vegetables. Thankfully, Oscar and Molly were my kind of people—funny, a tad off color, and kind.

"You are so domestic now," Molly had teased Miles. Molly came as a bit of a surprise to me. She was supposed to be this award-winning stylist, yet she wore a sweatshirt and yoga pants without a hint of makeup. She even had gray roots in her mousey brown hair. But her personality was attractive, so that's all that mattered. And she didn't look like she wanted to stab me, unlike her friend Penelope.

Oscar, on the other hand, made up for Molly's outward lack of style. The hair guru was overly dressed for the occasion in a form-fitted royal blue jacket with matching pants and a white button up. His hair was gorgeous, dyed platinum on the top with dark undertones, and styled to messy perfection. He called everyone lovey, even Miles, but I had a feeling it was an inside joke between them. Either way, I loved his easy manners.

There was some definite tension at the table when we all sat down. Miles tensed under Penelope's touch, which admittedly I was happy about. I noticed too how Oscar and Molly shook their heads at their friend as if they wished she would keep her hands to herself. That was a wish I could full-heartedly support. It didn't help that once Penelope sat down, she gave me one of those smiles that said *game on*. I wasn't playing games and refused to participate in any she might start. I planned to focus on Chloe and Henry. Miles seemed to be of the same mind.

"How was school and football practice today?" he asked my daughter while I served Henry and cut up his chicken into bite size pieces.

Chloe took a sip of her water before answering. "They were both good. You should have seen the save I made. I had to dive and when I caught it, I slid so far across the grass." She was all grins talking about it.

"I don't think the grass stains are coming out," I commented.

"If you don't come home dirty, you didn't work hard enough." Miles beamed proudly at Chloe.

"Mom and Emma worked us hard tonight. We play our toughest opponent on Saturday."

"I look forward to watching the match," Miles said. "Did you hand in your rough draft?"

By now, Molly, Oscar, and Penelope were staring at their friend in disbelief and looking between each other as if they weren't sure what to make of our usual dinnertime talk.

"Not yet. It's due tomorrow. Could you look it over one more time? Please?"

"I'd be happy to." Miles dished himself some roasted vegetables. It was then Miles realized his friends were all staring at him in awe. "Is there a problem?" he asked.

Molly's round face broke out into a large grin and she spat out a very girlish giggle. "Blimey, Miles, you've changed."

Miles cleared his throat before picking up his fork and shoveling his food in.

"That was not a criticism, mate," Molly added in.

Miles gave her a friendly nod.

"Tell us, how is the book coming along?" Oscar asked.

"Yes, darling." Penelope rubbed his arm, slow and sensual. "Tell us about your work. I've been so worried you would be uninspired working in this dreadful small town." She threw me a placating look. "No offense. I'm sure it's lovely, just not what we are all accustomed to."

Was it too early to say I hated her? "None taken."

Miles wiped his mouth with a napkin and lowered it slowly while he formulated a response.

Penelope dear, who reminded me of a pixie vixen, kept ahold of his arm. Her violet eyes transfixed on Miles, trying to lure him under her spell.

Miles didn't fall for it; instead he gazed at me. "I've been more inspired here than ever before in my life. I believe I have done some of my best work."

Penelope's hand dropped like a lead ball.

A look passed between Molly and Oscar that said *isn't that interesting.*

I gave Miles a reassuring smile. "It's amazing."

"You let her read it?" Penelope sounded appalled.

"She is my assistant," Miles stated matter of factly. "And my biggest fan." He winked at me.

That did not go over well with Penelope, who clucked her tongue but had no words.

Molly flashed her a look that said *behave*.

Penelope took a deep breath and dished herself some chicken.

I'm not going to lie, she scared me.

"Have you named this book yet?" Oscar asked.

Miles gave me the same proud look he had given my daughter moments earlier. "Actually, Aspen did, but I can't release it until my editor approves it. But it's brilliant."

I thought back to Miles's reaction when I got home from my day out with Henry on Monday. I swore I thought he was going to kiss me again. To say he loved *Ascending Stones* was an understatement. He went on and on about how brilliant it was. That it captured the essence of the book. How both Isabella and Dexter were learning how to rise above what occurred at the stone castle, but they were figuratively learning how to scale their emotional walls. Miles had cupped my face in his hands. He peered into my eyes like he had so much he wanted to say to me but couldn't put it into words. His lips parted and he'd leaned in. Like an idiot, I'd closed my eyes, waiting to taste him again. Instead, I was treated to a peck on the forehead and Miles scampering away.

Penelope gripped her knife. "Well, Aspen, aren't you just full of surprises. Is there anything you can't do?"

"I'm not very good at underwater basket weaving or accepting patronizing compliments, but I'll keep practicing." I smirked to the sounds of several snorts and sniggers at the table. I probably should have held my tongue, but like I said, I wasn't going to play her game.

Penelope's nostrils flared and I swore I could see her mentally counting. Then she petted Miles. I think to remind herself what was at stake. Was Miles willing to be her victim, I meant, lover? Or was he already? I wasn't getting that vibe. The only time he had touched her was that initial hug when they arrived. Other than that, it was only her hands on him.

"Oh, this is going to be a deliciously fun weekend." Oscar rubbed his hands together.

I wasn't sure how much fun it was going to be, but after dinner, Oscar, Molly, and I played a rousing game of Hi Ho! Cherry-O with Henry at the coffee table, while Miles helped Chloe with her paper at the island. Penelope sat on the couch wrapped up in her black cloak, drowning herself in wine, acting as if she were in some third world country. She kept staring at Miles like she'd entered the Twilight Zone. I wondered what she expected to find. And hello, if she thought this house and Carrington Cove were on the edge of civilization, she was crazy.

"So, Aspen, tell us some more about you." Molly helped Henry count his cherries. "Have you always wanted to be a nanny?"

"No," I laughed.

"I love Nanny," Henry informed everyone.

Miles whipped his head my way. He looked both disturbed and delighted that Henry loved me. As quick as he had looked my way, he turned back to help Chloe, who was full of light from the compliments she'd received from Miles. He was proud of his protégé's work.

"I love you, Henry," I made sure to tell the little man in my life, really the only man in my life.

He scrunched his face at me and threw some cherries in the air.

"You have other career aspirations then?" Penelope inserted herself into our conversation. More liked pleaded with me to tell her it was so.

"I'm happy where I'm at." It was true. Taking care of Henry was the best job I'd ever had. I knew it wouldn't last, which I tried not to think about because it killed me. And honestly, I had no idea what I wanted to do career-wise after my contract was over. Definitely not go back to the bank.

"I could never be a *childminder*," Penelope scoffed in her condescending voice.

"She's much more than a childminder," Miles defended me.

"Yes, I forgot she's your *assistant*," Penelope said maniacally.

"She's also a teacher and she tells fantastic bedtime stories." Miles flashed me a smile.

Penelope drained her glass.

I tucked some hair behind my ear, feeling uncomfortable being the center of attention. "Please tell me about yourselves. Miles said you've all been friends for a long time."

"We could tell you some wild stories about your boss." Molly wiggled her eyebrows.

"Not in front of the children," Miles warned.

Molly reached across the coffee table and patted my hand. "Later, darling."

"I look forward to it." I found myself wanting to know everything about Miles.

Penelope sat up and discarded her cloak as if it were on fire. "While we are on the subject of better days, is there a pub in town?" she asked me.

"Sure. There are a few bars."

"Brilliant. Miles, let's go have a drink and relive some of our glory days."

Molly and Oscar were shaking their heads again. "Foolish, foolish girl," Oscar whispered under his breath.

Miles rubbed the back of his neck and blew out a large breath. "Penny, I can't. It's almost Henry's bedtime and I have some work to do. We'll *all* go out for a drink tomorrow night, and Saturday night Aspen will take us to her friends' comedy club."

What he meant by "all" was the four of them. I told Miles I would keep Henry tomorrow night while Chloe was with my dad at the dance. My parents would keep Henry and Chloe Saturday night so we could go to High On Laughs and see Jenna and Brad perform along with some other top-notch comedians from across the country.

Penelope's face dropped. I thought she might burst into tears. Part of me felt sorry for her even if she was half evil. More like half in love with Miles. I could see where that could drive you insane. He was intoxicating.

"Well," she picked up her glass and bottle of wine. "It's not like I flew halfway across the world to see you. I'm going to retire. I'll see you in the morning."

"Good night, love," Miles said, not bothering to argue with her.

She waited for him to stop her and when he didn't, she dramatically swept up the stairs.

"Don't mind her," Molly told me, "she's a bit off her trolley now. She's never dealt well with disappointment."

"Or competition," Oscar purred.

Chapter Thirty

I FELT LIKE I was walking on eggshells Friday morning. Especially when I brought Henry in to Miles for their dance party and found Penelope already there, sitting on his desk in a skintight black body suit. I guess black was her signature color. Like I said before, she wasn't necessarily gorgeous, but there was something about her that was appealing. She carried herself well and she had that artistic vibe going for her. Even her asymmetrical haircut played into her persona. Her stunning violet eyes didn't hurt either.

When I walked in, Miles was taking my sketch out of her hand and placing it back on his desk where it belonged. Penelope threw me a snide look.

"Good morning." I tried to pretend that it was business as usual. I set Henry free and he ran to his uncle.

Miles took Henry up in his arms. "Good morning, mate. Did you sleep well?"

Dang. Miles was even more attractive with Henry in his arms. At least I thought so. Penelope's slackened mouth said she was horrified.

Henry shouted, "I want to dance!"

Penelope rubbed her finger against her ear. For goodness sakes, he wasn't that loud. Had she never been around a child?

Penelope reached out and petted Miles's arm. "Only five more years until you can send him to boarding school."

I gasped and held onto my chest. Miles wouldn't do that, would he?

Miles's eyes hit mine. He swallowed hard several times.

Penelope offered me a smug smile. "Is something wrong? Afraid you'll be out of a job?"

"Enough, Penny." Miles stood with Henry in his arms.

I wasn't worried about job security. I was sick thinking about the little boy I loved so much being all alone at a boarding school.

"Are you ready, love?" he asked me.

Distracted, I pulled out my phone to record his dance.

Miles used his phone to pull up a song by the band Wings called "Silly Love Songs."

Penelope came and stood next to me. Oh joy.

As soon as Miles turned up the music and before I could hit record, she whispered in my ear, "Don't think he'll be content to play house with you forever."

She stalked off before I could tell her that at least he wanted to play with me. That sounded kind of kinky. Maybe it was a good thing that didn't come flying out of my mouth.

I watched and recorded Miles's silly dance. The song repeatedly said "I love you" throughout. I foolishly wished that maybe someday he would point at me and repeat those words. But I was happy he was directing them all at Henry.

When they were done, Henry ran back to me saying, "Let me see. Let me see." He loved watching himself on the screen. I handed him my phone and caught Miles's attention across the room. "You're not thinking of sending him to boarding school, are you?"

Miles gave me a pained look. "That is several years away, and nothing has been settled yet."

"So you're thinking about it?"

He released a heavy breath. "Aspen, my life has been turned upside down the past several months. And you won't be around forever. I have to keep my options open."

I wasn't ready to let it go. "But boarding school?"

"They can be quite lovely."

"Surely not as good as being with you."

He flexed his fingers several times. "Aspen, you don't know that. I'm not the man you wish me to be."

"How do you know what I wish for?"

He lowered his head. "Because I know you, and it's the same thing I wish for." He took his seat at the desk. "Now, if you'll excuse me, I have a lot to accomplish."

I stared at him for a moment. Did he truly wish for the same thing as me?

Henry tugged on my hand. "Again." He handed me the phone.

I picked him up and kissed his head, wishing I could do it every morning until he was at least old enough to drive a car. But from the sounds of it, I wouldn't be getting my wish. Like Miles said, I wouldn't be around forever. The thought stabbed me in my heart.

I left Miles to his brooding ways and took Henry to the cottage with me.

Chloe was bubbly this morning. She was feeling good about her report and she was looking forward to the dance tonight. She had her beautiful dress laid out on her bed so she could admire it while she got ready for school.

I loved having both kiddos at the table eating my blueberry pancakes. Chloe was so good with Henry and he was the happiest when he was around her. I didn't blame him; she was amazing.

After I dropped Chloe off at school I stayed in town as long as I could. Anything to stay away from Penelope, and if I was being honest, Miles too. Unfortunately, it was too nippy to stay at the park for long and Henry wasn't in the mood for the library again. He begged to go home so he could play with his trains. How could I say no to his cuteness? Seriously, I could kiss his cheeks all day long.

When we arrived back at the house, I was grateful to find only Oscar and Molly sipping tea at the island. Apparently, Penelope was off taking pictures of the landscape. I was surprised she wasn't in Miles's office trying to seduce him.

"Can I make you something to eat?" I offered the pair since I had to make Henry's lunch anyway.

Oscar set down his teacup. "You are a doll, that would be lovely."

Molly's eyes followed me wherever I went, from placing Henry in his booster chair and giving him some fruit snacks to tide him over to when I walked over to the refrigerator. "You are certainly different from Miles's usual type."

"Quite right you are," Oscar agreed with her.

I opened the refrigerator and stuck my head in it. Can we say awkward? "Um . . . he's my boss."

"He must be a wicked boss. Wicked Mr. Wickham," Molly said, making them both laugh.

I set down the ham and cheese I retrieved from the refrigerator on the island and tried not to make eye contact with Oscar and Molly, but they weren't going to let this go.

"Does she remind you of someone?" Oscar asked Molly.

"Oh, yes, now that you mention it. She's practically the spitting image of the only woman Miles has ever loved," Molly replied with glee.

That got my attention. My head popped up and was greeted with two mischievous grins.

Oscar ran his finger around the rim of his cup. "It's like Isabella has come to life."

"No wonder our mate has transformed into a domestic god. He's met his match." Molly dared me to challenge her.

Oh, I would be. "We have a professional relationship." They didn't need to know any different.

Their laughter pealed through the house.

"Please, lovey," Oscar could hardly contain himself, "the sexual tension between you two is delicious."

"Now we know why he didn't dash back to London like we all thought he would despite the promise he made to Sophie," Molly added.

Oscar gave me a good once over. "Looking at you, he may never come home."

"That's not true." I began arranging bread for grilled ham and cheese sandwiches. "Do you mind if we change the subject?" I tried to keep the pain out of my voice, but I didn't do a very good job. They had no idea how I wished Miles and Henry would stay.

"Oh, dear, we've upset you. I'm sorry," Molly said. "It's just, you don't know what a transformation has taken place in Miles. You have had quite the effect on him. Let me say it is a good one."

I set down the butter knife I was getting ready to use. "What was he like before?" I couldn't help but ask.

Oscar reached over and stole a piece of sliced cheese. "He was always a good mate, but a bit self-absorbed."

"A bit?" Molly ripped a corner of cheese off Oscar's slice and helped herself. "He missed Penny's first wedding because she got married during one of his polo matches."

"She was married?"

"Twice," they said in unison.

"What happened?" I asked.

"Besides her loving nature?" The sarcasm oozed out of Oscar. "She's never gotten over Miles."

I gripped the island's edge. "They dated?"

"Off and on for a couple years a long time ago," Molly responded. "For Miles's part, he was up front with her and he let her down gently."

I turned on the griddle. "Maybe they'll finally work things out." My stomach turned at the thought. Not only did I not want Penelope with Miles, I hated to think of her as a parental figure for my sweet Henry. She'd ship him off to boarding school for sure.

They fell onto each other, chuckling.

"Listen to her." Molly snorted.

Oscar reached his hand out to me. "Lovey."

I cautiously took his well-manicured hand.

He held my hand between his own. "I don't know the exact arrangement between you and our mate, but believe me when I say the man is besotted with you. Perhaps even with the new life he is living here in the Wild West. It will be interesting to see how it all works out."

Things certainly took an interesting turn.

Miles came down to have lunch with us. He kept casting me furtive glances from across the table while his friends regaled me with tales of them closing down pubs, singing for their dinner in poorer days, all the way to holidays in Monte Carlo where Miles was stalked by several cougars in their sixties. While we were all laughing about how Miles had to hire security to save him from senior citizens, Penelope walked in with a camera case slung across her shoulder and a look that said she wished I'd never been born. I was thankful my mom called, giving me the excuse to walk into the kitchen and answer my phone. Granted, Penelope could still see me, but the kitchen was full of weapons in the event I needed to protect myself from her.

"Hello." I kept my eyes on Penelope, who was rubbing Miles's shoulders. She was making everyone uncomfortable, even Henry, who threw a fruit snack at her. I loved that kid. It was a good aim too. It landed in her hair, making her squeal. I had to hide my smile.

"Honey, it's Mom. I have some bad news." This was never a good conversation starter. My heart started pounding wildly thinking of all the possibilities, from my siblings being in an accident all the way to my mom hating Miles's book. She was currently reading *A Rose for Every Season.*

I turned around against my better judgment, praying Miles wouldn't let his ex-lover hurt me. "What's wrong?"

"It's your dad. He's an idiot."

Oh. That was a relief. I mean, not that I was happy to hear my father was an idiot, but it was better than a paralyzing injury or heart attack. "What did he do?"

"I've told him a dozen times not to eat at the gas station near his office, but does he listen? No. He got an egg salad sandwich of all things there yesterday. He's been up all night having it come out of both ends, if you get my drift."

Loud and clear. Yuck.

"Honey, he's so sorry, but he's in no shape to take Chloe to the dance tonight. He'll make it up to her."

I leaned against the refrigerator. "Is he sure he can't take her?"

"He fell asleep on the bathroom floor and he's still running a fever. I know this means a lot to her, but I'm sorry, honey, it's not possible."

"Okay," I choked out. "I hope Dad feels better soon."

"We'll try and make it to her game tomorrow if we can. I have another report for Miles." Of course she did.

I hung up, feeling ill.

"Everything all right, love?"

I jumped. I hadn't realized Miles was standing behind me, too close for my own good. My entire body zinged and zanged. I gazed up into his tell-me-everything eyes.

He hesitantly reached out and wiped an errant tear off my cheek. "What's happened?"

"My dad got food poisoning and he can't take Chloe to the daddy-daughter dance tonight. She's going to be crushed, especially after Leland's brief appearance and then him skipping town. She was looking forward to dressing up."

Miles pressed his lips together. I could see the wheels turning in his mind. "What if I took her?"

I could hardly believe I'd heard him right. "You have plans tonight. I don't want to ruin those for you." I peeked around him at his friends staring at us, one was shooting daggers at me with her eyes while the other two were egging me on.

He glanced back at them for a moment before focusing right back on me. "Chloe is more important."

He had no idea what those four words meant to me. I flung myself against him and wrapped my arms around him. "Are you sure?"

He enveloped me in his arms. "Absolutely."

"Thank you." I breathed him in.

"It's my pleasure."

It was then I realized I belonged in his arms. How I longed to stay there, but I knew he was unsure, so I untangled myself from him. I was never again placing myself in a man's arms who wasn't one hundred and ten percent sure that's where he wanted me to stay. "I'm sorry for . . . uh . . . you know . . . touching you . . . I mean, hugging you." Why did I always sound like an imbecile in front of him?

He leaned in and whispered in my ear, "You have my permission to touch me anytime."

I didn't get to respond because Penelope cleared her throat so loud I thought she might have coughed up a lung. "You're abandoning us for the night?"

"We can go out for a late drink when I return from the dance." Miles tried to placate her.

"Wait." I thought of something Chloe might find important. At her age, embarrassment was the worst and Miles's dancing was, let's say, unconventional. "Do you know how to dance properly?"

Miles wickedly grinned before taking my hand and pulling me to him. Okay, I know I just said I would never place myself in his arms again unless I knew he was sure, but for the record, he put me there, not the other way around.

He held my right hand out while his free hand rested on my back. He stepped forward and back then twirled me around before bringing me in very close to his body, proving he had some moves. "You're not going to dance like that with Chloe, right?" I asked, breathless.

"That move was for her mother only. I will treat her as if she were my own daughter." He released me.

He was seducing me with his words. I stood on my tiptoes and kissed his cheek without even a second thought. "You don't know what that means to me."

Miles rested his hand on the cheek I kissed. "I think I do."

I was about to get lost in his eyes, but Penelope was tsking and tapping her boots so loudly against the wood floors, it was going to give us all a headache. "So, what are we supposed to do while you're out playing father dearest?" she spat.

Oscar clapped his hands together. "We will help the lass get ready of course. She will be the belle of the ball."

Chapter Thirty-One

MILES WASN'T LYING when he said he had talented friends. Oscar and Molly came to the cottage and made my daughter feel like she was a movie star. Penelope opted to stay in the main house to pout and drink. Fine by me. She wasn't really invited anyway.

Molly had Chloe slip into a smock before they seated her in front of the vanity in the master bath. There they went to work on her. Molly did her makeup, giving her a natural look that only enhanced her beauty, while Oscar wanded, curled, and twisted her hair into perfection. When he was done, she had a lovely low bun updo with tiny blossoms placed sporadically throughout her hair.

Once I had her all to myself and got her into her dress, I couldn't hold the tears back. I stood in awe of her. "You are so beautiful."

She looked down at her dress and heels then stared at herself in the full-length mirror in my bedroom. "I feel like a princess."

"You look like one too." I wrapped my arms around her from behind. "Are you sure you don't mind that Miles is taking you?"

She didn't even have to think about it. "I'm sorry grandpa's sick, but I'm glad Miles can take me. He's treated me more like a daughter than my own dad."

"He's a good guy."

"Mom," she looked at me through the mirror, "are you and Miles dating?"

"No," I answered quickly.

"Oh," she said, disappointed. She turned and faced me. "How come?"

"Honey, he's my boss."

"Yeah, but he's more than that. He and Henry are like our family now."

I smoothed her cheek with my hand. "In some ways, yes."

"I can tell he makes you happy."

"No one can make you happy." I kissed her brow.

"That's not true," she stated boldly. Miles was right, she was cheeky, and I loved it. "You make me happy and I know I make you happy, so why can't you admit Miles makes you happy?"

"It's complicated."

"No, it's not. You both like each other."

"Yes, we do." I couldn't lie to her.

"Then do something about it."

"What should I do about it?" I couldn't believe I was asking my twelve-year-old for dating advice.

She flashed me her cute, crooked grin. "Tell him how you feel."

I hugged her. "Honey, it's never that simple."

I could feel her rolling her eyes against me. "You're just scared."

Yep.

Miles saved us from our conversation by knocking on the cottage door. Oscar opened it and let him and Henry in when Chloe and I walked out. We were swapping kids for the night.

I wasn't prepared for how good he would look in a suit and tie. I hardly noticed Henry clinging to my legs for staring so hard at his uncle. It was like the black suit was invented especially for him. I literally had to bite the insides of my cheeks before I took Chloe's advice and told him exactly how I felt, right down to wanting to grab the lapels of his jacket and kiss him like the first time, but forever. The corsage he held in his hand only made him more attractive. He insisted on picking up the one my dad had ordered for her. Chloe was right. He made me happy.

Molly straightened Miles's red tie for him. "Darling, you look smashing."

Yes, he did. I wanted to smash myself against him. I couldn't think like that. I was a mom.

Oscar got out his phone. "We need pictures. Lots and lots of pictures."

Miles approached me and Chloe. He threw me a wink before he addressed Chloe. "You look very pretty tonight," he complimented Chloe. He took the cream rose wrist corsage out of its plastic container. "Can I have the honor of placing this on you?"

She held out her left hand. "Yes, but don't be so formal in front of my friends. You'll freak them out."

Miles chuckled while placing the corsage. "Duly noted."

Chloe admired the roses around her wrist. "Thank you. You really are the best."

Miles stood a little taller. "Your grandfather did pick it out."

"Yeah, but you picked it up and you're taking me last minute."

"Pictures, pictures," Oscar called. "Let's get some of Miles and Chloe and then some of the four of you. You all are too adorable for words."

I held Henry in my arms while Chloe and Miles got their pictures taken. They were doing goofy "dad and daughter" poses. They stood back to back and made silly faces. It was enough to make me want to fall in love with the man.

"Now the four of you," Oscar motioned for us all to stand together.

I ran my fingers through my hair. "I think pictures of Chloe and Miles are good enough. I'm a mess."

"Have you lost the plot?" Molly felt my forehead. "Have you seen anyone as fetching as her?" Molly asked Miles.

Miles looked me over from head to toe in my mom clothes—jeans and a sweatshirt. "I've never seen anyone more lovely."

My cheeks flushed red. Chloe gave me an I-told-you-so look. Molly pushed me toward Miles. Miles put his arm around me while I held Henry, and Chloe took Miles's other side.

Oscar patted his heart. "I'm getting all verklempt." He snapped several pictures. "I'm tagging you in all these photos, Miles, my social media pages need a boost."

"How do you feel about that, Aspen?" Miles asked.

"I'd rather not have Chloe subject to all your adoring fans."

"Understandable," Oscar agreed. "In that case, we need one of just you and Miles."

"No. No. No. I look like a slob compared to him."

"Nonsense, lovey," Oscar insisted.

Chloe took Henry from me and gave me a mischievous grin.

"Just take one of Miles by himself, or how about I take one of you, Molly, and Miles," I suggested.

"We're old news," Molly commented. "The two of you will garner much more attention." She wiggled her brows.

Miles whispered in my ear, "Just one, please?"

"Fine," I sighed through my shivers.

"Close together," Oscar instructed.

Miles put his arm around me, and I looked up at him as he gazed down at me. I didn't realize Oscar had even snapped a picture.

"If that doesn't say it all." Oscar showed his phone to Molly who fanned herself. Oscar held the phone up to us and he was right, my feelings were spelled out in one look. It said, *I'm willing to climb the wall again. Will you be my climbing partner?* Miles's gaze said, *What am I going to do about you?* That was a good question.

Penelope thought she had the answer to it. She decided to pay me a visit after everyone left and it was only Henry and me. Henry had fallen asleep on my couch while we watched *Toy Story.* I wouldn't have answered the door had I known it was her. I thought maybe it was Chloe or Miles, but I should have known better since they both had keys to the cottage. I supposed it was wishful thinking. I was anxious to see how their night had gone. Chloe had texted me some pictures of some of the other dads getting autographs from Miles. A lot of men did read his books, but you wouldn't know it by the women who followed him online. You would have thought he was writing romance novels.

When I opened the door, Penelope was standing there with mascara stains under her eyes. "Can I talk to you?" she hiccupped.

I felt sorry enough for her that I let her in.

She settled into the comfy chair across from the couch where I sat watching over my slumbering angel.

"Why are you here?" I asked, point blank. I wasn't going to pull any punches with her.

She wiped her eyes and flipped her angular hair. "I came to warn you that this isn't real. The Miles you think you know is a façade."

I tried not to squirm in my seat. I didn't want to give her the satisfaction of knowing her words bothered me. "What makes you say that, other than your jealousy?"

"You think I'm jealous of you? I do photoshoots for *Vogue* and *Cosmopolitan*. I travel the world capturing the rich and famous. Why would I be jealous of a childminder?" she choked.

I folded my arms. "You tell me."

She pulled her thin black sweater around her. "I'm not jealous," she lied, "because this isn't real. Miles loves his work and freedom. And I don't care how much you resemble his precious Isabella; he'll always love her more than you. You don't know him like I do. He runs from commitment at every turn. You should have seen the state he was in when he got landed with his nephew." She pointed at Henry. "He's all kisses and stories now, but mark my words, it won't last. As soon as he can, he'll ship the brat off to a prep school."

"Don't call Henry a brat," I snapped at her. I wasn't going to let anyone talk about my Henry that way.

She sneered at me. "Yes, I saw that picture you drew. The one Miles gushes over like you're bloody Picasso. But I see right through it. You think loving his nephew will make Miles love you? By his own admission, he's not capable of loving anyone but himself."

"That's where he's wrong."

Her laugh bordered between mirthful and evil. "Listen to you. You are a naïve poppet." She stood up. "Do yourself a favor and open your eyes. As soon as he doesn't need you anymore, he'll move on. He always does."

I stood too, ready to see her out. "It sounds like maybe it's you who needs to move on."

My words were much braver than I felt. What if she was telling the truth? His words kept playing in my head that he didn't want to hurt me and all he could offer was friendship. Maybe this was why. But it didn't add up. His actions said otherwise. Take tonight, for example. He saved my daughter from devastating disappointment. And he loved Henry. I saw it in eyes. Sophie wouldn't have left Henry to him if she thought he was incapable of love.

Penelope's lips curled into a snarl. "Don't worry about me, love, it's you who has the most to lose here."

Would I be the loser again?

Chapter Thirty-Two

I DIDN'T SLEEP well at all, so I gave up tossing and turning around five in the morning and decided I would properly thank Miles and make him some orange scones for breakfast. By all accounts Chloe had the best time. Apparently, Miles was the life of the party, getting them all to do a Congo line and the Macarena. Chloe giggled in my bed about it until she fell asleep there. She hadn't done that in forever. I watched her sleep most of the night as Penelope's words ran through my mind. It wasn't only my heart on the line, it was Chloe's too. I could tell she was becoming fond of Miles. That she wished for a father figure like him in her life.

I think Chloe was right—I needed to tell him the truth, but after his friends went home. Well, one friend in particular. I was tempted to back out of going to the comedy club with them tonight, but my friends were curious about Miles's friends, especially the ex-lover. I'll tell you this, she had some nerve. You would never catch me staying at Leland's house, and that's not only because he couldn't afford a house.

Miles said he would take care of Henry this morning when he woke up, but I couldn't help but head over to check on him. I missed the tyke, and there was nothing like his sweet smile first thing in the morning. I let Chloe sleep in since her game wasn't until mid-afternoon. I arranged some scones on a plate and wrote a thank you card for Miles before I made my way to the main house. The trek each morning on the cobblestone path was getting colder and colder. My hoodie and athletic pants were barely adequate to keep me from shivering.

When I walked in through the mudroom, I was surprised to hear voices so early on a Saturday. More surprising was to hear my name. I stopped and listened more intently. It sounded like Miles and Oscar were in the kitchen.

"Bloody hell, what a mess you've created for yourself. Why don't you just fire Aspen already then?" Oscar asked.

My breath ceased, waiting to see what Miles would say.

"Believe me, if that would solve the problem, I would do it now."

The plate and scones dropped to the tile floor, making an earsplitting clang when the plate broke in several pieces. *Dammit.* I stood there looking at the broken glass and crumbled scones, shaking, not sure what to do. He wanted to fire me? Penelope was right. I was a naïve poppet. In my panicked state, I left the mess and headed for the door.

Miles and Oscar came rushing in to investigate before I could escape. Their wide eyes looked between the mess on the floor and me.

I didn't even bother looking at Oscar, it was only Miles who needed to hear what I had to say. "I quit."

I ran out the door before I could even comprehend what I just did. But on some level, I must have known since I burst into tears. The ramifications began to swirl in my mind as I ran toward the cottage. The most beautiful place I had ever lived. The place where my daughter slept peacefully, not knowing her mom was disrupting her life. And then there was Henry. How was I going to leave him? A loud sob escaped me.

"Aspen," Miles called after me. "Please, stop."

Not happening. I had to pack and disappoint my daughter. After that I needed to figure out what was wrong with me. Or buy a cockroach. Probably both.

Miles caught up to me. He grabbed my hand moments before I made it to the cottage's front porch. "Bloody hell, woman." He turned me toward him. Did I mention he was only wearing pajama pants? He chased after me barefoot and half-naked. By how perky his pecks were and all the goosebumps that covered him, I would say he was uncomfortable to say the least. I was so heartsick, though, I didn't even care how beautiful his body was or that he must have been freezing.

He pulled me toward him, though I put up a fight. "Aspen, what's happened? Why would you quit?" His teeth chattered.

"I figured I would beat you to the punch. I heard you tell Oscar you wished you could fire me." I yanked my hand away from him.

He scrubbed his hands over his face. "What you heard was taken out of context."

"Was it? Because Penelope said this would happen."

His jaw clenched. "Please, let's go inside and discuss this."

"No. It was a mistake to think I could work for you. I can't do this anymore. I can't pretend that I don't have feelings for you. That I don't want to entangle our lives, romantically, emotionally, and every other way. But I'm going to believe you and leave before you hurt me."

Miles's shivering ceased. He stepped closer. "Why do you think I said I want to fire you? I hate having that bloody contract between us, but I know it's what keeps you safe from me. If you think for one second that I don't want you, that you don't keep me up at night wishing you were sharing my bed, wishing I could be the man you deserve, then you are sorely mistaken. Never before has a woman bewitched me the way you have."

He ran the back of his cold hand down my wet cheek. "From the moment I met you, I knew there was something special about you, more than just reminding me of Isabella. Your goodness became more apparent as I've watched how you've taken care of Henry and me."

He drew closer to me, taking my face in his shaky hands. "Then the night we kissed." He leaned down as if he wanted to relive it. Our breath mingled between us. "I thought I could simply walk away from it unchanged, but I can't stop thinking about you. The connection was something I'd never felt before. In that kiss, you so willingly gave yourself to me and I realized you deserved that in return. Aspen," he whispered, "I don't know if I can be that man. Like your ex-husband,

I've been a selfish bastard my entire life. I would never subject you to someone like him again. And like my father, I can't keep my eyes off the nanny. What kind of man does that make me?" He dropped his hands and backed away.

"You're not Leland or your father."

He hung his head. "I'm afraid I am."

I took his hand in mine and held it against my heart that was about to beat out of my chest. "Believe me when I say you are no Leland. He would have never canceled his plans to take Chloe last night, and she's his flesh and blood. He wouldn't have stopped that night we kissed. He would have taken all he could get, not caring that he planned to break my heart. And how can you say you're like your father? He was a married man when he pursued your mother."

"That is one sin that I have not committed."

"What sins do you think you've committed?"

He pulled his hand away from me. The heavy breaths he released in the cold air lingered between us. "Most of my life I've done what I wanted, caring very little about others. There have been exceptions, but even then, I've still hurt them. Take Penelope, for example."

My forehead crinkled at the sound of her name.

"I couldn't commit to her the way she wanted. I haven't been able to commit to any woman for long."

"Maybe you haven't found the right woman."

"I have found her." His anguished eyes peered into my own. "She lives and breathes in front of me this very moment. I wish I could write myself to be the man you deserve. But we are not my characters, and as much as I wish it, I know I'm not the man you need."

"You're wrong," my voice cracked. "You've been the man I needed since the day you came into my life. No man has ever treated me with such deference. You have made me feel like your equal despite our very different financial situations. More importantly, you helped me recognize my worth. And the way you've treated my daughter has meant more to me than you will ever know. I know you aren't a perfect man, but you are a good man. I see it in everything you do for Henry, Chloe, and me. And maybe it's not your nature to think of others before yourself, but you are trying and that in and of itself says more about who you really are. It makes you the man I not only need, but want."

His entire body shook, but not from the cold, it was as if he could hardly believe what I was saying. "I don't want to try only to end up failing you. I won't hurt you."

I released a heavy breath. My hopes were dashed. "If that's how you feel, then you already have. I'll work for you until you can find a nanny to replace me," I could barely say it through the raw emotion coursing through me and pouring down my face. The thought of leaving Henry and Miles was a pain I had never known.

Miles took my hand. "Aspen, please reconsider. Henry needs you. I need you. We can remain friends."

"No, Miles, we can't. I'm always going to want to be more than your friend. And I want to be more than needed. I need to be wanted. I deserve a man who will risk it all for me."

"You are mistaken if you don't think that I want you. I have never wanted anyone more. If I could, I would give anything to be with you."

"Then give anything."

He gave me a pained stare. His beautiful chest was raising and lowering at a mad pace.

I waited and watched him shiver in the cold. His mouth parted several times as if he was going to speak, but in the end, he walked away. I didn't watch him go. I refused to witness another man walking away from me.

"Are you going to put Henry down today?" Emma asked while we were doing backward jogging with the girls to help them warm up before the game.

The answer was no. I was never putting him down even though he was getting heavy. I was going to snuggle him every second until he got a new nanny. Stabbing pain in my heart accompanied that thought. Which induced more tears. I felt like I'd cried all day.

Emma tugged on my arm and stopped jogging. "Will you please talk to me?"

I had been refusing to since we arrived. I didn't know what to say. I hadn't even told Chloe yet. Even though she knew something was wrong, she was so disappointed Miles wasn't coming with us after he promised he would be here.

Emma pulled me to the side. "Aspen, what's going on? Where's Miles?"

"Probably still locked up in his office." Oscar and Molly had informed me that as soon as he came back into the house after our little discussion, he ran straight up to Henry's room and promised him he would make it all better before asking Molly to bring Henry to me. Then he warned them all not to bother him and shut himself in his office.

"What happened between you two?"

"I told him the truth about how I feel, and he doesn't want to try," I blubbered. "I think it's time to have a cockroach named after him."

Emma went to hug me, but instead looked over my shoulder and grinned. "You might want to hold off on that."

"Why?"

She pointed behind me. "Because your boss is headed our way. And, dang, does he look good. He's got the David Beckham vibe going on in that stocking cap and tight jeans. Me-ow." She unceremoniously took Henry out of my arms.

"Hey, give him back."

She flashed me a devious smile. "I have a feeling you aren't going to want anyone between the two of you."

"You don't know what you're talking about," I disagreed.

"I don't think I'm the wrong one here. Turn around."

Like a child, I refused. Emma nudged me, though, until I complied. Holy mother, she was right, and I wasn't very happy about it. I didn't need him looking like a walking men's cologne commercial. Suddenly the forty-degree weather felt like the Bahamas. Emma pushed me forward. "Go."

I couldn't move. I was completely mesmerized by the man walking with a purpose holding a black folder in his hand. Did he bring his manuscript with him?

My mom interfered. She maneuvered her way down the bleachers, waving her report at Miles. "Oh good, you came. Aspen said you wouldn't be here."

I cringed.

Miles paused to speak to her at the edge of the field. I couldn't hear what he said, but he pointed in my direction and Mom nodded before looking my way and giving me two thumbs up. Not sure what that meant. I was about to find out.

Miles approached, making sure to keep eye contact with me. It held me in my place in the middle of the soccer field. When he landed next to me, he was smack dab in the middle of my personal space, intoxicating me with his smell and the thunderous aura that surrounded him.

"Hello, darling," he said as if he hadn't left me crying just hours earlier.

"What are you doing here?" I stuttered. I thought we had already hashed out our fate, yet here he was. Was he chasing after me?

"I promised Chloe I would be here."

"Oh." Of course. I was never worth the chase.

His lip twitched. "I also brought something for you." He held up the black folder. "It's a new contract I drew up. I hope you find the terms amenable." He handed it to me.

I stared at it, not sure what to make of this. "I told you, I quit."

"I don't accept your resignation."

"I can't work for you. I need to get back to the girls." I turned to leave.

He grabbed my hand and pulled me to him. We are talking up-against-his-body, sharing-body-heat close.

"Please don't," I begged him. "I can't be close to you and know I can't have you." I started to pull away.

He wasn't letting go. "Aspen," he whispered my name as if it was a secret he wanted to keep. "If you truly want me, I am yours."

I blinked an inordinate amount of times trying to let what he said sink in. "I thought you didn't want to try."

"No, *my love,*" he ran a finger down my tear stained cheek, "I'm *afraid* to try; there is a difference. But I'm more afraid to be without you. I don't know if I can be me without you anymore."

That was probably the most beautiful thing anyone could say to me. "Why the change of heart?"

"I realized it was the first time in my life I couldn't walk away. No woman has ever affected me the way you have. If you give me the chance, I will do *anything* and everything in my power not to muck this up. Though I fear I will hurt you on occasion, but never on purpose."

I ran my hand across his stubbled cheek. "I'm not expecting perfection."

He took my hand and kissed my palm. "That is a good thing, because if you accept the new contract, you will need to sign a clause stating you acknowledge that I'm getting the better end of the deal."

"When did you have a new contract drawn up?"

"Darling, I am a writer; I wrote it myself, today."

Was that why he locked himself in his office? I took the folder from him, eager to read it. I opened it up to find a single sheet of paper.

THIS AGREEMENT is made as of NOW and going forth FOREVER between Miles Wickham and Aspen Parker, whose last name may be subject to change upon further review.

WHEREAS Miles Wickham desires Aspen Parker to be employed as his Nanny and Personal Assistant and Aspen Parker agrees to render such services, she must agree to the terms and conditions set forth.

Ms. Parker will agree to never call Mr. Wickham her boss. She may use the following terms: Lover. Boyfriend. Darling. My Love. Dear. Secret pet names are also acceptable.

Mr. Wickham requests one child-free night per week for adult only activities that will be decided upon by both parties. Mr. Wickham reserves the right to request more than one night when the occasion calls for it. Ms. Parker may also request child-free nights.

Ms. Parker will agree to use proper language when teaching Mr. Wickham's nephew. This includes but is not limited to: Pants will be called trousers. Soccer will be called football. The bathroom is the loo.

Mr. Wickham will provide kisses on demand as well as other types of physical affection. A complete listing will be provided upon acceptance of the contract.

Ms. Parker will promise to, as she has most capably done already, keep her employer and lover from being a complete arse. She will voice any and all concerns as they may arise.

Mr. Wickham will promise to do his utmost to be a man of his word and faithfully keep all the terms and conditions set forth in this contract, and any others the lovely Ms. Parker would like to negotiate.

By initialing here, Ms. Parker acknowledges that she is by far superior and that she is doing this of her own free will and choice. In return, Mr. Wickham will do his best to deserve her, climb any wall for her, and risk it all, even his heart.

I laughed and cried through the entire thing. I lifted my head to meet his anxious eyes. "I think this is the most beautiful thing you have ever written."

He leaned down and brushed his warm lips against my cheek. "Do you agree to the terms?" he whispered in my ear.

I didn't really need to think about it, but I thought he should sweat it out for at least a few seconds.

When I didn't answer right away, he leaned away with concern.

I dropped the folder and grabbed his coat, pulling him closer to me. "I'm all yours. Now, I demand that you kiss me."

"Mmm," he groaned, "I think I'm going to like this new contract." He brushed my hair back and took a moment to gaze into my eyes. "Aspen, thank you."

"For what?"

"For helping me be a better man, and for this." He leaned in and skimmed my lips once before pressing his against my own. His slow hands ran down my back and landed on my hips, bringing me closer to him.

I barely got a taste of him before Emma let Henry blow her whistle. She yelled, "Hey, no curve fondling—there's kids on this field."

We both gave her an apologetic grin.

She returned our smiles with one of her own and let Henry loose. He ran to me and I took him up in my arms, right where he belonged. Miles kissed his head and then mine. I swore I heard Sophie say, "Now they're yours. Take good care of them for me."

I had every intention to.

Chapter Thirty-Three

ISABELLA STARED UP at the abandoned castle and, for the first time, the crumbling stones did not haunt her. The truth had set her free.

Dexter took her hand and held it firmly in his own. "It's over."

She turned towards him and admired the man who had saved her life in more ways than one. She loved everything about him, from the way the cowlick on the top of his head perpetually went untamed, to the mischief that played in his chocolate eyes. But mostly, she loved the way he protected her heart, even from herself if he needed to. She rested her head on his broad shoulder. "This is just the beginning."

I wiped my eyes and peeked over the *Ascending Stones* completed first draft to find Miles nervously pacing the floor in front of the rather large Christmas tree the kids had picked out at the tree farm last week. Henry's new electric train went around and around it. My little man could spend hours watching it. Miles, always impeccably dressed in his black sweater turtleneck and trousers, looked beautiful in the glow of the white Christmas lights and fireplace.

I couldn't believe Isabella's journey had come to end. Together, she and Dexter had discovered it was his uncle who was the true killer. He was in love, more like obsessed, with Dexter's mother. In a fit of rage, the uncle killed Dexter's mother because he could never have her. He also killed the Alexanders, who turned out to be Dexter's grandparents. The uncle framed Isabella's father because he knew that he was

Dexter's mother's one true love. Dexter's father was honorable, like his son, and had married Dexter's mother to protect her from his evil twin. Miles had done an amazing job with all the twists and turns. I was guessing until the end who did it.

I tried to savor each word because I didn't want it to end, not only because the writing was amazing, but because I owed so much to Isabella. Because of her, I learned to forgive myself and was willing to take a chance on love again. And who better to take that chance with than Isabella's creator? I know Miles said that Isabella came to him, but I think she always lived inside of him. She was the part of him who yearned to break free from his family's shame. A shame that was never his to bear.

"I'm finished," I informed Miles.

He immediately stopped his pacing and raced to my side on the couch. "Well?" He was as eager as a child on Christmas morning.

I placed my hands on his stubbled cheeks and kissed him once. "It's brilliant. I have a new favorite book."

His hands cupped my face. "Are you in earnest, darling?"

"I would never lie to you."

"It is one of the many reasons I love you."

"I love you, too. Should we go and get the kids? I'm sure my mom has them in a sugar coma by now and it's almost Henry's bedtime. I don't want him to be grouchy tomorrow." The kids had spent the day with my parents making Christmas cookies and shopping, giving me the day to read. Miles wanted my opinion before he sent the completed manuscript to his editor.

Miles nuzzled my neck, making me rethink picking up the kids right at that moment. "There has been a change of plans. The children are spending the night with your parents."

I tipped my head back, so he didn't miss any spots on my neck. "What will we do with our time alone?" My tone suggested what his answer should be.

"I'm glad you asked. I have some research I need you to help me with."

That was not what my tone indicated. I leaned back with a

crinkled brow. He had to be joking. "You just finished the book and we've hardly seen each other because you've been so busy writing."

"I know, my love, but I feel like it needs an epilogue and I need your help."

"It's perfect the way it is." I pulled him to me. My lips played above his, begging to be kissed.

"You are tempting, darling, but this is important." He pushed off the couch and stood.

I stared up at him in shock. He was serious.

He held out his hand to me. "I promise I will make it up to you." A bemused smile played on his lips.

I placed my hand and my trust in his. "Okay. Where are we going so late?"

"The Ranch, so dress warmly."

I still couldn't believe we were spending our first night alone in the last few weeks doing book research—for a book that was done, mind you. But there was something cozy about being bundled up in the car listening to Christmas music and staring at my handsome boyfriend. Boyfriend was weird for me to say. I mean, I was a mother of an almost teen, and Miles was forty. Boyfriend seemed juvenile and didn't adequately describe what I felt Miles and I shared. Our connection ran so deep that at times we spoke each other's thoughts before either one of us could express them.

"You're still planning on speaking at career day next week, right?" Chloe had asked him instead of me, because let's be honest, his job was way cooler than mine. Though the perks of mine were hard to beat. Cute kid that adored me and a dashing boss whose kisses made not only my toes curl but my entire body zing.

Miles reached over and rested his hand on my thigh. "I'll be there. My publisher is having some books from their middle grade line shipped for the occasion."

"Chloe will be excited about that."

"Have yours and Chloe's passports arrived yet?"

"Did I forget to tell you? They came yesterday. I can't believe we will be spending Christmas in London."

Miles caressed my thigh. "I'm anxious to return and to have you and Chloe with Henry and me. Oscar and Molly have requested we spend Christmas day with them."

"I would love that. What about Penelope?" I hesitated to ask. Last time I saw her was after Miles and I decided to give this a go. She threw a better temper tantrum than Henry and flew out the door saying it would never last. I was going to do my best to prove her wrong.

Miles cleared his throat. "She will conveniently be on holiday in Rome."

That was music to my ears. "What a shame."

Miles laughed. "You will not go entirely unscathed. My father and my siblings are hoping to meet you." Miles tried to keep the edge out of his tone.

I rubbed Miles's hand. "I would be happy to meet any of your family."

"You say that now, darling. You may rethink our entire relationship after you meet the motley crew."

I took Miles's hand between my own. "I'm sorry, but you're stuck with me. We signed a contract remember?"

He glanced over at me. "That I do, my love."

"So, what are your plans for the epilogue?"

"You'll see." He wagged his brows.

"Why so mysterious?"

"I'm just trying to keep the magic alive in our relationship."

I laughed at him, but magical was a good way to describe what we had together. It was by no means perfect. Miles was set in his ways and he was still adjusting to not only dad life, but being a partner. For the most part he was amazing, and he tried his best to be present, but it didn't come naturally for him, and more than anything, I think that frustrated him more than it ever frustrated me.

Sometimes it was hard for me too. Especially letting Chloe grow up. Miles was less cautious by nature and he had to remind me at times to let go of the reins I had held so tightly. Of course, that made Miles Chloe's favorite. It gave me holy envy, but I wouldn't have it any other way. I was happy Chloe had a Miles in her life. Every girl deserved one.

When we pulled into the Ranch in front of the main house, it looked as if we were late to a party we hadn't been invited to. I recognized Shelby and Ryder's truck, and Jenna and Brad's minivan— they were really embracing parenthood. We tried to talk Jenna out of it, but she loved the roominess. Bobby Jay's truck towered above them all. I assumed that meant that Emma and Sawyer were probably around too. I wasn't sure if I should feel slighted or not.

"I'll get your door," Miles interrupted me before I could decide if I wanted to get out. He hustled around and opened my door. He took a moment to peer into my eyes. "Aspen, I do love you."

I tilted my head. "Is there something I should know about? Are you all right?" He was acting awfully strange.

"Everything is perfect. You're perfect." He leaned in and brushed my hair back before kissing my forehead. He lingered for a moment before trailing soft kisses down my cheek. With each touch, my pulse ticked up. His lips teased my own, skimming them, taking small tastes here and there until they came crashing down on mine. His tongue invited my lips to part. As always, my lips immediately accepted his invitation. My hands ran through his hair. He pushed me farther back in the car while thoroughly exploring my mouth. I liked this research trip. But I loved him and how he made me feel. His kisses made me know I was wanted and adored.

He groaned against my mouth. "As lovely as this is, we have some research we should really get to."

He stood upright and pulled me along with him.

"Where are we going in the dark?"

"You'll see." He buttoned up my coat and wrapped a scarf around my neck. "Are you warm enough, darling?"

I took his hand and leaned into him. "Always, when I'm with you."

He kissed my head and we took a trail leading away from the main house. I pushed out any jealous thoughts of being excluded and tried to focus on being in the moment with Miles. While the path was clear, snow covered most of the ground. The glow of the moon made it glisten in the dark. It was like walking in a winter wonderland.

Miles was quiet but attentive, making sure to keep me steady on the gravel path. Several times he looked down at me with an adoring gaze. It didn't take long for me to realize we were heading for the amphitheater. Something was off, though. If I wasn't mistaken, I saw a shimmer of light in the distance. I didn't remember there ever being any lighting in the amphitheater. The closer we got, the tighter Miles held me to him.

Just as we were on the cusp of our destination the source of light came into view. The pergola was lit up in hundreds of twinkle lights. Pink rose petals covered the snow-covered ground beneath it. I stopped and placed my hand over my mouth. "What is this?"

Miles placed his gloved hand on my cheek. "This is how Dexter's and Isabella's story ends and ours begins, I hope." He led me to the pergola.

I paused on the outer edge. This was hallowed ground. Ground I never thought I would step foot on. Miles recognized my hesitation. He removed his gloves and placed them in his coat pocket before cupping my cheeks with his warm hands. "My love, finish this walk with me. Let us say goodbye to our past demons here and now."

Hot tears leaked down my cheeks and fell on his reassuring hands. I nodded and let him lead me the rest of the way. There we stood together under the pergola. The twinkle lights made it feel as if we had entered a fairy land.

Miles bent on one knee and took me by the hand.

"Aspen, the truth is that you are like a dream come to life. In every second we share together, you captivate me and scare the bloody hell out of me all at once. I know I will never be the man you deserve." He used the same beautiful words from the first time he kissed me. "Despite how unworthy I am of you, I would like to propose a new contract, even more binding than the last one." He reached into his pocket and pulled out an enchanting filigree ring that sparkled under the lights. He held the beautiful ring between his finger and thumb before offering it to me. "Please do me the honor of agreeing to be not only my wife, but mother to my nephew. I, in return, will promise to be your faithful husband and loving father to Chloe and Henry."

I was so choked up I could hardly utter, "Yes. Yes. Yes, to all of it."

He placed the ring on my finger before standing up and kissing me gently. His tenderness bled through my lips. "I love you, Aspen," he whispered against my mouth, this time as if it was a secret he no longer wished to keep to himself. "Shall we go celebrate with *our* children and your family and friends? They are all waiting for us in the main house."

I kissed his lips. "I think I would like to privately celebrate for a little bit longer."

"I am happy to accommodate you," he groaned.

Best. News. Ever.

Epilogue

Eight Months Later

YOU WOULD HAVE thought we were running a fancy day care instead
of getting ready for a wedding—my wedding, to be precise—with all
the babies and children running around. We had overtaken Emma's
old bedroom in the main house at the Ranch. I smiled at the chaotic
scene around me. Emma was nursing her daughter, Shannon Elaine,
while Chloe held Shannon's twin, Dane Anders. Meanwhile, Shelby
was changing her daughter, Maribelle's, diaper for the second time in
a half hour. To add to the fun, Henry was in his tux chasing Elliott
around with a plastic sword. Jenna was doing her best to keep the
chaos down as much as possible, running here and there in her pink
organza bridesmaid dress. I chose pink for my wedding colors to
honor Emma's mom.

Thankfully, Oscar and Molly were there to do our hair and
makeup. Molly had even designed my dress. The gorgeous trumpet
antique lace dress with the most romantic train was hung up in the
bathroom, away from the children.

Oscar was putting the final touches on my braided crown updo.
He left some loose pieces to fall around my face. "You are breathtak-
ing, lovey." He smoothed the last curl.

Molly applied a pink tint to my lips as the final touch.

I stared in the vanity mirror, hardly believing this was happening and that I could ever look so elegant. Henry took a break from chasing Elliott and crawled onto my lap. "I'm bored," he exclaimed.

I kissed his nose. "It's nice to meet you, bored."

"Mum, my name is not bored."

I loved when he called me mum. I think he started doing it because that's what Chloe called me, but whatever the reason, I cherished it. I felt like it made Sophie happy. Of course, Henry still talked about his mummy and daddy, and we encouraged it. Miles made sure to tell him stories about Sophie every day so he would never forget her.

Elliott took Henry's sword, so Henry was off again on the chase.

I stood and took little Dane from Chloe so Oscar and Molly could work their magic on my beautiful daughter, who was now officially a teenager and boy crazy. Boy band posters littered her bedroom walls and I was monitoring her texts like a mad woman. I kissed my daughter's cheek before she could get too far.

"You look beautiful, Mom."

"Thank you, baby girl." I smiled, thinking of the present Miles had for her later today after the ceremony. He was going to ask Chloe if he could officially adopt her. I had to stop thinking about it or I was going to ruin my makeup. For the first time in Leland's life, he was going to do the right thing and relinquish his rights to Chloe. It had taken forever to track him down. I had to go through Kylie's parents. Sadly, I think he was relieved that's why I was contacting him. It made me more grateful for the way Miles loved Chloe as if she were his own.

While I bounced little Dane, who was already a whopping fifteen pounds at four months old—I swore Emma produced cream for her twins—I watched Emma nurse Shannon, who was petite compared to her brother. I longed to be in her place. Miles had asked if we could have one of our own, even though he said it scared the hell out of him. I couldn't wait to accommodate him.

Emma smiled up to me, tired, but happy. "I've become a cow."

Shelby plopped down next to her on the couch and began nursing

Maribelle, who no doubt would grow up to be as beautiful as her mother. She already had the crown of gold and big blue eyes. "Think of all the calories you're burning." Shelby tried to put a positive spin on it. Shelby, who was already back in her size two jeans. We would hate her if we didn't love her so much.

"I'm just happy I can drink Dr. Pepper again. The babies love it." Emma laughed before she took a swig of her nearby drink. I think the first thing she asked for after she delivered her twins was a Dr. Pepper.

Jenna joined us with Elliott in her arms. His arms were flailing every which way while he tried desperately to escape. "I'm going to take this kid to his dad. Where are all the guys, anyway?"

"I think they are at our place," Emma said.

"Ugh," Jenna complained. "I'm not walking over there in my heels. I'll call Brad and make him come here."

"Tell all the men to come here," Emma suggested, "so we can finish getting ready. And tell Brad to tell Sawyer I need my Spanx, like all of it. And nursing pads. That sounds attractive, doesn't it?"

We all laughed at her.

My three best friends all took to staring at me at the same moment. I knew what they were trying to say. None of us could believe I was getting married. But more importantly, I could see in their eyes how happy they were for me. It meant the world to me. Thankfully, Jenna added some levity to the moment before the tears came and I ruined my makeup.

"I can't believe you are marrying Mr. Wickham, Jane Austen's bad boy. It sounds so wicked and yummy."

Amid our laugher there was a knock on the door.

"Darling, are you in there?"

"Speaking of wicked, someone is anxious," Shelby drawled.

I still couldn't get over his accent. I rushed to the door and only opened it a fraction. Enough to see he was holding a white box and how ridiculously gorgeous my soon-to-be husband looked in his black tux that fit him like a glove. I wanted to reach out and pet him.

Miles tried to peek in. "Are you dressed?"

"I'm wearing a robe."

"That is unfortunate," he faux frowned. "Can I speak to you in the hall?"

"Isn't it bad luck to see me before the wedding?"

"Darling, I don't believe in that rubbish. Please, I have something for you."

My curiosity was piqued. I slid out the door and into the hall.

Miles took a moment to take me in. "You are lovely. I would run away with you now, but I fear your mother."

I was afraid of her too today. Last I saw, she was barking orders at the wedding coordinator, making sure everything was perfect. She had even dragged my sister into it. I was hoping to have Vanessa and my mom help me get ready. But Mom was so overjoyed that the day she thought would never come was happening—her daughter was finally marrying someone who wasn't a loser—she couldn't be bothered with trivial things like hair and makeup.

"Best not to test her nerves," I agreed.

Miles held the box out to me. "I have a pre-wedding gift for you."

I took the box. "Does this mean you have a post-wedding gift?"

He pulled me to him and held me tight. "Yes. It's called the honeymoon. I hope you've packed little to nothing at all."

"I can't wait to unwrap that gift." A week in Belize of only the two of us.

"Me neither, darling." He brushed my lips before reluctantly letting me go. "Please open it."

I lifted the lid to find a book, my favorite book. "When did you receive this? I thought it wasn't coming out until November?" I set the box down on the floor and cradled the hardbound book in my hands. It was gorgeous. The cover still said it was a thriller with the cemetery cover, but in the background, there was a stone wall with a ray of light descending on it. It spoke beautifully to the theme of the book. I ran my hands over the title, *Ascending Stones.*

"This is an advanced copy. It came last week. I've been saving it for this moment. I hope you enjoy the dedication."

I gently opened the book and carefully turned the pages. I was struck with the loveliest of words. My makeup wasn't going to survive.

To my wife, best mate, lover, and climbing partner.

"It's beautiful," I choked out. "Thank you."

His thumb wiped away a few of my tears. "What have I told you about thanking me for telling the truth?"

I leaned into his hand. "I love that you called me your wife."

"I hope you don't mind that I jumped the gun a bit."

"Not at all."

"Well . . . what do you Americans say? Let's get this show on the road." He kissed my head. "Meet me under the pergola. I'll be the one standing there undressing you with my eyes." He strutted away chuckling to himself.

As always, he was true to his word.

On the arm of my father, I walked the rose petal strewn path behind my daughter and my son. Chloe held Henry's hand while Henry waved to everyone like this was his big day. In the audience, so many faces who had been part of my journey stood out to me. Dane, who was holding his namesake, bouncing him to keep him from fussing. Beside him were Sawyer's dad and his wife, Bridgette, who was holding baby Shannon. She looked to be in grandma heaven. Frankie, the woman of the hour who had made the most delicious cake and cupcakes for the reception afterward, gave me a little wink.

On the other side of the aisle stood Marlowe and Bobby Jay, who were planning their own wedding. A destination wedding in Hawaii. The pergola was too trite for Marlowe. Next to Marlowe stood Macey, who I think finally figured out what she had in Jaime. They both looked at each other with stars in their eyes.

My mom was prominent on the first row, beaming with pride and waving at her grandchildren. My sister stood next to her. Vanessa thought she was too old to be a bridesmaid. My brother and his wife were there as well. One of the most surprising guests was Miles's father, Baron Greaves. He was a stately looking man in his tuxedo with tails. His height and silver hair added to his presence. His facial expression bordered on grateful and pensive. I knew he was happy Miles had invited him, but his relationship with his son was an uneasy one filled with layers and layers of intricacies that may never get worked out. But I think they both wanted to try.

Once the path turned, I was hit with the most beautiful sight. Miles, first and foremost, who *was* undressing me with his eyes. But surrounding him were all our friends who meant so much to us both. Emma, Jenna, Shelby, Molly, Oscar, Sawyer, Ryder, and Brad, who begged us to let him marry us. He'd been dying to have an excuse to get ordained online to perform weddings. Who better, I thought, than my lovable goofball friend? He knew what this day meant more than most people, so it was fitting.

My father, with tears in his eyes, kissed my cheek before placing my hand in Miles's. Miles tenderly brought me to his side under the pergola covered in pink climbing roses. He gently pressed a kiss to my lips. Our tears mingled with each other's. "You look divine," Miles whispered before we faced Brad to become man and wife. And there under the pergola, we climbed another wall and began a new chapter in my favorite love story. A story that began with a not so wicked boss.

DELETED SCENE

Comedy Club

"DARLING, I WISH we were alone," Miles whispered in my ear before he pressed a kiss to the side of my head.

That zinging feeling whenever his lips touched me was never going to get old. "We promised our friends we would come," I reminded him quietly. "Besides, Molly and Oscar are leaving in the morning."

It's not that I didn't wish we were alone too, I did—more than anything. But Oscar and Molly, who sat on the other side of Miles, waiting for the acts to begin at High on Laughs, were really looking forward to all of us hanging out tonight. Dear Penelope, on the other hand, had jetted off after storming out of the house when we all returned from Chloe's soccer game. To say Penelope was less than thrilled that Miles offered me a new contract was an understatement. She threw a temper tantrum complete with stomping feet and one good scream when Miles kissed me as soon as we had walked in the house. While I wasn't sorry to see her go, I did feel sorry for her. Losing Miles would be devastating. I thought for sure I had this morning. I still couldn't believe this was real. Miles and I were truly going to give this *couple* thing a try.

Miles groaned. He was doing a terrible job hiding his disappointment in front of his friends. "That was before I finally got my head out of my arse and decided to let you have your way."

I leaned away from him, brows raised. "My way?"

He chuckled and tapped my nose. "Believe me, my love, from the moment I met you, I've wished for this."

"Says the man who made me sign a contract stating he didn't want to be romantically entangled with me," I teased.

He leaned his forehead against mine. "All for your protection."

I skimmed his lips, wishing to have more than just a taste, but since we were in public and my nosy friends sitting in front of us kept turning around and staring at us, I kept it short and sweet. "I'll take my chances."

"You don't know how happy I am to hear that." He sat back and draped his arm around me.

I settled against him and shook my head at my friends, who were all unabashedly gawking at us.

"Y'all are the cutest," Shelby said from Ryder's lap. A moment not curve fondling his wife was apparently a moment wasted, according to Ryder.

"They are too adorable for words," Oscar agreed. He and Molly were looking around trying to soak in the atmosphere, from all the old movie memorabilia, to the wall signed by every comedian who had performed there. They were impressed by some of the names.

"Well, it's about time," Emma chimed in. She gave Miles a pointed look, bordering on serious and playful. "Make sure you deserve her. Jenna's always wanted to bury a body, and my dad owns acres and acres of land."

Her threat didn't faze Miles. "If I do anything to hurt her, please do what you must."

Emma nodded satisfied. "I like you."

Jenna hustled over. She and Brad had been standing near the stage, ready to begin their emceeing duties. "Did I hear my name?" she asked.

Sawyer gave Emma a squeeze. "My wife was just informing Miles you were thinking of going into the body burying business together."

Jenna flipped her curly brown hair. "Heck, yeah. Watch yourself, *mate*," she teased Miles. She pointed her finger at me. "You should watch yourself too. Brad and I have a surprise for you lovebirds tonight."

Molly rubbed her hands together while flashing Jenna a conspiratorial grin. "That sounds positively delightful."

"Oh no, no, no," I protested. I knew all about their kind of surprises and it always ended up with one of us on their stage doing anything from bad Spice Girls karaoke to kissing strangers. "Miles and I are audience members only tonight." I snuggled in closer to his side.

Jenna faux laughed. "Famous last words. See you on stage. Love you." She flitted off to join Brad.

"Is she having a laugh at us?" Miles asked.

I bit my lip. "Maybe. I hope. We can leave if you want." I didn't trust Jenna and Brad, at least not in this regard.

"Excellent idea." Miles started to stand.

Oscar placed a hand on his shoulder and pushed him back down. "Not so fast, mate. Believe me, I understand your motivation for privacy at the moment given the beautiful creature by your side, but it's our last night in town and I have a feeling we will be seeing less and less of you in the future." He leaned around Miles and reached out to take my hand. "You don't mind, do you, lovey?"

How could I say no to that? I placed my hand in his and hoped it conveyed that not only did I not mind staying for his and Molly's sake, but that I hoped we would all be a part of each other's lives. I wasn't looking to steal Miles away. Though secretly I hoped he would want to stay in America. At least for a while, or possibly until, you know, Chloe graduated from high school. Then if he wanted to whisk me away to the UK, I would probably be amenable to that. I was getting way ahead of myself. Funny how Miles had that effect on me.

"You do realize the danger you are placing Miles and me in if we stay," I responded to Oscar lightheartedly, but meant every word. When it came to comedy, my friends took no prisoners.

Oscar patted my hand. "I have no doubt you two will rise to the occasion. Besides, lovey, our chap here," he let go of my hand and patted Miles on the back, "did a bit of acting during our university days. He was quite smashing."

I turned my attention toward Miles and tilted my head. "Is that so? What other hidden talents do you have?"

He leaned in and brushed his lips across my cheek. "I would be happy to show you those in private."

Oh, holy mother. I needed to blow down my blouse.

"Now look what you've done," Molly reached over Oscar and swatted Miles, "you've embarrassed the lass."

Miles's brows furrowed. "Did I embarrass you, darling?" He sounded worried.

"No, darlin'," Shelby answered him for me. "She's not embarrassed, she's downright twitterpated."

I whipped my head toward Shelby. "Thank you, Shelby." The sarcasm ran deep, making everyone laugh.

"Don't worry about Jenna and Brad," Emma commented. "It can't be any worse than the time they pulled me on stage for that made-up sketch to see how Sawyer would react if another guy kissed me."

Sawyer cleared his throat. "Let's not talk about that." Obviously, it bothered him still. I knew it had that night too, by the sour look on his face. I thought he was going to storm the stage and punch the guy. Yet Emma still hadn't believed that Sawyer had feelings for her.

I wasn't sure I agreed with Emma's assessment that it couldn't be worse than that, but I didn't get to voice my opinion. It was time for the show to begin.

The house lights lowered while the spotlight for the stage illuminated some of my sneaky best friends.

Miles paid no attention to Brad and Jenna. He pulled me close to him. "Did I embarrass you? That was not my intent."

I placed my hand on his clean-shaven cheek, touched by his concern for my feelings. "I know that. However, I would like to explore those talents of yours later."

Miles ran a finger down my cheek. "You are making it very difficult for me to stay."

I reached up and took his hand. "I already know it will be worth the wait."

"Aspen," he said low, "we aren't waiting anymore."

I settled against him, safe in his arms. I knew he wasn't talking about leaving the comedy club early or even about sex. He was referring to living our lives unafraid of making past mistakes. We both knew we'd make mistakes just as much as we knew what we had between us was no mistake.

"All right, all right, all right," Brad spoke loudly into his mic. The crowd got quiet and we focused our collective attention on the stage. "Who's ready to get this party started?"

The crowd roared.

Brad flashed a wicked grin at his wife. "Baby, listen to that crowd," he said more than pleased. "Why don't you tell them what we have in store for them tonight."

She swiped the mic from him and nudged him with her hip. "Love to, handsome."

Jenna glowed in the spotlight. I always admired her curves and confidence. She was showing them off nicely in a denim jumpsuit that only she could pull off.

"Sooo," she began, "our headliner is running late. I guess now that he's starred in two movies, he's feeling a bit full of himself, or . . . maybe his flight was diverted because of bad weather."

There was a collective groan in the audience.

"No worries though," Jenna threw me an evil look, "we have an even bigger celebrity in our audience tonight who has graciously volunteered to entertain us while we wait."

Everyone in the crowd started looking around for the supposed celebrity while I gripped Miles's leg. I couldn't believe my friends. Well, I could, but come on, this was our first night out as a couple. My friends should be breaking him in slowly, not shoving him into the fire. Miles, on the other hand, was both pensive, shifting in his seat, while also looking a bit smug being billed as bigger than the comedian/movie star we had all come to see.

The spotlight was directed right at us, blinding us. Brad and Jenna both pointed at Miles.

"Ladies and gents," Jenna's voice hitched up a notch, "we give you the one and only New York Times number-one bestselling author and the master of thrillers himself, Taron Taylor."

The guy behind us shouted, "Dude, no way! His books are so trippy."

"Stand up," Jenna instructed Miles.

Miles rubbed his legs before reluctantly standing and giving a wave.

Several females around us ogled him and commented about loving his dance routines on Instagram. A few even squealed like high school girls. Lots of pictures were being taken. Flashes filled the room.

Miles went to sit back down, but Jenna and Brad weren't done with him or me.

"No, no, no," Jenna stopped Miles. "Don't be shy, grab your gorgeous girlfriend and come on up here."

Several women in the audience sighed in disappointment to find out he was taken. That's right, ladies, he was all mine.

Miles turned and offered me his hand. "Stage or the exit?" He left it up to me.

"Get on up here, Aspen," Brad cheered me on.

All our friends began encouraging us, more like taunting us, to get up there.

My teenage self would have gone up in a second, but the mother in me was voting for the exit. My inner voice, however, reminded me that moms could have fun too. Fine. I took Miles's hand.

He helped me to my feet, and we wended our way down the row and up to the stage. The spotlight and the crowd followed our every move. By the time we reached the stage, my cheeks were burning.

"Don't they make a beautiful couple?" Jenna asked the crowd.

Lots of cheering ensued.

Miles held our clasped hands up together, playing into it. It was the first time I truly saw Miles for the celebrity he was. Managing his online presence never gave me a full appreciation for his star status. People would have never cheered for so long or so loud if I was with, let's say, an accountant.

Brad lowered his hands, telling the audience to quiet down so he could speak again. "In honor of our famous guest tonight, we have come up with a very special sketch called *Adult Bedtime Stories.*"

"Ooooh," the audience was intrigued.

"Before your minds start taking a trip down the gutter, we will be keeping this PG." Jenna ruffled my hair.

The audience groaned.

"Okay, PG-13," Jenna said playfully. That lent to more cheers.

I grimaced while Miles looked me over from head to toe as if he wouldn't mind acting out a sexy scene. Thankfully, I knew Jenna and Brad were a lot of talk. They tried to keep their shows from being overly crude.

"So here's how it goes," Brad turned the attention back to him. "I will be the narrator for our author and hero here." Brad patted Miles on the back. "And my hot wife will be the voice of our heroine, Aspen. Our victims . . . er . . . participants will have to act out what we say." Brad turned toward us. "Sound good?" he asked.

Um . . . not even remotely. I raised my hand to object, but Jenna grabbed me while Brad took a hold of Miles. Miles was pulled to one side of the stage while I was practically dragged to the other.

"Please don't embarrass me," I begged Jenna.

She patted my cheeks condescendingly. "Never."

Right.

"You'll be thanking me, I promise." She gave me one more pat.

I highly doubted that. I gave Miles an I'm-so-sorry look before Brad started the ridiculous sketch. Miles returned it with a reassuring smile. I had to say it did make me feel better. He always did.

"Once upon a time," Brad began, "there was a so-so looking Brit."

The audience snickered at Brad's big, big lie.

Miles didn't let it bother him, in fact he faced the audience and spread his arms out so everyone could get a good look at him in his fantastically fitting slacks and button-up, further proving Brad's assessment wrong.

I didn't care that every woman was ogling him, just as long as no one threw their panties at him.

Brad stepped in front of Miles and continued. "Our average looking Brit finally got smart and decided to come to the winning side of the pond, otherwise known as America."

Miles's frowned. He had some strong opinions about the Revolutionary War. The audience, though, found Brad highly amusing. Laughter rang through the club.

Brad stepped to the side, letting everyone see Miles before giving him a push toward me. "As luck would have it, the Brit met an exponentially better-looking woman than him."

Jenna gave me a shove toward Miles.

Miles eagerly reached for my hand and pulled me to him, making the crowd say, "Aww."

"It's the first thing he's gotten right all night," Miles whispered in my ear.

It was sweet he thought so, but I didn't agree. Miles was probably better looking than anyone I knew.

"But," Jenna walked toward the center of the stage, "our heroine, while charmed with the debonair Brit—"

Brad pretended to shove a knife in his heart. He wasn't fond of how physically attracted Jenna was to Miles.

"—she was afraid." Jenna turned around. "Act afraid," she instructed me.

Ugh. Fine. I just wanted to get this over with. I turned dramatically from Miles.

Some women in the crowd booed.

"Thankfully, though," Brad interrupted the booing women, "the Brit knew she was the best thing that was ever going to happen to him, and he fought valiantly for her."

"It didn't hurt either," Jenna added, "that his accent made everything he said sound sexy." Truer words had never been spoken.

Brad and Jenna waited for Miles to act his part.

Miles did his role justice and swept me off my feet, holding me tight against him.

The crowd loved it. I did too.

I threw my arms around his neck and peered into his beautiful eyes wishing we were doing this in private. Though I had to admit this was kind of fun.

"Ooo la, la," Jenna fanned herself. "Our heroine could hardly breathe when she found herself in our hero's arms." That about summed up how I truly felt.

Brad wagged his brows. "Our hero, on the other hand, was hoping for some heavy breathing between the two."

Miles's grin said he agreed.

"Keep it PG-13, babe," Jenna reminded her husband.

Brad wrapped his arm around Jenna. "Okay, fine, our hero confessed his love before kissing her passionately."

I felt the entire crowd stare intently at us, waiting for Miles to quote unquote *confess his love.*

My face turned red while I bit my lip. "You can skip the first part," I whispered.

Miles leaned in until our noses touched. "What if I don't want to?"

My heart stopped. What? Did that mean what I thought it meant? He couldn't, right? We just started dating. Though we did live on the same property and we spent a lot of time together. But love? Were we ready for that? My heart started beating again, this time erratically. Excited about the prospect.

When I didn't answer—more like couldn't answer—Miles brushed my lips with his own. "Darling," he whispered, "I've been falling in love with you from the moment we met."

Oh. Wow.

If you enjoyed *My Not So Wicked Boss,* here are some other books by Jennifer Peel that you may enjoy:

My Not So Wicked Stepbrother
My Not So Wicked Ex-Fiancé
All's Fair in Love and Blood
Love the One You're With
Facial Recognition
The Sidelined Wife
How to Get Over Your Ex in Ninety Days
Narcissistic Tendencies
Honeymoon for One- A Christmas at the Falls Romance
Trouble in Loveland
Paige's Turn

For a complete list of all her books, visit her Amazon page.

About the Author

Jennifer Peel is a *USA Today* best-selling author who didn't grow up wanting to be a writer—she was aiming for something more realistic, like being the first female president. When that didn't work out, she started writing just before her fortieth birthday. Now, after publishing several award-winning and best-selling novels, she's addicted to typing and chocolate. When she's not glued to her laptop and a bag of Dove dark chocolates, she loves spending time with her family, making daily Target runs, reading, and pretending she can do Zumba.

***

If you enjoyed this book, please rate and review it.
You can also connect with Jennifer on social media:
Facebook
Instagram
Pinterest

To learn more about Jennifer and her books, visit her website at
www.jenniferpeel.com

Made in the USA
Monee, IL
04 August 2021